Sir Walter Frederick Miéville

Under Queen and Khedive

The Autobiography of a Anglo-Egyptian Official

Sir Walter Frederick Miéville

Under Queen and Khedive
The Autobiography of a Anglo-Egyptian Official

ISBN/EAN: 9783337099565

Printed in Europe, USA, Canada, Australia, Japan

Cover: Foto ©Raphael Reischuk / pixelio.de

More available books at **www.hansebooks.com**

UNDER QUEEN AND KHEDIVE

*THE AUTOBIOGRAPHY OF
AN ANGLO-EGYPTIAN OFFICIAL*

BY

SIR WALTER MIÉVILLE, K.C.M.G.

LONDON
WILLIAM HEINEMANN
1899

TO THE MEMORY

OF

MY FATHER AND MOTHER

CONTENTS

CHAP.		PAGE
I.	EARLY LIFE	3
II.	EGYPT IN THE SEVENTIES	8
III.	CONSULAR CAREER—WORK	12
IV.	CONSULAR CAREER—PLAY	35
V.	SUEZ	42
VI.	MY FIRST OPPORTUNITY	56
VII.	KHARTOUM	72
VIII.	BOMBARDMENT	83
IX.	AS BRITISH DELEGATE	103
X.	CHOLERA	120
XI.	IN THE FOREIGN OFFICE	132
XII.	ABUSE	145
XIII.	CONFUTATION AND ENCOURAGEMENT	156
XIV.	THRUST AND PARRY	167
XV.	SMUGGLERS AND THE POST-OFFICE	180
XVI.	UNDER THE YELLOW FLAG	185
XVII.	TWO BATTLES ROYAL	196
XVIII.	THE YEAR OF JUBILEE	205
XIX.	THE MECCA PILGRIMAGE	213
XX.	THE PILGRIMS' WAY	227

CONTENTS

CHAP.		PAGE
XXI.	DEATH OF THE KHEDIVE TEWFIK	235
XXII.	MINISTERING ANGELS	240
XXIII.	VENICE AT LAST	251
XXIV.	THE NEW KHEDIVE	259
XXV.	A MEMORABLE EPIDEMIC	268
XXVI.	THE PARIS CONFERENCE	285
XXVII.	STRUCK DOWN	291
XXVIII.	VALEDICTORY	296
XXIX.	WINDSOR	302

UNDER QUEEN AND KHEDIVE

B

CHAPTER I

EARLY LIFE

As Mark Twain remarked in his inimitable 'Speech on the Babies'—"We have not all had the good fortune to be ladies—we have not all been generals, or poets, or statesmen; but when the toast works down to the babies, we stand on common ground." So also we cannot all be Wellingtons, Shakespeares, or Pitts; but whilst biographies of our great men are read with avidity, instruction, and profit, there is rarely present in the reader's mind the flattering feeling that, given the opportunity, he also could have done likewise—whereas, any one reading my unpretending reminiscences will have the comfortable conviction that not only could he have done like unto me, but much better. And possibly this simple record of my career may encourage and fire with a modest ambition some youth who, like myself, was born with neither a silver spoon in his mouth, nor with powerful ready-made friends. It has no pretensions to literary merit; it is meant but to serve as a record—I would fain hope a readable record—of

what I have thus far done with a life which happened
to be cast in somewhat stirring times.

I would add that I am fond of laughter, and have
extracted from life a full share of mirth and amusement; but if I have often cried from laughter, I
have never been ashamed of tears when some action
or manifestation of sympathy has touched that spot
—a weak spot—which exists in all of us, even the
most cynical and case-hardened. And I have in
these pages been at no more pains to stifle a sob than
to suppress a smile.

At school I did not particularly distinguish myself,
though I won a fair share of prizes both for work and
at play. I am afraid I did almost everything I ought
not to have done—was keen on slipper- and pillow-
fights; fell in love; checked the big fellows and took
many a licking; smoked "out of bounds," brown
paper or tobacco (cigarettes were not known to boys
in those days), and generally had a rattling good
time. And the inevitable result was that I got a bad
name—a very bad name—and often was punished for
escapades of which I knew absolutely nothing. After
four years, however, the head master, tired of punish-
ing me, hit upon a somewhat novel—and successful—
plan of inducing me to keep out of hot water. Every
twelve months (or was it every term?) Prefects and
Sub-Prefects were chosen from among the senior or
extra-steady boys—and these monitors had certain
duties and privileges, and wore a square inch or so of
ribbon on their coats as a sign of their standing and
authority: the Prefects a blue, and the Subs. a red

ribbon. Well, one winter's day the whole school (some two hundred boys) was assembled in the big school-room to witness the ceremony of the making of these swells. It used to get about pretty well who were to be the new Prefects, and who the new Subs., and thus little surprise was felt as name after name was called out, and the boy received from the head master his blue or his red badge of office. We knew how many officers were to be made "to complete establishment," and our early information as to who they were to be proved on this occasion fairly accurate; but when all but the last boy had been called up, there was a pause—a seemingly intentional pause—and then *my* school number was called out. For a moment there was a dead silence—a silence born of sheer astonishment—followed, as I advanced to the master's desk, by a ringing cheer from my comrades.

Tranquillity was soon restored, and feeling hot and uncomfortable, I heard myself thus addressed by the rev. gentleman, our head master—

"I have, after much thought, decided on giving you this piece of red ribbon because, although you have given your masters great trouble, and have frequently had to be called to my study" (giggling, which was promptly suppressed), "you have, I believe, a high sense of honour, and will not disgrace the office which you are now called on to fill."

I murmured something unintelligible, and went back to my seat full of good resolutions, and cheered to the echo by the whole school; for there was something that appealed to the better nature of enemies and friends alike in the fact of a regular scapegrace being thus put upon his honour.

I tried hard for the next few weeks to keep out of mischief, but I much fear that I should have had to again assume the kneeling posture of penitence in the head master's study had it not been for a serious illness which necessitated my removal from the school.

I was nursed back to life by my mother, and then it was decided that I should not return to school, but must begin in earnest the struggle for daily bread. So I looked out—answering heaps of advertisements —for something to do, and ultimately secured a billet worth sixty pounds a year, and budded forth into the traffic of the world as a bank clerk.

On my life at the bank I need not dwell. I may say, however, that it was not one of uninteresting drudgery and simple book-keeping, for I was attached to the coupon and exchange department, and the head thereof, seeing that I was keen and fond of figures, took me in hand and taught me the principles of arbitrage or the science of exchanges. His motive in coaching me appeared to be to have ready at hand a trustworthy under-study, who could replace him when absent. I had on the whole rather a hard time endeavouring to make my modest pay go as far as possible; but, looking back to those somewhat hungry days, I am glad I went through the experience, for it enlarged my sympathies and taught me the value of keeping private accounts, a habit to which I have

ever since adhered. Likewise this early apprentice-
ship to the science of banking has been of invaluable
help to me in dealing with matters financial.

When I entered on the battle of life, I did so
without misgivings ; I looked things—then as now—
straight in the face ; and, happily, the struggle has
not been a long one—though frequently keen, weary-
ing, and worrying. In less than two years from the
date of my entering the bank, what turned out to
be my chance was offered to me, and a new career
opened for me, as on the 30th of July, 1874, I set
sail from Southampton in the P. and O. steamship
Geelong, Captain Charles Fraser, for Alexandria.

I had been appointed to a clerkship in her
Britannic Majesty's Chief Consular Court for Egypt.
Pay small—£150 a year, increasing £10 annually to
a maximum of £200. Yet, being but nineteen years
of age, it seemed to my youthful inexperience such
a splendid beginning that I counted my fortune
made.

CHAPTER II

EGYPT, the land of "bookhra"[1] and "backsheesh,"[2] where sunshine is the air they breathe, the blue sky the perpetual canopy, all-begetting Father Nile the water of life, and its fertilizing mud the carpet under the naked feet of the fellaheen, the most good-natured and unsophisticated of peasantry—who have tilled the soil since the Pharaohs wrote their tragedies across the face of the world—this Egypt was in 1874, when I first set foot on her hospitable soil, rapidly nearing the verge of bankruptcy.

The Khedive Ismaïl, genial, astute, and a man of large ideas, had, owing to reckless extravagance and to the ease with which he found he could borrow vast sums from Europe, brought his country well-nigh to ruin.

Ismaïl meant well, of that there is no doubt, and many of the improvements he planned and even partially carried out have since been completed, and remain as benefits to his people. But the evil effects

---

[1] To-morrow, or procrastination.
[2] Tips, or palm-oil.

of Ismaïl's extravagance and reckless methods of finance were far-reaching, and were the direct cause of wide-spread misery, injustice, cruelty, and corruption.

So long as Egypt could easily raise loans in the capitals of Europe all went well ; but when money became more difficult to obtain, Ismaïl looked to his Chancellor of Exchequer, or "Moufettish," for supplies. This financial magnate looked in his turn to the governors of provinces, who applied to the deputy-governors, the mayors, sheikhs, and omdehs. And of course the money ultimately came from the patient, long-suffering peasant-farmer.

Now this system worked badly, and of itself bred new abuses, new evils, fresh corruption.

Let us suppose that the Khedive called upon his Finance Minister for £100,000. The Minister, possibly fearing that difficulties might occur in collecting the whole sum, and certainly anticipating no embarrass-ment in disposing of a few extra thousands should the amount be exceeded, issued his orders to the governors of provinces for the collection of, say, £120,000. Then the governors, to show their zeal, and peradventure also with a lurking desire to net a little profit for themselves, would write to their several subordinates for a still larger sum than that required of them. And so it came about that the tax-payer would have to provide some £150,000— though the Khedive had only asked for (and only received) £100,000. The remaining £50,000 went to enrich the numerous go-betweens, and so the whole administration became corrupt from top to bottom.

Now it will easily be understood how disastrous for the country was this irregular and casual method of levying taxes. In season and out of season the tax-gatherer would pounce on the peasant, and were the peasant recalcitrant, flogging would be resorted to. The end of it was that the victim, in cases where he really had not the wherewithal to satisfy the unjust demand, would in desperation borrow from the village usurer—a Jew, a Greek, or a Syrian—who, after the manner of his kind, was always at hand where his cruel trade could be carried on. The money-lender did not haggle about security, he contented himself with exacting extortionate interest, and, later, were his loan—his pound of flesh—not paid in full, he simply annexed the poor peasant's few acres. Indeed, paradoxical as it may seem—and Egypt is a land of paradoxes—thrift was by its very fact a source of insecurity.

Justice for the natives was non-existent, save for those who could afford luxuries—for justice, like immunity from taxation, was only to be had by those who could pay.

Irrigation, which plays such a vital part in the agricultural welfare of flat countries such as the Delta, was likewise carried out only with a view to the benefiting of the great landowners—not for the country at large. And if a peasant-proprietor did obtain water it was only on sufferance, as the dog picking up the crumbs from his master's table.

Government officials, unless possessed of private means, often had no other choice open to them than peculation or privation—for salaries in those days were generally many months in arrears.

This being the state of things when I landed as a youngster in Egypt, it were almost superfluous to say that I arrived at a time when matters were likely to reach a head, and the valley of the Nile about to become the scene of stirring events.

CHAPTER III

CONSULAR CAREER—WORK

AT dawn on the 12th of August 1874, the good ship *Geelong* found herself some fifteen miles from the low coast of Egypt, and those of the *Geelong's* passengers who had risen early were able to make out the tall lighthouse built by the great Mohammed Ali on Eunostus Point. On nearing the coast we perceived, first, the Khedive Ismaïl's Ramleh Palace, then Fort Pharos, and finally the Harbour Palace on the promontory called Ras el Teen, the Cape of Figs.

I soon got ashore and drove to the Consulate—no one was moving except a subordinate official, who showed me to the room that for seven years was to be my home. Save for an old bedstead it was practically unfurnished, and looked most cheerless. I tried to keep up a good heart, and the chief constable of the Consular Court, in which I had been appointed second clerk, kindly provided me with some breakfast; after which meal I made the acquaintance of my chiefs and fellow-clerks.

I need not introduce the reader to all the members of the Court and consular staffs, but I must make an exception in the case of Mr. Henry Hunter Calvert, the Vice-Consul, whose rooms adjoined mine, and with whom I am glad now to remember I always lived in charity and amity. I will leave it to an abler pen than mine to describe my old and valued friend by copying a letter which appeared in *The Times*.

"His death," says the letter, "will carry sorrow into every Anglo-Egyptian family. No member of the colony was more beloved. The white-headed old gentleman, with his kindly, genial ways, was welcome in every house, and his coming was always an especial jubilee to the little folk of the family. Many a time have I seen him greeted by a crowd of small faces crying out, ' Mr. Calvert, Mr. Calvert, you have come to tell us another story ! ' He was not only a man of loving and lovable ways, he was a man of science, and an excellent man of business. His knowledge of conchology and botany was famed throughout the Levant. His collection of shells, the result of years of patient labour and long days of deep-sea dredging in an open boat off Alexandria and in the Red Sea, unique in its way, was burnt with the Consulate after the bombardment. He was a great botanist too; he had exhausted the desert flora, and rare plants in Kew Gardens bear his name. ' You must ask Mr. Calvert,' was the invariable close of any discussion as to any shell or flower in our colony. Last, though not least, he made an excellent Vice-Consul. The whole of the commercial business of the Consulate, no small work in a great port, was conducted by him with admirable regularity, and there are sailors as well as master-mariners all over the world who will remember kindly the polite old gentleman who checked their papers and gave them clearances at the Alexandria Consulate. It is sad to think of a useful and a happy life cut short by a sudden and large increase of responsibility which the old man's morbidly sensitive and conscientious nature was unable to carry."

Officially I had but very little to do with Mr. Calvert, as my work was of a different nature to his, and rarely commingled therewith ; but I saw him daily, morning, noon, and night ; and I hope and believe that I am the better man for having been thrown so constantly into his cheery company.

Of my duties and labours during the six months following my arrival in Egypt I will say nothing, as I was working with a temporary chief—a most worthy gentleman who rejoiced in the title of legal Vice-Consul, had a stilted handwriting and walk, was addressed as "Doctor" in virtue of his having obtained the degree of LL.D. at Malta, but who did not understand the genus to which I belonged. I could recount many quaint episodes as to my relations with this estimable Acting Judge, but I refrain from doing so, as I purpose in this book to set down nought that could offend or cause pain ; and I confess that if on the one hand my temporary Chief did not understand me, it is equally certain on the other that I did not half understand and appreciate his many excellent qualities.

The following February there appeared on the scene Mr. (now Sir Charles) Cookson, H.B.M.'s Consul at Alexandria, and Judge of the Chief Consular Court for Egypt. I worked under him, and was practically his secretary for six years—till May 1881. He trained me, bore with me, and befriended me, and in return I tried hard to render him loyal, faithful service.

A man of experience, a man of parts, a kindly gentleman, an upright Judge, Mr. Cookson lost no time in finding out what his future secretary was made of, and in making the most of such material as he found to his hand. I put down much of my ultimate success to the thorough training and just treatment I received from Mr. Cookson : I have always taken every opportunity of declaring this, and now once more do I acknowledge gratefully my indebtedness to my first kind Chief. To others also am I much indebted, but not in the same sense nor in the same degree, as Mr. Cookson knew me at a time when my character was being formed, when being of a malleable nature whatever good there was in me could be either made or marred.

But amidst the peaceful doings there was a thunderbolt being forged for my pate in Downing Street. Within twelve months of the date of my arrival in Egypt I received from the Foreign Office an intimation that before I could be confirmed in my appointment I must obtain a certificate of educational qualification from the Civil Service Commissioners, or in other words pass the Civil Service examination.

This was rather a blow to me, the French examination being particularly stiff, one requirement being that I should satisfy a French gentleman, to be named by the examiners, that I could converse fluently in French on any subject. This test was to last three-quarters of an hour. One has but to recall what one's school French was, in order to realize the hopelessness of this ultimatum.

Under the circumstances I pleaded for six months delay before presenting myself for examination. Fortunately this breathing-time was allowed, and I made the most of the respite, working at the language from five to six hours a day. During the whole period I had of course my official work also to attend to, and thus my days were well occupied, and my nights often rendered restless by the vain strugglings of a tired brain with dazed searchings after the intricacies of French grammar.

I employed a professor—who came to me for an hour on three days in each week—and the poor grey-haired old gentleman fully earned his fees, for I nearly always had more translations and essays ready for him than he could find time to correct ; but I made a point always of learning by heart two or three speeches which I repeated to him, that he might teach me the proper accent, pronunciation, and ges-ticulation. Throughout the six months of preparation, I altogether eschewed English literature, and plodded through French newspapers, read my Bible in French, and, as a relaxation, procured for myself translations of my favourite English novels, for, knowing them well in my native tongue, I soon learned to read them in French with a certain amount of pleasure, though not always understanding all the words and idioms.

As the time neared, by dint of work and perseverance I had managed to gain a little superficial grip on French, but I knew only too well I was still far from proficient enough to satisfy the French barrister who, I discovered, had been picked out to converse with me for the stipulated forty-five minutes, and on whose willingness to sign a declaration that I had during that time talked fluently, my future career would depend. Almost at my wit's end, I suddenly thought of a brilliant idea. I ascertained by the most painstaking and elaborate diplomacy the great man's pet hobbies, his leanings in politics, his favourite newspaper and the histories of the *causes célèbres* in which he had been on the winning side. This done, I learned by heart a conversation and pretty speeches on all these subjects, speeches which I took care to rehearse to my long-suffering French master, until every accent and gesticulation was absolutely French. At last the eventful day of examination came; and the charming member of the French Bar and the trembling candidate exchanged greetings; then I made my effort calmly and volubly, gabbling away glibly enough of course, and getting him well away at the very start from a critical attitude towards me, speaking with apparent ease on his favourite themes; and he was no doubt charmed to find that, though an Englishman, and a young one to boot, I had studied

the politics of France, and had had the intelligence to
see that the side which he, the barrister, had taken, was
the side of right, and that all other parties, cliques,
divisions or sub-divisions, were hopelessly and stupidly
in the wrong ! !

Then *he* began to talk—with passion and vehe-
mence—and I knew I was safe. After he had been
going a good while, I ventured to remind him that
the required forty-five minutes had expired, and that
I hoped I should be allowed to continue the conversation at some future time, but I feared that it was
now my duty to wait on my Chief. Then placing paper
and pens before him, I begged, in nervously forcible
French, and with comically forced gesture, if he conscientiously could do so, that he would make out the
certificate to satisfy the Civil Service Commissioners.
The dear old gentleman sat down and penned such a
certificate as must, I think, have given the official folk
at home an idea that I was a coming member of the
French Academy ! And not only did I thus pass
easily for my test, but I am convinced that all unwittingly I learned French in the very best way. I
laid the foundation of an ease and facility in French
which has since become of inestimable value to me.

Looking back to this happy time of youth and hard
work, it seems that there is but little about my first
six years of probation which it is necessary to record.
Yet, as showing a resolve to overcome adverse circumstances (for I hold it will be conceded that poverty
is a circumstance adverse to rapid success), I ought
perhaps to set forth how I managed all through these

early years to double my official income, and it sadly wanted the doubling.

I have elsewhere stated that a grateful country had agreed in return for my services in a foreign land to throw away on me the noble sum of £150 of the tax-payers' money, and that this lavish generosity was not to stop short even there, but an annual rise of £10 was to reward me as the best years of my life rolled by. The phrase may read a trifle sarcastic, but is really only a playful way of recalling the un-varnished truth: speaking quite seriously, I admit that her Majesty's Consular officers are a great deal better paid than the majority of their brother officials in the service of other European countries. Be this, however, as it may, the stubborn fact remains that £150 a year does not go a great way. One half the world does not know how the other half lives, but taking mankind as a rule, one may safely conclude that there exist always private calls on the purse—met bravely or grudgingly—which are rarely, if ever, spoken of, and for the most part unknown even to one's most intimate friends. I was no exception to this rule, and when I add that I had made unto myself a law never to owe any man a sixpence, and yearly to put something by—however insignificant the amount—it will be patent to the most ordinary comprehension that one of the first things for a man meaning to rise was to look about for legitimate ways of bringing extra grist to the mill. When I say *legitimate ways*, I mean legitimate to me, for being in her Majesty's service my field was limited. Many things open to others were closed to me. However, fortune favours the determined, and I soon became initiated into the mysteries of "copying records."

The Court to which I was attached was the *Chief* British Consular Court in Egypt, but if suitors were dissatisfied with the judgments delivered, they could appeal to the *Supreme* Consular Court held at Constantinople. Now for purposes of the appeal a "Record" of the case was necessary, and this Record consisted of the documents in the case, and of the "Judge's notes." The said documents and notes could not be sent in the original, and so had to be copied. These copies had to be made by officials of the Court, and were paid for by the parties appealing, according to a fixed official scale. The lion's share of the fees went to the Court (and so into her Majesty's Treasury) for "certifying" the copies to be correct, and the remainder went into the pocket of the clerk who made the said copies. There was fairly keen competition between three of us as to who should get the most copying, but I soon out-distanced my friendly rivals, and throughout the time I was attached to the Court managed to secure the bulk of the extra work. The reason of my success was threefold : first, being accustomed to copying despatches I wrote very legibly in the clear hand that is called a " Foreign Office " hand ; secondly, I never disappointed a lawyer when I promised that he should have the Record to send by a certain mail, for, living on the spot, I could copy long after hours, stop when my servant announced my evening meal (I had almost written "dinner," but in those struggling days it was *not* dinner), and peg away again later, writing often, when pushed, half through the night ; thirdly, I was more familiar than my fellow-clerks with Mr. Cookson's handwriting, and this was a distinct advantage, as, however much I respect my excellent Chief, there is no disguising the fact that at that time his " fist " was no easy reading. Indeed, a story was current in those days—and it is needless to say I encouraged barristers practising in the Alexandria Court to believe in its truth—that Mr. Cookson had three handwritings ; the best decipherable by the outside public, the next best by himself, and the worst by Miéville alone. As a fact Mr. Cookson wrote a clearer hand than many, but there is no smoke without fire, and it's an ill wind blows nobody any good, and thus I came to profit by this exaggerated tale. But this brings me back to the second part of the Record, namely, the " Judge's notes." The practice in Consular Courts in the Levant was for the Judge to make most copious notes of the proceedings and of the evidence during every trial. When a Judge sat morning and afternoon, and when a trial lasted several days, the Judge's hand got tired, and naturally his handwriting became less and less legible. Now when I first copied a Record, I found myself obliged constantly to ask the Judge to help me to decipher his notes. This was annoying to him, and not all joy for me ; so it came about that when trials were on, I used to sit in the Court as much I could, especially towards the termination of each sitting (when the Judge's hand would be most tired, and his writing least legible), and thus having myself heard the evidence I could with comparative ease read the Judge's notes. It was naturally a great help, if, when copying the Record, I came across words that were somewhat illegible, to possess a general idea of the context, and to have heard at the time the words themselves from the witnesses. So a legend grew that I could read what the Judge himself could not decipher.

I have said that when " pushed" I used to write half through the night. The occasions were rare, the incentive—money. From time to time it so happened that if the Record could be sent off to Constantinople by a certain mail, the case would be heard many weeks, if not some months, earlier than it would be were the Record to go by the following mail. This was owing either to the impending absence on duty, or on leave, of the Appeal Judge, or to the approach of the Appeal Court's vacation. If the parties were in a hurry, the counsel engaged would come to me and offer an extra fee over and above the usual scale, to get the Record copied in time for a certain steamer. This meant that instead of daily devoting some three to five hours of my spare time (for in office hours I was fully occupied) to copying dry-as-dust legal agreements, affidavits, evidence, or what-not, I had to squeeze eight to twelve hours' extra work out of the twenty-four. Once or twice after promising a Record for a certain date, I found I had miscalculated the number of words to be copied ; and then the squeeze became a tight squeeze, but I never once disappointed counsel.

But copying is weary work for an active-minded man, and I was glad when more intelligent occupation came in my way.

My second source of additional revenue was in acting as " Clerk to a Commission." The High Court of Justice in England now and again issued edicts or orders (we are not concerned with the proper legal term) to have evidence in cases pending before it "taken on commission." A commissioner was appointed with the necessary powers ; the witnesses were duly summoned before him ; the parties appeared by their counsel ; and due and regular note was taken of the proceedings and evidence by the clerk appointed to the commission.

The commissioner (usually a local Judge—British, of course) received generally ten guineas for the first, and five guineas for each succeeding day ; and the clerk (who had none of the dignity, but a good deal of the work) five guineas the first, and two and a half guineas the following days. The clerk's work was onerous, and his post a responsible one, as, if the Record was not in order, the whole proceedings were quashed, time wasted, and the expense practically doubled. On the other hand, I readily admit that the remuneration was generous. I think that my good friend Judge (now Sir John) Scott first gave me, or obtained for me, the post of clerk to a commission.

Keenly desirous of doing myself credit and justifying his choice, I took some pains to make myself acquainted with the ins and outs of the pro-cedure by which the commission should be fulfilled, and I soon found that it was not all plain sailing, but that certain *formulæ* and technicalities had to be looked up and remembered. In the end I undoubtedly became an efficient clerk, as the following incident I may be forgiven for assuming fully bears out.

In the year 1878, or thereabouts, Judge Scott was appointed commissioner to take certain evidence. The barrister interested in the case came to me, and proposed that I should be the clerk to the commission. " But," added he, " I shall only pay you half the usual fees, as I think it is preposterous to pay a clerk five guineas the first day, and two and a half guineas a day afterwards."

" Then," replied I, " go and get your cheap clerk elsewhere," and even his forensic eloquence could not get me to alter my decision.

Well, the day fixed by the commissioner arrived in due course, the Court was constituted, and the new (and cheap) clerk introduced, but he knew not how to begin, or how to continue, and the first half-hour was passed most unprofitably. Then the commissioner lost patience, and said to counsel—

" This gentleman does not know his work ; why did you not engage Mr. Miéville, who has served on commissions before ? "

" I did ask him," answered the barrister, " but he declined to act."

" Well, go and ask him again ; you have already wasted our time, and now we are forced to adjourn."

Judge Scott was not a man to be denied, so off came the eminent counsel bewigged and begowned to see poor humble me. Careful as he was, not to tell me exactly what had happened, I made a pretty shrewd guess at the truth, when he said that I was to come at once to act as clerk and that he would give me the entire fees as usual. Then two devils entered into me, the spirit of vengeance and the demon of greed ; and I replied—

" No, Mr. ——, you cannot play fast and loose with me like that. You tried to get me to give my services for half fees, now you say you will give me the usual remuneration. Why ? Simply because in all probability your cheap clerk isn't worth his salt. I decline your offer, and what is more, I refuse to act as clerk to the commission unless you *double* the ordinary clerk's fees."

Furious wasn't the name for his emotions ; rage and language filled the air, but, disconsolate, he had to retire. I learned later that Judge and counsel had a private confab, and that the Judge chuckled and chortled when the learned counsel shamefacedly owned to the real truth. Ultimately the biter had to avow he was the bitten ; *my terms were accepted ;* and my reputation for standing no nonsense firmly established.

A third source of additional revenue—a source at the same time of much benefit to me in after years, by reason of the experience it gave me in diplomatic ways, methods, and usages—was that derived on several occasions from acting as secretary (in addition to continuing to carry on my ordinary Court work) to her Majesty's diplomatic agent in Egypt. In those days the British agency was always during the summer months located at Alexandria, in a delightful house, known, from the charming grounds in which it stood, as " The Garden."   It is gone now, and on the old site has arisen a great pile of buildings erected for a Jesuit College.   My first Chief was General (now Sir Edward) Stanton, who employed me to help him, as his own secretary was ill.   I was young—scarcely of age—and quite inexperienced, and my knowledge of French was not all it should have been, though I had given much time during the previous six months to mastering it—I needed practice, and I got it.   I soon learned the ways of the agency, and had a most interesting five months' work, amongst other matters being privy (ciphering and deciphering telegrams for the most part) to the negotiations which terminated in the purchase of the Khedive Ismaïl's Suez Canal shares by the British Government for four million pounds sterling.   When it is remembered that the said shares are to-day worth six or perhaps seven times the price for which they were purchased, it will be seen how great is the debt which the nation owes on this account alone to Benjamin Disraeli, Earl of Beaconsfield.   And this without taking into consideration the power, political and commercial, which the possession of the shares has given to England in respect of the great waterway on the direct route to India and the Far East.

That summer-time dwells in my memory, and one of the figures that stood out most clearly was the kindly personality of that charming gentleman, Cherif

Pasha, then, I think, Egypt's Prime Minister. He has gone to his long rest, but has left an able son to perpetuate the family, whose aim has been to render loyal service to Egypt and her rulers.

A year or two later another diplomate reigned at the agency, and he in his turn requested Judge Cookson, my official Chief, to allow me to temporarily act as secretary. Permission was at once generously accorded, but Mr. Cookson was, I think, somewhat surprised when I, instead of thanking him and expressing my readiness to again take on the agency work, asked him to inform me what the new agent was prepared to give me by way of remuneration. Now I must explain that at the same time General Stanton proposed to me to help him, I had never given money a thought, being only too glad to be initiated into the mysteries of the higher branch of the service, and when he ultimately sent me a small cheque in recognition of my work I felt fully rewarded, for had I not learned much and profited by the daily lessons and training I had received? But once thoroughly conversant with the agency work, I looked at the matter through quite a different pair of spectacles, and felt also that the labourer—particularly a skilled labourer—was worthy of his hire. Well, Mr. Cookson interviewed the new diplomate on my behalf, and the answer I received was that the pay would be at the same rate as that given me by General Stanton. In vain did I urge on Mr. Cookson that when I went to General Stanton I had everything to learn, but that now I knew all

the ropes and should be of real service to a new-
comer, and in vain did my Chief lay this view before
the diplomate. At last I said, "I will go to the
agency if you order me to do so, otherwise I won't
unless I get £25 a month, the secretary's full salary."

My good friend, Mr. Cookson, who always had my
true interests at heart, thought that this was going
too far ; however, I pointed out that the work of the
combined posts was pretty severe in the hot weather
(he knew only too well that this was true, for he often
acted as British diplomatic agent) ; that I was not
feeling over well ; that I was entitled to leave of
absence ; and that if I gave up my holiday to Europe
I expected to be well paid for the sacrifice.   The new
agent took the intelligence of my contumacy badly,
very badly ; but he was on the horns of a dilemma :
if he did not accept my offer I should leave for
England, and he knew that there was no one else
available who knew the work and who could be
trusted ; if he referred the matter home, the Foreign
Office would be sure to point out that an ample
allowance was made for a secretary, and further that
it could surely make no difference whether the allowance went to a permanent or to an acting official.
So Dignity yielded, and Impudence triumphed.
Needless to say, I took care to wear modestly the
laurels of victory ; and I must in fairness add that
my new master took his reverse like a man ; bore
me no grudge, but thereafter proved a firm friend
and staunch well-wisher.

Other opportunities of adding to my income

cropped up from time to time; once, for instance, I was asked to translate into French (for a small consideration, of course) the memorandum and articles of association of an English limited liability company doing its business in Egypt. Curiously enough I am now a shareholder in the concern, and a member of the London Board of Directors—*tempora mutantur*.

Then the representative of the British Postal authorities being at one time without an assistant, asked for me to replace him during his leave of absence. So it fell out that I was for some four months in charge of what was officially known as her Britannic Majesty's Packet Agency in Egypt—and for the next six months continued to work as assistant to the titular Packet Agent, Mr. Jabez Leach. The extra salary I drew was at the rate of £230 a year; the work was easy in a sense of only taking up a few hours on two (or sometimes three) days in each week, but required accuracy and strict attention to business while it lasted. It was however irksome, inasmuch as, often as not, the mails arrived at night; and bitterly cold it often was, standing in winter-time on the old Gabarri Quay, checking, by the aid of a lantern or "fanoos," eight hundred to a thousand sacks of mails as they were hurriedly borne past me from truck to lighter, and from lighter to train, on the stalwart shoulders of the dusky, good-natured native labourers. For the Packet or Post-Office agents were in those days practically responsible for the transit of the Overland Mails through Egypt, the agent at Alexandria taking delivery of the bags from the P. and O. steamer, and

seeing the mail safely into the train, while the agent
at Suez checked the bags as they came out of the train
and handed them on to the steamers for India, China,
and Australia.

But again, *tempora mutantur*, for all this has been
altered for some fifteen years now, the mails for the
Far East going at the present time with the vessel
through the Suez Canal, and not being landed in
Egypt at all.

I have, I think, thus indicated sufficiently how by
keeping my eyes open and by steady application, I
managed during my years of probation to make both
ends meet fairly easily, to keep out of debt, and each
year to put a small store away for a rainy day. I admit
that the store *was* small, very small ; but still, as I
hinted before, I had private calls on my purse, and
even if my nest-egg was but the size of a tom-tit's egg
the first year, it had grown by the sixth to the
grandeur of a barn-door fowl's.

The sinews of war had to be come by : I could not
beg ; to steal I was ashamed ; so I had to earn by
hard work a few extra bawbees. But I only did so
as a means to an end ; if I was to succeed I felt I
must be to some small extent independent, so as not
to be obliged to take the first billet offered to me
because I could not afford to refuse it, though possibly
aware that if I waited I might get something better.

And now I am off at a tangent, and shall relate two
or three episodes connected with the old Court.

As my memory goes back to these years I come
into touch with the word " murder," for I once sat

close under the dock in Court while the prisoner was sentenced to death. My feelings were far from pleasant. . . . Again, in later years, while chatting to a friend at the Club, the fact that man's lust for blood is only dormant in some of us, was brought home to me, for a young man, a stranger to me, rushed into the reading-room where we were sitting, and came straight up to us and cried excitedly— "Arrest me, arrest me, for I am a murderer, I have just killed a man up-stairs!" Unfortunately the young fellow's self-accusation proved only too true, and I had to keep him in custody—feeling somewhat perturbed and uncomfortable—while my friend went and telephoned for the police. Being alone with a murderer is not an agreeable sensation.

During the time I was employed in the Consular Court a most unpleasant thing happened to me. I was sitting one morning in my official room, which communicated with that of the Judge, when an old gentleman, not an Englishman, but what is called a British protected subject, was ushered in. He seemed in some distress, and entertained me with a long rigmarole about his troubles, winding up by an appeal to me to use my influence with his Honour the Judge to have the trial of his case put down at an early date, or something of that sort. I felt a little sorry for the old fellow, though I cannot now recall exactly why I sympathized with him, or what he wanted, and I assured him that I would gladly do what I could, but that the Judge was most certainly not likely to be induced by anything I might say to modify any order he might have made, or any conclusion at which he might have arrived. My answer seemed, however, to satisfy the old gentleman ; for, as he got up, he thanked me warmly, and, before I understood what he was doing, pressed into my hand *a roll of twenty-franc gold pieces.* For a second or two I failed to comprehend what he meant (for it must be remembered that I was new to the East); then the blood boiled in me, and I threw the packet of coins straight at his head, bounced into the adjoining room, and denounced to the Judge, as well as I could for rage which almost deprived me of the power of speech, the old would-be corrupter of my honesty. I believe he for many years bore the marks of his own napoleons on his visage. And the funny part of it all was, that he could never be made to understand the enormity of his crime. He had bribed all and sundry in the Levant from his youth up : why then should a young Englishman take such dire offence ? Doubtless I was too hasty, and later I felt sorry for him, and ashamed of myself for having used force ; but there are occasions when the provocation excuses even violence and loss of temper. He is dead now, and gone where there is no giving of bribes.

One further incident and the scene changes, and the time of probation is over.

Confined to my bed in my little room in the consular building (which had for so long been my home, and in which I had passed many happy hours, and much weary time also), with gentle genial old Mr. Calvert bearing me company, a knock came suddenly at the door. We both cried "Come in," and our Chief, Mr. Cookson, entered, evidently the bearer of good news. He did not beat about the bush, but said at once—

"Let me congratulate you, for you have been chosen to replace Mr. West as Acting Consul at Suez."

The phrase was unfortunate in that it was not quite clear for whom the congratulations were intended. It seemed naturally, however, to refer to Mr. Calvert, the Vice-Consul and senior officer, who had besides acted as Consul at Suez on a previous occasion.

So he thanked Mr. Cookson, and said how glad he was to be going, as he delighted in collecting Red Sea shells.

Mr. Cookson seemed confused, and stammered out—

"But, my dear Calvert, *you* are not to go, it is Miéville who has been chosen."

The situation was a little awkward ; but the kindly nature of the true gentleman did not let Mr. Calvert dwell on his own disappointment, and my two kind Chiefs quite overwhelmed me with congratulations. I felt very sorry for Mr. Calvert ; but I am sure it was all for the best, and he did not relish undertaking unaccustomed responsibilities, and, had he gone to Suez, arduous duties would have been thrust upon him. Before I left that place the dark clouds which foreshadowed the Arabi rebellion were massing on the political horizon.

When my good friends left me to myself, I was soon lost in a sea of speculation, in which one thought was uppermost: How soon should I be convalescent, and able to embark on the new quest which I hoped might end in my winning my spurs?

CHAPTER IV

CONSULAR CAREER—PLAY

" Some happy souls there are that wear their nature lightly ;
these rejoice the world by living, and receive from all men more
than what they give.   One handful of their buoyant chaff excels
our hoards of careful grain.   Justly : for one man's joyous
laugh augments earth's joys—is all men's gain.   Scorn not
the gift of gladness given to those bright souls.   It is from
Heaven."—OWEN MEREDITH.

IT must not be thought that during these years of
probation it was " All work and no play."   On the
contrary, I think that by reason of my work being
hard I enjoyed play as much, if not more, than most
men.   For instance, during these first six years I did
my full share of travelling.   After my second year,
I took a trip to Messina, Alexandretta, Beyrouth,
Baalbec, and Damascus.   The voyage (in a small and
not over-cleanly steamer) was scarcely agreeable, but
though the sea was rough, the captain of the vessel
struck but a poor bargain, for he "found" or victualled
the ship, and a passenger with my appetite could not
have left much margin for profit.   Ashore I was much
struck with the mystical Druzes of the Lebanon, and
the extraordinary rapidity with which they managed

to spread any news affecting their well-being to distant villages and strongholds. On the voyage back to Alexandria we had as passengers a band of Moslem pilgrims bound for Mecca ; and one evening at sunset I was sitting on deck absorbed in a book, when, suddenly raising my head, I found myself hemmed in by the pilgrims, who, with an old man (possibly a priest) kneeling in front of and leading them, had organized a service, and were praying, with faces turned to the Holy City, to Allah. " There is no god but God ; and Mohammed is His prophet." Involuntarily I bared my head ; I am aware that it was no more the right thing to do than it is to take off one's hat in a mosque or synagogue, but I firmly believe that instinctively the little congregation (poor and ill-educated as the majority of them were) realized that I had meant the action as one of respect for the religious exercise in which they were engaged, for thereafter throughout the voyage the poor fellows would now and again invite me—though in their eyes I was but a despised Nazarene—to share a pomegranate, or smoke a cigarette with them. And, as we smoked, the great lessons of toleration and consideration for others, especially for those of alien creeds, sank deep into my heart.

In the spring of my third year I spent my leave of absence in England.

In my fourth year I made a most interesting journey, in company with Mr. Cookson, to Joppa, Jerusalem, Bethlehem, Jericho, the Dead Sea, and Jordan. The trip caused some little excitement in Egypt at the time, for we left Port Said in a native fishing-boat, and instead of reaching Jaffa in ten or twelve hours as we expected, we encountered terrible weather, and were so long on the voyage that it was feared we were lost. The late Lord Vivian telegraphed repeatedly to Port Said and Jaffa for news of the missing smack, and we heard later that two other fishing-boats *did disappear during the same storm.*

Next year I again went home—going and returning by the long sea route. The return voyage was made memorable by the fact of the vessel on which I was a passenger—the s.s. *Thessalia*—rescuing another vessel, the s.s. *Yorkshire*, in mid-ocean. We observed the *Yorkshire's* rocket of distress on the evening of the 10th October, and stood by her till the next morning. Then, after many abortive efforts, we managed to pass a line to the *Yorkshire*, but hawser after hawser (twelve-inch ropes, and four-inch wire hawsers) snapped like thread; the heavy seas running making further attempts that day quite useless. The *Yorkshire* drifted some sixty miles from where we had first found her, but we stuck by her, and at noon on the 12th October, two new ten-inch Manilla hawsers were made fast to her, and without further mishap we towed the disabled steamer one hundred and sixty miles into the beautiful Spanish port of Ferrol. The *Yorkshire* had broken her main shaft, and had been drifting about in the Atlantic *for more than a month* before we had fallen in with her.

So much for holiday travels; there were other pleasures and pastimes in Egypt. Race-meetings there were from time to time, tennis-parties almost every day, dinners and dances galore, for Alexandria and its European suburb Ramleh are hard to beat for open-handed and open-hearted hospitality. I was especially fortunate in finding on my first arrival some very kind friends—connections by marriage—in the members of a clever and entertaining Swiss family called Simond. These genial, hearty people welcomed me with open arms, and introduced me to all the leading families of the Greek, Italian, and French colonies. In this I was especially fortunate; for this early foregathering with peoples of all nationalities not only helped me, in time, to become something of a polyglot, but made it possible later on for some wag to describe me as " English by birth, Swiss by extraction, Egyptian by adoption, and cosmopolitan by nature."

There was chess, and backgammon, and billiards. Then on the long hot tiring summer afternoons, when any movement seemed a fatigue, I would spend hours sailing—in a friend's cutter, or in the fast native craft —about the spacious harbour and down past the Quarries of Mex to Marabout.

Our cricket was played on a sandy, stony ground, destitute of any vestige of turf or grass, and the pitch itself was but beaten down and rolled, and covered, when in use, with a strip of cocoa-nut matting. Good fielding was very difficult, as stray stones would often turn off a ball and cause the fielder to misjudge it; but the innate love of cricket, so strongly implanted in the average Englishman's breast, overcame all difficulties, and many hundreds of good matches did I witness on the old club ground. Local and club matches excited much interest—Alexandria *v.* Ramleh, Married *v.* Single, Smokers *v.* Non-smokers, and so on.

And now, discreetly as a lady's postscript to this chapter, shall I venture to tell the plain truth, and say that in my leisure hours I derived some of my greatest pleasure from ladies' society ?—God bless 'em—and was in fact inclined to have a flirtation wherever a "petticoat" would tolerate me ; for flirting is impossible "all by one's lone," or, as the Bishop replied to sweet seventeen, when she asked his lordship to explain a *faux pas*—"Well, my dear young lady, it is never a *pas seul.*" I will not recount how many times a year I used to propose, nor how broken-hearted I was after every fresh refusal ; the gentle reader must be content with one love story. Of course I was always in love, but I once thought I had really found "the only girl I ever *really* adored" (excluding all former "only ones"). Invitations had been issued for a donkey-picnic by moonlight at the Palm-grove, a few miles beyond Ramleh, and the day before the great event I was walking with *the* angelic being, and after the usual sweet nothings I said to her—

"Dearest, I *know* I shall propose to you at the picnic to-morrow night, and if I do, for goodness' sake refuse me, for, as you are well aware, *I have nothing a year, and no boots !*"

She smiled blandly at the low state of my exchequer, begged me *not* to make a fool of myself at the picnic, but promised that if I did she would spurn my advances—as requested. The eventful evening arrived ; the guests assembled at our hospitable hostess's house (or joined the cavalcade at Bulkeley station) ; donkeys were fought for and mounted ; and the party enjoyed a fizzing fine ride. I had secured a capital " moke," and had got its stable-companion for my " fair one "—for if you want to be near a certain young lady during a donkey-ride (Colonial papers, please copy), the best and safest plan is to get two donkeys that are used to keeping together.

We reached the Palm-grove all in good time, and soon paired off. A few minutes later I found myself lying at the feet of my angel under a small group of palm-trees. The undulating desert bathed in moon-light, the feathery palms, the very moonlight itself, and, above all, the near proximity of a young and beautiful maiden, soon made me lose my head, and as I plucked the grass and sprinkled my angel's dainty little boots therewith, I was so overcome by a paroxysm of spooniness that prudence went to the winds, and I proposed in due form, and with all the warmth and ardour I could command. But my angel kept cool.

"What about 'Nothing a year, and no boots'?" she said.

" Don't remind me of that foolishness," said I ; "you know I did not mean it, and now surely you can see I am in frantic earnest?" But my angel was not to be moved ; in vain did I implore her to think it over, and answer me on the morrow; in vain did I shower upon her the most endearing epithets; in vain did I beg her not to wreck my hopes, my future, my life.

I was heartbroken and disconsolate for close on a week. But I could never tolerate suicide, so did not attempt it.

Within a year my angel was married, and I am bound to confess I enjoyed myself amazingly at the wedding, though I was *not* cast for the leading part of bridegroom. And within the same twelvemonth I, too, put away foolish things, and had proposed in all seriousness; and what is more, I was accepted. I did not this time admit my impecuniosity, and the lady evidently had no glimmering of what a handful I should prove to be. Still I *was* accepted, and the rash lady is, I am proud and happy to relate, my present charming wife.

CHAPTER V

THAT I, a young clerk, should, at the age of twenty-six, have been selected by Lord Granville, at the instance of Sir Edward Malet, the Queen's representative in Egypt, to take charge of her Majesty's Consulate at Suez, was a gratifying evidence that I was becoming not only known to those in authority, but regarded favourably by them. To the uninitiated the appointment may appear not so momentous; but to me it was all-important, and that for two reasons. I knew only too well how difficult it was for an understrapper to get full credit for his work: my immediate superiors were always most kind in bringing my name forward officially; and twice Mr. Cookson most handsomely acknowledged my services. As early as the 25th February, 1876, he had mentioned me in despatches to the late Lord Derby, then her Majesty's Principal Secretary of State for Foreign Affairs.

Yet, in the very nature of things, a secretary cannot receive mention or recognition except in a very general way. This was the chief reason why I considered the Suez appointment so important, because there I should be master, and the credit (or discredit) for any and everything done during my term of office must of necessity be placed to my account. Hundreds of good men in public offices all over the world are often the real authors of capital despatches, or of successful policies or plans of action, yet, because they are not the head, or in independent positions, their names never appear ; but the despatch is signed by, or the policy attributed to, the head. It may be urged that a just Chief is sure to make some mention of the part played by the veritable author. As often as not, however, the Chief fails to remember who did originally have the happy thought ; or even if he honestly tries to render a just account, the Secretary of State, or other bigwig, in ninety-nine cases out of a hundred, thinks little of it except to reflect on what a good fellow the Chief is, to try and share his triumphs with his subordinate.

Reason number two for my rejoicing was of a more private nature : I had become engaged to be married. On the 10th January, 1881, I had asked a most charming lady to become my wife, and ten days later my engagement to Miss Theodora Johanna Taylor, grand-daughter of Janet Taylor, the eminent authoress of so many standard works on navigation, had been announced. It was thus a stroke of luck getting a step so soon after the eventful matrimonial plunge, and the knowledge that I was working for another did not lessen my resolve to do my best in my new post.

Suez, when I took over charge of the British Consulate, was a dead-and-alive sort of town, yet some of the old residents, proudly remembering its former glories, cherished the idea that, notwithstanding its decayed state, it was still not far removed from being the hub of the universe. In the good old days of the Overland Route, Suez had been the headquarters of the transit trade between the East and West. The Peninsular and Oriental Steam Navigation Company then maintained there a large depôt called Ansari, and curious stories of little fortunes having been made in connection with the handling of the vast stores of provisions, material, and so on, which the Company kept there, now and again found voice even in my time, some dozen to a score of years after the events happened. Then came the opening of the Maritime Canal, and the rapid decline in the bustle and prosperity of Suez. Even the town itself has been practically left stranded high and dry on the shores of its once busy creek, for the Canal only skirts Suez, and its waters mingle with those of the Red Sea at a point nearly three miles from the old town. Gradually it sank into a mere port of call, then down the scale one step further into a "jump-off place," and to-day what little business is transacted, is no longer carried on at Suez, but is done at Terreplein, a thriving little colony composed of Canal officials, steamship agents, and quarantine magnates, which is situated on a spit of reclaimed land at the mouth of the Canal.

I entered on my consular duties at Suez early in

May 1881, and soon my hands were very full trying to arrange certain petty local differences which existed among the members of the British colony. One may venture now to characterize the local differences as "petty"; but had I so designated them at the time, I should most certainly have brought the Consulate about my ears. They were burning questions—questions of more importance to the English at Suez than all the serious matters of political import which may at that date have been agitating Europe. And the Burial-ground Key controversy was the most momentous of all.

In reality it was trivial and childish in the extreme, but it cost me a world of trouble. The dispute related to the guardianship of the keys of the British burial-ground. The cemetery was out in the desert a mile or two from the town, and was walled in with a view to preserving the graves from desecration by evil-minded anti-Christians. It thus became necessary for a key to be kept at some convenient place in the town, where residents desirous of visiting the tombs of their dead relations or friends might obtain it before setting out. For ten years the place chosen had very properly been the British Consulate; but some six months before my arrival at Suez, the key had, for some occult reason, been withdrawn, and placed in charge of one of the burial-ground trustees, residing at some distance from Suez proper. This caused endless trouble and loss of time : hence the controversy.

It is difficult to convey any adequate idea of the

bitterness of the conflict between the party who wanted the key deposited once more at the Consulate, and the friends of the trustee, who had obtained some little importance (local and temporary) through having become the key's custodian. This gentleman's partisans were naturally loth to witness the dimming of his glory. I managed at last to bring about an understanding by effecting a compromise. Unfortunately the war had raged so fiercely that rumours thereof had reached the outside world, and the leading English newspaper in Egypt, *The Egyptian Gazette*, mentioned the matter, and ended its account by the following paragraph—

"Though there may be persons who consider H.M.'s Consul as the proper custodian of the key, still let us hope that they will be satisfied with the concession made, and not re-open a question which has already caused enough unpleasantness. We cannot conclude our notice without congratulating Mr. Miéville on bringing about so satisfactory a result."

But to let the matter rest at the bidding of a local journal was not what the trustee and his party desired. So a letter was written setting forth that congratulations should not be addressed to me, as the *question had been settled before my arrival.* This letter, which was signed "Resident Trustee," the editor of *The Egyptian Gazette* refused to publish, so the writer printed and circulated it at his own expense. This proceeding "drew" the editor, who, with his best quill pen, slew the trustee by pointing out that I took

charge of the Consulate on the 11th of May, and that
the meeting at which the arrangement of the difficulty
was effected was held just nine days later. This
incident, "all about nothing at all," will make it
clear that in a small town like Suez, where the work
is not really heavy, a Consul's lot is nevertheless not
always cast in a bed of roses.

From burial-ground to church is not a very far
cry, so I will here relate how it happened that I acted
as parson during my nine months' residence at Suez.
When I first arrived I was informed that there was
no church, and no clergyman, but that her Majesty's
Consul read Service on Sundays in a room in the
principal hotel set apart for that purpose. Now
Consul West, for whom I was acting, was a man well
over fifty years of age, of a splendid presence, and
doubtless filled the *rôle* of chaplain to perfection. I
had my doubts as to being able to do likewise, so I
explained to a few of the old residents that considering my youth, and that I was only an *Acting*
Consul, the colony might deem it more fitting for one
of themselves to read the Service. This view appeared
to give much satisfaction, and my proposal was at
once accepted. So seemingly I had killed two birds
with one stone, for I had freed myself from Sunday
"duty," and at the same time gained a reputation for
a conciliatory and proper feeling towards my elders.
But when the old residents welcomed my self-efface-
ment, they had not present to their minds the difficulty
and delicacy of choosing *which of themselves* should
fill the vacant place. As far as I could glean—and

before long I heard all the different stories—they found it impossible to agree among themselves. We will take it that the leading old residents numbered half-a-dozen; we may further presume that two, Mr. Wahed and Mr. Etneen, were pre-eminently fitted for the position of acting parson; but of course Messrs. Tellata, Arbaa, Hamsa, and Sette could not be expected to recognize the superiority of either Mr. Wahed or Mr. Etneen. Then Mr. Tellata was objected to because he was a Plymouth Brother, Mr. Arbaa because he was deaf, while Mr. Hamsa opined that he had a right to be chosen, having on a previous occasion taken the Service in the Consul's absence. Poor Mr. Sette, a peace-loving soul, mildly ventured to suggest that as no objections had been urged against him, he would, if requested, undertake the duties himself. But this suggestion was too much for the other five; Sette, indeed, not to be thought of! So Mr. Sette was told that he lived too far off. Then a new series of proposals was brought forward. Wahed suggested that the senior among them should be elected, but was promptly and sarcastically informed that age was surely not in itself a sufficient qualification. Etneen voted for the oldest resident, but the five *next oldest* inhabitants saw that this plan would put them all out of court, and so pooh-poohed it. The compromise of all six taking the Sunday duty in turn met with scant favour, as it would include the Plymouth Brother, and the deaf Mr. Arbaa, so in the end it was unanimously decided that I had no business to shirk what

was, after all, at least by usage, part of my duties as
Consul. Thus it happened that on the first Sunday
morning after my arrival I received an urgent request
to conduct Service. Fearing a crisis in the church,
needless to say I did not comment on, or appear to
notice, the sudden change of front ; and during my
stay at Suez I did my utmost to act my part with all
due reverence.

But other duties fell to my lot in connection with
Church matters, and in two instances I gave such dire
offence to a small—a very small—minority of the
members of the British colony (of my *nationals* as
the technical phrase has it in diplomatic parlance),
that I was reported to the late Bishop Gobat, Bishop
in Jerusalem ! So it came about that there was even
heresy and sedition in my bed of roses.

Both the cases for which I was reported had
reference to my reading the Burial Service over the
bodies of persons not entitled to the Office for the
Dead.

I find the first incident in a private letter I wrote
at the time—

"*Suez, 7th of August*, 1881.—I had a very trying
day yesterday, but I hope I acted rightly. In the
early morning (7 a.m.) a gentleman came to me and
told me of the death of his first-born child, a babe of
three days old. He was greatly distressed, as his
wife was still dangerously ill, so I said that to save
him trouble I would myself see about the little grave
and the funeral. Then he spoke to me about reading
Service over the body ; he was aware, he said, that

the Prayer-book enjoined Ministers not to do so in cases where persons die unbaptized, but he added that it would be a great comfort to himself and his sick (possibly dying) wife if I would do so notwithstanding the prohibition. The rubric lays down the law clearly enough, leaving no room for doubt, yet I was undecided. After all I was not a cleric, but a layman; and it struck me that in a delicate and painful personal question of this sort it would be well to endeavour to *put myself in his place*. After so doing, I came to the conclusion that considering the parents had had *no chance* of calling in a clergyman to baptize the child when they knew it was dying, I should be justified in consenting to read, so I sent the grief-stricken man away the bearer of a comforting message that may, I trust, have somewhat softened the trial of the bereaved young mother.

"Then came protests from the sticklers and the goody-goody; but I had given my promise, and nothing would induce me to go back on my word, not even the threat of reporting my irregular conduct to the Bishop.

"So at half-past five the same evening (you know how quickly interments have to take place in this hot climate), the simple *cortège* wended its way on foot across the desert. The road lay across the desolate plain for about a mile and a half; on our left rose the lonely Attaka mountains, and as we trudged westward the setting sun mercilessly shot towards us over the hot sand his still powerful rays.

*   *   *   *   *   *   *

*"' We brought nothing into this world, and it is certain
we can carry nothing out. The Lord gave, and the
Lord hath taken away; blessed be the Name of the
Lord.'*

*"' Man that is born of a woman hath but a short time
to live, and is full of misery. He cometh up, and is cut
down, like a flower; he fleeth as it were a shadow, and
never continueth in one stay.'*

* * * * * * *

"The little procession arrived at the cemetery at
six o'clock, and I read such portions of the Service
as seemed to me most fitting. I managed to read
clearly, and we committed the body of the poor
child to the ground, 'earth to earth, ashes to ashes,
dust to dust; in sure and certain hope of the
Resurrection to eternal life.'"

Then came the complaint. The sticklers' protest
was duly sent; but the Bishop, and likewise the
Foreign Office, to whom the matter was also referred,
refrained from taking any notice of an irregularity
which, on the face of it, could only have been prompted
by feelings of humanity.

The second case which provoked wrath, concerned
not the burial of an unbaptized and innocent child,
but the burial of an excommunicate.

Late one evening a message was brought to me
that I was needed at a dying person's bedside. I
obeyed the summons without loss of time, and found
a poor woman, who had for some time led at Suez a
notoriously evil life. She was anxious about two

things. First, she wanted me to make her will
(which I at once did); and secondly, she desired the
assurance that she should at her death receive decent
and Christian burial. Unhesitatingly I undertook
that all should be done as she wished, and after a
few words of comfort and sympathy I returned to the
Consulate. Now it will readily be understood that
when I promised to give the poor woman Christian
burial, I certainly gave no thought to rubrics or
canonical law: I saw before me but a fellow-creature
whose last hour had come, and who for her comfort
needed an assurance which I could give. But
according to "one of the elect," I should not have
taken into account suffering humanity; but because
the dying woman belonged to the frail sisterhood, I
should, on the contrary, have remembered the letter of
the law and refused consolation. And this Christian
gentleman, when he heard the poor Magdalen had
breathed her last, came to me (in all sincerity and
truth, I am willing to believe), and pointed out that I
had no business to read over the poor creature the
Church's Order for the Burial of the Dead. I proceeded to explain the circumstances, but the dissentient would not be satisfied, and again was I
threatened with the Bishop. Consuls, however, are
but human after all, and the interview, conducted so
far by me with patience, grew somewhat stormy, and
I finally routed my gentleman, tackling him on what
he evidently considered his own special ground, and
quoting Scripture at him: "Well," said I, "'let him
that is without sin cast the first stone at her;' I am

not sinless, so I shall do unto the woman as I would be done by."

Solemnly and reverently did we that afternoon lay our sister to rest, and many there were (some who attended from curiosity, others from nobler, kindlier motives) who, standing round the grave, heard the words of St. Paul—

"*As is the earthy, such are they that are earthy: and as is the heavenly, such are they also that are heavenly. The dead shall be raised incorruptible, and we shall be changed. For this corruptible must put on incorruption, and this mortal must put on immortality: then shall be brought to pass the saying that is written, Death is swallowed up in victory.*"

Many other difficulties occurred during my stay at Suez, and I had lots of unpleasant duties to perform. My magisterial duties especially were not at all to my taste, and I hated having to sentence sailors to terms of imprisonment: Providence had given me too tender a heart for that sort of work. Then, as will be seen from the following two extracts from private letters written by me during the summer of 1881, I had other interests to attend to, besides those of British shipping and the British colony.

In Letter No. 1, I find—

"I have taken over charge of the Vice-Consulate of his Majesty the King of the Netherlands. I have done so (with the consent of our Government) to oblige a friend who is going on leave. It is not an important post, my chief work in connection with it being with reference to Javanese and other Dutch pilgrims, who come up to Suez for trans-shipment to Jeddah on their way to holy Mecca. There are, however, sometimes as many as four thousand Dutch (Javanese) pilgrims in a season."

In another letter, dated October 28, 1881, I find—

"I have mentioned having had some trouble with my Dutch work lately; it has been in connection with the deplorable disaster which on the 5th instant befel a vessel called the *Koning der Nederlanden*, bound homewards from Batavia. Near the Chagos Archipelago (Indian Ocean) she sank, and 213 persons, consisting of passengers, soldiers, and crew, were packed into seven boats and left to the mercy of the waters. One was picked up by an English ship in Lat. 5° 25′ S. and Long. 67° 18′ E., and brought on here. Thirty-eight souls were saved in her, including three ladies and one baby four months old. The fate of the other 175 persons is not yet known."

I ultimately learned the following details of the disaster :—On the evening of October 4, the engines of the *Koning der Nederlanden* suddenly began to race, and the engineer declared the propeller-shaft to be broken. All attempts, however, to ascertain the exact nature and extent of the damage failed owing to the roughness of the sea, but within an hour water began to stream from the store-room and powder-magazine into the after-hold, and so increased in volume that, a little later, the lower fires were submerged. Early next morning it was resolved to leave the vessel, and all the boats were provisioned, the smaller ones for three weeks, the larger for four weeks.

At 7.30 a.m., on October 5, the last boat left the ship in charge of the captain, and at noon the vessel sank. Four out of the seven boats were picked up, and 124 souls saved. I fear nothing was ever heard respecting the fate of those in the remaining three boats.

But though settling local differences at Suez, and doing my magisterial work to the satisfaction of my official Chiefs helped in a way to bring me to the front, and make me known to them, yet it was not sufficient to raise me from the ruck or to insure my promotion in the service. However, everything comes to him who knows how to wait, and before the end of the, to me, eventful year I was to have my chance; but that is another story—a story which marks such an important turning-point in my life that I think it must go into a fresh chapter.

CHAPTER VI

MY FIRST OPPORTUNITY

THE dominant features in the political outlook on my arrival in Egypt in the year 1874, were corruption, oppression, and incipient bankruptcy, and the figure and personality of the Khedive Ismaïl then stood out head and shoulders above all others.

The seven succeeding years had, however, seen startling changes.

Ismaïl had gone a step too far in flouting Europe, and had in June 1879 been forced by Turkey, at the instance of Great Britain and France, to abdicate. I took leave of him on board his magnificent yacht *Mahroussa* in the harbour of Alexandria on the eve of his going into exile, and the feeling uppermost in my mind was one of profound pity; for, with all his faults, he was an accomplished gentleman, possessed of a wonderful intelligence akin to genius, and commanding regard and sympathy.

Ismaïl's eldest son, the kindly Mehemet Tewfik, succeeded to the Khedivial throne: Great Britain and France had stepped into the financial breach, and through the medium of an inadequate institution, known as the Dual Control, were endeavouring to remedy the crying evils which had sprung up and multiplied exceedingly during Ismaïl's long reign. The Dual Control initiated many excellent reforms, and strove hard to uproot the abuses which were rampant in every Government administration. But the Dual Control had no effective power at its back, and in any case time would have been required before the full effect of the reformer's hand could have been realized in the country districts.

So it came about that discontent continued, and a quasi-National movement grew up, whose party-cry was "Egypt for the Egyptians." And the threatening figure that now began to loom on the political horizon was that of " Ahmed Arabi, the Egyptian."

Arabi was a tall, stolid man, heavy-looking both in face and figure, yet pleasant and courteous withal. Many said he was a mere puppet in the hands of wire-pullers and of Toulba, his coadjutor and *fidus Achates*, but I incline to think that while Toulba's intelligence was the quicker, Arabi's will and purpose were the more tenacious.

This Colonel Arabi Bey, the peasant-soldier, had throughout the year 1881 been posing as representative of the Egyptian army, and as its champion for the redress of grievances, and had come to be recognized by most of his brother officers as a leader. He had, on the 9th of September, surrounded the Khedive's Palace with some three thousand revolted soldiers, and had demanded the dismissal of the Ministry (who, he alleged, had sold Egypt to the

English); the creation of a representative chamber; and the raising of the strength of the army to eighteen thousand. And it was only after the Khedive had given his consent to the dismissal of the Cabinet that the troops were drawn off to their respective barracks.

It will thus be seen that the native soldiery were ripe for anything; that in their eyes Arabi Bey was stronger than either the Khedive or his Ministers, and even the little garrison at Suez had become affected.

I do not think I shall be considered indiscreet either by the Foreign Office or by my old Chief, Sir Edward Malet, if I venture to let the despatches I then addressed to him as to the disturbance at Suez tell their own tale. In the first place, they were written a good eighteen years ago, and certainly contain nothing of a confidential nature. The official language does not, it is true, by any means make the most of the incident, yet it was strong enough, as I afterwards heard, to let first Sir E. Malet, then Lord Tenterden, and finally Lord Granville see that as Acting Consul, notwithstanding my youth, I could in an emergency keep a cool head, have the courage of my opinions, and not scruple to act up to them without waiting for instructions from head-quarters. I held, and still hold, very strong (some may think revolutionary) views on the question of instructions. In nine cases out of ten, to ask for instructions is tantamount to shirking responsibility; of course I mean in cases where the senior officer has to judge solely from information supplied by the very junior who asks for advice. Surely a man, who is a man and not a ninny, should, being on the spot and in a position to know the whole ins and outs of the problem to be solved, be able to form as sound an opinion as another (though admittedly a cleverer man), who has only a written and possibly incomplete account of the matter to guide him in coming to a conclusion. This by the way,—now for the narrative as contained in the following despatches addressed by me to Consul-General Malet.

At Suez on the 17th December, 1881, I wrote—

"I have the honour to report that I was informed in the course of this morning that a disturbance had taken place at the Governor's Palace.

"I have since learnt that it occurred under the following circumstances—

"A soldier attached to a quarantine station on the Maritime Canal was early this morning found dead near the encampment to which he belonged, a distance of some five miles from Suez. The body was discovered by a subordinate officer in charge of the station, an Italian subject, who immediately went and reported the circumstance to the Governor, adding that the body bore marks which led him to believe that the deceased had been shot. The Deputy-Governor, Rachid Bey, who is also Prefect of Police, at once told off two soldiers to accompany the officer, that he might point out to them where the body was; but the soldiers thereupon strongly demurred, saying that it was commonly known that the Italian officer owed money to the deceased, and that he was probably himself the murderer. They then insulted Rachid Bey, telling him that he was not fit to be Deputy-Governor if he allowed the officer a chance of escape by sending him to point out the whereabouts of the body—and one of the soldiers went so far as to strike Rachid Bey. The soldiery also threatened that they would not allow the body to be brought to the hospital or buried, but that it should be taken to their Effendina, Arabi Bey.

"Ultimately Rachid Bey, the Deputy-Governor, accompanied by a doctor and by the necessary clerks, proceeded to the spot indicated by the Italian, the said officer being himself kept under restraint at the Mohafissah (Governor's official residence). Many of the soldiers of the town followed, in order, it is presumed, to be present at the inquiry.

"In order to make you clearly comprehend the situation, I would here remark that the soldiery were predisposed to become excited by such an incident, as a few days ago an Arab officer of the Egyptian despatch vessel *Sakka* was found dead (presumably murdered) near the Docks, and the supposed assassin is still at large.

"At one o'clock my Italian colleague called on me and informed me, that on hearing of the detention of the officer he had sent his Consular Dragoman to the Mohafissah to seek an explanation, and that his Dragoman had been refused admittance by the guard on duty. In answer to a question which I put to him, he said that he had not himself been to the

Governor, as he feared that by so doing he might unduly excite the soldiers, who would think he had come to deliver the accused.

"At 4 p.m. the corpse arrived at the Gouvernorat, and after a discussion of an hour and a half's duration, the comrades of the deceased were persuaded to allow of the body being transported to the hospital, from whence it was taken to the cemetery and quietly interred.

"With the exception of a few isolated cases of mild assault, committed on curious persons who hovered round the Governor's Palace, the town throughout the day has been perfectly quiet, though towards evening greatly exaggerated rumours have been mischievously circulated.

"11.40 p.m.—At 10.25 p.m. I received your telegram asking whether it was true that a military riot had to-day taken place in Suez, to which I at once answered that the soldiers had shown insubordination towards the Governor, but that the town was now perfectly tranquil, which reply I have now the honour to confirm.

"I have reason to believe that some greatly exaggerated accounts of to-day's incident have been, and may be, forwarded to Cairo prompted by the, in my humble opinion, totally false fear that Christians and Europeans generally were threatened and in personal danger.

"In conclusion, I feel it my duty to inform you, sir, that I do not consider undue importance should attach to the mention of Arabi Bey's name by the soldiers, or to the fact that Rachid Bey was assaulted. The first was invoked when the men were suffering from excitement on hearing of the death of their comrade, and the latter was committed by a soldier whom a few days previously it had been Rachid Bey's duty to severely censure.

"I may add that the Italian officer is no longer under restraint at the Mohafissah, but has been removed to the Governor's private house until the feeling against him shall have subsided."

Next day I wrote—"I should have at once telegraphed to you on hearing of the disturbance at the Governor's, had I not felt confident that the soldiers would act reasonably after the first excitement at hearing of the second murder had somewhat abated. Also I was deterred by the knowledge that the soldiers were watching the telegraph-office, and would only be encouraged if undue importance had been given to their insubordination by long accounts of their doings going at once to Cairo. I honestly believe that my having made light of the matter helped in a measure the bringing about of a satisfactory conclusion.

"The consular body here, which is mostly composed of traders and Syrians, were only too ready to make matters worse by exaggerating the real importance of what had happened, and I did what I could quietly to allay the fear that the demonstration would result in an attack on the Europeans.

"Had the Greeks and the other scum congregated at the Mohafissah when the body was brought in, it would have encouraged the soldiers to persist in their early (morning's) idea of taking the body to-day (Sunday) to the Effendina or to Arabi Bey. Happily this was averted. I trust most sincerely that you will not think I have acted wrongly in refraining from at once telegraphing to you. It could have done no good, and it might have done harm, for the populace felt reassured and remained tranquil when they heard that the English Consul said all would be well if they kept quiet."

Later in the day I said—"I have the honour to acknowledge the receipt of your telegram, dated Cairo 3.30 p.m., informing me that the Italian Vice-Consul here had telegraphed to Cairo saying he had heard that the soldiers had threatened the Governor that unless Arabi Bey arrived to-night at Suez, and the Italian officer suspected of murder was executed, they would massacre the Europeans, and asking if I thought there was any cause for anxiety.

"At 8.10 p.m. I despatched my reply to the effect that having seen the Governor, he had assured me that he apprehended no disturbance, and that personally I was convinced there was no cause for alarm. I added that the commissioners who had been appointed to inquire into the matter had just arrived. This message I have now the honour to confirm, and in continuation of my despatch of yesterday to report the following additional particulars.

"No disturbance of any kind occurred last night. During the evening of yesterday, the Governor, Raef Pasha, sent Rachid Bey to inform the Italian Vice-

Consul that he should be happy to receive him. Mr. Vice-Consul Vitto at once waited on the Governor, and his Excellency pointed out that until after the inquiry into the death of the soldier, it might be better if he would allow the Italian officer to remain as a guest in his Excellency's house, as, being an important witness, he would in any case be required to attend the inquiry, and until the feeling entertained against him by the soldiers had subsided, it would be more prudent for him to remain with his Excellency than at the Italian Vice-Consulate or elsewhere.

"This afternoon I called on the Governor at his private residence, and he told me he had received a telegram from Cherif Pasha, announcing that a commission had been appointed to inquire into the matter of the soldier's death, and urging on the deceased's comrades in arms to remain quiet, and justice would be done. I mentioned that the soldiers in the town were saying that Arabi Bey was coming to Suez, and his Excellency admitted that this idea did exist, and explained it by saying that on hearing that a commission had been appointed, some of the soldiers at once came to the conclusion that Arabi Bey was sure to be one of the commissioners. His Excellency, in speaking of the Italian officer, told me that the inquiry would doubtless establish his innocence, as three soldiers of the same encampment as the deceased had declared that the officer was with them in the tent during the whole of the night on which the supposed murder took place.

Raef Pasha then repeated what he had said to Mr. Vitto, and concluded by assuring me emphatically that the soldiers under his command were now quiet and obedient, and that he apprehended no recurrence of insubordinate acts when it became known that Arabi Bey was not on the commission.

"On the arrival of the train several soldiers congregated on the station platform, which immediately adjoins the Governor's Palace, but no demonstration was made.

"I must beg you, sir, to allow me to add that whether or no the ultimate decision of the commission be deemed satisfactory by the soldiers, it is my conviction that no danger to Europeans as a body is to be apprehended."

On the 19th of December I wrote—"With reference to the subject of my despatches of the 17th and 18th instant, I have the honour to inform you that I had this morning a long interview with my Italian colleague. He recounted to me his version of the circumstances from the commencement, and he told me that he had been instructed by his Consul-General, Mr. de Martino, to take part in the proposed inquiry, but that he had up to that time (10.30 a.m.) received no communication on the subject from the Governor. Mr. Vitto further mentioned that he had yesterday sent a telegram to Mr. de Martino to the effect that he had been informed by the French Vice-Consul of an intended massacre of Europeans should Arabi Bey not arrive by that day's train, but he allowed that our French colleague had only heard the rumour from his Cavass.

"The French Consul at Port Said, a Mr. Gilbert, has arrived here on a mission to inquire into the truth of his Suez colleague's impression that the safety of Europeans is in danger. I called on the French Vice-Consul this afternoon, and while with him met Mr. Gilbert and Mr. Vitto.

"Mr. Gilbert in the course of conversation stated that in his opinion the situation was not of such gravity as he had imagined from what he had heard at Port Said, but that he feared for the public safety, and that he should telegraph to the French Consul-General giving as his opinion that the garrison of Suez should be at once changed. He said that Mr. Vitto was likewise of his opinion, and he invited me to telegraph to you in the same sense.

"In studiously courteous terms I, in reply, pointed out that I could not share his opinion as to there being danger of violence being shown to the Europeans of our town, and that although not unwilling to report to you a *résumé* of our conversation, I could not for the moment pledge myself to telegraph to you in the sense indicated. For, I urged, there was (as I felt sure that all must admit) no immediate danger, and I added, that it would be scarcely just to the soldiers to remove them for an act of insubordination which, however grave in the eyes of Europeans, could not be viewed in this country in the same light as in the case of a similar breach of discipline in a highly civilized army. I qualified this remark by admitting

that I saw no objection to the garrison being changed
later on, but that I felt to demand their immediate
removal would be at least premature when taking
into consideration the whole circumstances; and I
expressed a hope that my colleagues would wait
until after the inquiry before forwarding such a request to the respective diplomatic representatives of
their Governments

"I could but feel that it was a matter of some
delicacy to ascertain the ground or sources of information which had led Mr. Gilbert to come to the conclusion that the public safety was in danger; but he
allowed that this conclusion was quite a matter of
opinion, and I therefore did not hesitate to avow
that I had of course reported the facts fully to you,
and that you, sir, would doubtless appreciate the situation and recommend to the Ministers such steps as
you might consider necessary.

"I did not seek to disguise that it would, in my
opinion, be ill-advised to endeavour before the termination of the inquiry to (secretly or otherwise) send
away (*éloigner*) or remove the Italian officer from his
present safe quarters with the Governor, but that Mr.
Vitto had assured me that this step was not contemplated. I allowed also that should the soldiers after
the inquiry still entertain a strong feeling against the
Italian, even though the evidence thoroughly established his innocence, it might then be necessary
to prefer a joint request to have the garrison or some
portion of it removed. Notwithstanding this difference of opinion, I am glad to say, sir, that I parted
with my colleagues on the best terms possible.

"Not having been able to entirely dispel from my mind the knowledge of former recent difficulties in regard to the Egyptian Army, I think it due to you, sir, to confess that though such considerations are, I conceive, somewhat out of the range of my functions as her Majesty's Acting Consul, they have in a measure availed with me in my decision to decline at present to submit to you as my conviction that the garrison of Suez should be at once removed.

"I fully appreciate the responsibility that rests with me of doing all in my power to ensure the safety of the British residents here, as well, of course, as that of the European community at large, and I need hardly assure you, sir, that I shall at once telegraph to you if I opine that the public security is endangered. But, on the other hand, I deem it equally my duty to abstain from requesting your high intervention unless I honestly believe that there is occasion so to do."

And on the following day (20th December) I continued—

"It is with much regret that I heard to-night that it is privately proposed by certain members of the British community here to hold a meeting on the subject of the insecurity of Europeans, which, it is contended, exists in general throughout Egypt, and in particular in the town in which they reside, in consequence of the predominance generally of military influence and alleged fanaticism. It is purposed to address to you a strong representation, begging that some measures may be taken to provide in all towns in Egypt a force sufficient to cope with and overcome the local garrisons in case of need.

"As her Majesty's Acting Consul, and fully and anxiously alive to the responsibility that would attach to me should I neglect to advise you the moment I apprehended any disaster, I still feel bound to repeat the assurance which I have already conveyed to you, that I do not consider British or European life or property any more in danger in Suez than it may be considered to be in Cairo or Alexandria, and you, I am aware, are in a position to correctly judge the extent of the risk (if any) run by Europeans resident in those towns."

Then on the 21st December I penned the last despatch of the series—

"I have the honour to report that I have to-night learned on good authority that the commissioners appointed to inquire into the recent disturbance among the soldiers in connection with the supposed murder of one of their comrades, have to-day condemned eight of the Suez garrison to imprisonment in chains, and have adjudged twenty-three others guilty.

"The eight former have actually been imprisoned here, but the remainder are still allowed to fulfil their regular duties, as otherwise there would not be the requisite number of soldiers needed to carry on the ordinary service.

"It is proposed to send the whole of the thirty-one men convicted to Cairo to undergo their several punishments, but I have not been able to ascertain when it is intended to despatch them.

"I further understand that as regards the question

of the assassination, the commission have not yet terminated their investigations, but that the evidence up to the present tends to establish the innocence of the Italian officer, and to point to a Bedouin together with an Arab of the town as the perpetrators of the crime. It is also reported that some of the soldiers here are still loth to admit that their suspicions against the Italian were unfounded, and are therefore now seeking to prove that the above-mentioned Bedouin and his accomplice were but the creatures employed by the Italian. This report I give under some reserve.

"I am glad to be able to add that the town is perfectly quiet, and that I apprehend no demonstration on the part of the troops on account of the sentences which I now record."

*   *   *   *   *   *   *

On December the 22nd Sir Edward Malet wrote to me privately, and was good enough to conclude his letter with the following sentence—

"I entirely approve of your attitude since the beginning of this affair. Cherif Pasha (the Prime Minister) told a person this morning, who repeated it to me, that I was the only (diplomatic) agent who had been correctly informed as to what was really going on."

Matters soon afterwards quieted down at Suez, and the garrison was changed without any fuss by the simple expedient of changing three or four men at a time, and by giving others leave of absence, and sending them to different stations at the expiration of their holidays.

Sir Edward Malet sent home to the Foreign Office copies of my despatches, and doubtless, like the kind loyal Chief he was, he wrote even stronger praise of me behind my back than he had addressed to me personally; the result was that within a few days of reading the correspondence, Lord Granville made up his mind that I was the sort of man then wanted in the Soudan, and on the 10th of January, 1882, I received from the Foreign Office the following telegram— "Lord Granville offers you the appointment of Consul at Khartoum. Salary, £600."

Letters of congratulation flowed in during the next few days, but I will only quote extracts from those addressed to me by my immediate Chiefs.

Sir Edward Malet wrote—"I congratulate you heartily on your getting the post. I was very glad, in the first place, to recommend you for it, and then to see that you got it."

Mr. Cookson's letter was also most cordial—"I think," he wrote, "there can be no doubt whatever about your great good fortune in getting such a step in advancement. The appointment is one which will be continually bringing you before the Government and the public. I am really proud of my pupil (if you will condescend to be called so now), and especially that your late conduct at Suez should have so fully justified the choice made of you. *Macte esto virtute nova.* You will be glad to hear that *every one* in Alexandria is delighted at your promotion ; this is the best proof of your deserving it."

CHAPTER VII

ON the 11th of January, 1882, I accepted the appointment, as will be seen by the following private letter written by me on that date—

"This morning I sent the following telegram to Lord Granville's private secretary—'Please inform Lord Granville that I accept the Consulship at Khartoum, and kindly convey sincere thanks for honour conferred.'

"Setting aside for the moment the possible drawbacks, let us look sensibly at the advantages. By accepting the post offered, I, at the age of twenty-six, pass over the heads of all the Vice-Consuls in the service, numbering some four hundred and fifty, and gain a rank equal to that of a Colonel in the Army, or a Captain in the Navy of three years' standing. My appointment is also a great mark of confidence, and an honour rendered peculiarly pleasing from the fact that I did not even apply for the post. There were, I understand, very many who did apply. I personally know of three. Then Khartoum is probably the one place at the present time where a man will, if successful, have a chance of distinguishing himself. The duties will be in the interests of *humanity* (suppression of slave trade, etc.), and my every act will be carefully noted and commented on by the English Press. I must not, however, be too sanguine of success. Firmness and courage mingled with tact and prudence will be required. The responsibility will be very great, almost *awfully* so. To succeed I must be able to hold the scales of Justice with a very even hand. I shall be surrounded by men who will ever be working against me, some of whom will, and some who will not, conceal their disgust at the object of my nomination. Khartoum again, taken as a commercial town, is the centre of what *must* be one of the world's greatest markets, and as soon as I am established there as Consul, the European colony will, I doubt not, increase exceedingly, and then will follow naturally facilities for getting to Cairo and the Red Sea ports. As to health, I believe that a man (or a woman for that matter) can live anywhere if he will only adapt himself to the climate and take ordinary care. Besides, the climate of Khartoum is tolerable, if not actually good."

I then without loss of time set about obtaining information as to the journey. I had by me the copy of a letter written by Mr. Kemp, the engineer attached to General Gordon's expedition in 1874. The letter, which was dated from Fashoda in 1874 (Fashoda at that period was reckoned a fourteen days' journey from Khartoum), ran as follows—

"The road from Souakim to Berber is through

an arid mountainous country: as far as Ariab it is covered with dwarf trees of stunted growth. The wide plains are partly sand and partly black basaltic stone. From Voback to Berber the plain is generally sandy, the wells are mere holes scratched in the beds of rivers. During November heavy showers fall, but they are soon soaked up. Price of camel-hire from Souakim to Berber, 1½ napoleons. Hire of boat from Berber to Khartoum, 7 or 8 napoleons. The Nile rapids are dangerous to pass at night. Packages for camels ought to weigh about 150 or 120 lbs. The climate is very dry and cold at day-break. The worst part of the journey between Souakim and Berber is the latter half, the wells being so far apart. The stations from Souakim are—

1. Handoutok.	3 hours.	Gordon took 3 hours.
2. Handoukh.	10 ,,	,, ,, 5 ,,
3. Goloos.	10 ,,	,, ,, 7 ,,
4. Haribre.	10 ,,	,, ,, 7 ,,
5. Hyab.	10 ,,	,, ,, 9 ,,
6. Mattah.	6 ,,	,, ,, 3 ,,
7. Ariab.	16 ,,	,, ,, 9 ,,
8. Voback.	24 ,,	,, ,, 23 ,,
9. Berber.	24 ,,	,, ,, 22 ,,

" Distance from Souakim to Berber by road, 288 miles. Sheep can be bought *en route*.

Gordon left Suez   22 Feb. 1874 ; arrived Souakim   26 Feb.
  „   „ Souakim 28 Feb.   „   Berber   8 Mar.
  „   „ Berber   9 March   „   Khartoum 13 Mar."

Friends also kindly gave me the benefit of their experience.

Mr. Bewley (now Colonel Bewley Bey) wrote to

me from Souakim. After congratulating me he said—

"I have never been to Khartoum, but I have heard so much about it from people passing here who have lived there that I can form a pretty good idea of what the life is like there. Of course the best time of year to make the journey is during the cool weather, say from middle November to end of March, or beginning of April, after which it is too hot to march during the day, but with moonlight nights the journey can be performed by resting for six or seven hours during the day. Neither donkeys nor horses are procurable here—in fact they could not manage the journey, especially in the summer, as owing to the scarcity of water you have to go sometimes two days or more without coming to wells.

"I feel sure your wife will find camels less fatiguing than either horses or donkeys; camel-saddles can be bought here, and cost about $10: the Soudan ones are admirably adapted for ladies, in fact may be called side-saddles, and are infinitely more comfortable than the Cairo ones. If I might be allowed to make the suggestion, I think your wife would find Bloomer costume suitable for camel-riding ; several ladies that I have seen start from here have been so rigged, and I thought it a capital idea. Camel hire hence to Berber averages from 5 to 5½ Maria Teresa dollars.

"Souakim to Berber takes about ten to twelve days. If accompanied by your wife, bring a tent. Tinned provisions and soups you will find useful, as you will have very little time for cooking. From all accounts Khartoum, although undeniably hot in the summer, is not unhealthy except during September and October, after the inundation of the Nile, when, as the town lies very low, there is a good deal of stagnant water about, which gives fever: many people during those months go either to Berber or Moselemia, both of which places have salubrious climates."

Then the Rev. Robert W. Felkin, whom I had met years before when passing through Alexandria on his way, with other young missionaries, to Uganda, wrote to me as follows about the available houses, etc., in Khartoum—

"There are two houses only, as far as I know, which would do for you. One, the old German and English Consuls' house : *do not* go there ; it may look nice, but it is very bad in the rains ; the place in front is often a foot or so under water. The best house for you, though not so large, is 'Abou Kamse Mike's'—I stayed in it the last time I was in Khartoum. House-rent is very dear. I should not take any provisions at all save *tea* and soap for your own use. You can get all else, wine, beer, spirits, etc., at pretty reasonable terms : jams and marmalade as well ; also chairs, etc.; but you must take a table, mosquito-curtains, and I should advise two light iron bedsteads. Have all your boxes made long and narrow—they go better on camels—and *not a single nail* in them—all screws ; then you can take them to bits and make table, bookshelves, etc. of them.

Wood is worth its weight in silver almost, at Khartoum. As a rule a good camel will take five cwt. of luggage, but it all depends on whether they are good ones: those at Souakim are not first-class, as they have all come down with heavy loads, and are done up. If you want riding camels, you should order them beforehand. I should also advise you to get your wife a good angereb bed—made with a shade for the desert journey; the Arabs make them very well, but as you have had experience of these matters, I need say no more of them. You will want a couple of good large *filters*, plenty of quinine, and be sure and take 'Warburg Fever Tincture'; it is the best thing for any one who is not a doctor, and you will not find any good doctor in Khartoum. If you smoke, you can get good cigars in Khartoum, and tobacco, but no pipes. Needles, thread, tape, buttons, etc., are very dear, but there is a pretty good tailor and dressmaker. Be sure and take a sausage-machine, it is so useful, and salt for your own use. Ink is also a matter of importance; you get only very bad and very dear stuff there. As you will probably be travelling sometimes, do not forget a few good waterproof sheets, bags, and *bath;* also a good canteen. No good knives can be got in Khartoum, and a few English shilling ones are most useful as presents—worth twenty times the amount of other things."

I have transcribed these letters, Khartoum having once again come to the front, and there being much in them, though they were written so long ago as

1882, that may be useful to young fellows about to try their luck in the Soudan. In addition to the above letters, with their valuable hints, I greedily read every book on Khartoum and the Soudan, and was in constant though indirect communication with kind Dr. Schweinfurth, the great African traveller, who was at that time in Cairo.

By the 21st of January I had decided on the Souakim-Berber route. A little later (though it dates 1st of January, 1882) I received my first commission given under the hand and seal of the Queen.

Then followed instructions, in which I was informed that I had been appointed to my present post more especially to watch over and report on the slave trade traffic, with a view to its suppression, my experience in her Majesty's consular service in Egypt having given me a general knowledge of its nature and extent. It would be my duty to maintain the most cordial relations possible with the Governor-General of the Soudan, and with the other authorities with whom I might be brought in contact, and, so far as the exigencies of the service would permit, I was to keep the Governor-General acquainted with any information I might acquire in regard to the slave trade which would enable him to take measures for its repression. I was further to communicate to the Governor-General any laxity or corruption on the part of his subordinates of which I might have proof, but I was to be careful not to listen to unfounded accusations against them. Then while keeping the head-quarters of my Consulate at

Khartoum as the seat of Government, I was to be at liberty to move about from place to place in my consular district as might seem to me most useful for the obtaining of information of the movements of the slave traders. The Governor-General of the Soudan in the first place, and the Government of the Khedive finally, would be responsible for my protection, and I was to be careful to avoid any interference with the slave traders or the natives which might provoke hostility or tend to raise difficulties in the way of my free passage through my consular district.

On the 5th of February, 1882, I was directed to place her Majesty's Consulate at Suez (for it will be remembered that I was still Acting Consul in that town) in charge of the gentleman appointed to relieve me, and to return to England prior to entering upon my duties as her Majesty's Consul at Khartoum. This was indeed good news, as it would enable me to get married before proceeding to the Soudan. And this reminds me of a curious predicament in which I was placed at Suez as regards my marriage. I had contemplated matrimony while there, but found that it was out of the question, for the following reasons. First, I could not be married in Cairo, where my *fiancée* was residing, as I could not absent myself from my post for the five weeks' residence in Cairo consular district required by the law regulating the marriage of British subjects in Egypt. Secondly, I could not be married at Suez, as *I myself* was the only person authorized in the Suez district to solemnize marriages between British subjects; nor could the Consuls from Alexandria, Cairo, or Port Said come and tie the knot for me, as their Marriage Warrants were only good *for their respective districts*, and consequently did not authorize them to marry any one outside their special district under any circumstances.

I lost no time in getting home and reporting myself at the Foreign Office; and on the 20th February I was informed that Lord Granville wished me to make arrangements for proceeding to my post at Khartoum with as little delay as possible. His lordship was willing, the despatch added, to grant me leave for six weeks, but hoped that by that time I should have completed my preparations for my journey, and should be ready to start. This was not a too generous allowance of leave, considering that I had had no leave for three years, and was certainly not likely to get back from Khartoum for another three. But I quite understood that it could not be otherwise if I was to reach the Soudan before the bad weather should set in, and before the desert route to Berber had become exceedingly difficult and unpleasant to traverse. So I set to work with a will; telegraphed to Cairo, begging my future wife to come home; was presented at Court on the 9th March; married on the 28th, and after a very short honeymoon reported myself at the Foreign Office.

But while I was working with a will in order to be prepared to proceed to my post in due season, so as to be able at once to tackle the slave trade question with the vigour and energy of youth—not bad weapons with which to fight officials whose aim and object is to find out "how not to do it"—others were working, likewise with a will, to bring about a different state of things—namely, the cancelling of my appointment ; and, as far as I have ever been able to ascertain, the persons who were working against me were the very people whom one would have confidently thought would, on the contrary, have laboured heart and soul to help me to expedite my departure, namely the British and Foreign Anti-Slavery Society.

The first blow was struck in the anti-slave trade organ, which, in laying before its readers an extract from the Foreign Office letter of the 27th February announcing my appointment to the Society, made the following significant comment—

"Mr. Miéville is quite a young man, and we cannot help expressing some anxiety as to the possibility of his being unable to withstand the effect of the Soudan climate, and the inevitable hardships and fatigues which must be inseparable from the efficient duties of his office, which Colonel Gordon has so often said ought never to be faced by any man under forty years of age."

This string must have been harped on to good purpose, for later on I was instructed by the Foreign Office to visit an eminent physician (who, if my memory does not play me false, lived in Park Lane), and be overhauled by him. His report was to the effect that my constitution was not robust enough to justify his sending me to Khartoum; and ultimately

Sir Charles Dilke, on behalf of the Foreign Office, gave the following reply to a question asked in the House of Commons—"It has been decided on grounds of health to appoint Mr. Miéville to some other post, and to select another gentleman for the Consulate at Khartoum."

My feelings were difficult to describe. I was bitterly disappointed, yet at the same time glad ; I was sorry to lose such an excellent opportunity of doing interesting and humanitarian work ; I was glad that I had not to take my wife to such an out-of-the-way spot ; and I was lost in astonishment at the action of the Anti-Slavery Society, which, when a Consul had been appointed to Khartoum at their instigation, or at least as a result of their efforts to secure such an appointment, conscientiously objected to the man selected simply and solely on the grounds of his youth and the consequent possible shattering of his health. For I honestly believe that the Society had no *arrière pensée*, but acted straightforwardly, and as seemed right and best to them.

As things ultimately turned out, it appears self-evident that but for the Anti-Slavery Society, I should have had the sad privilege of being in Khartoum when in January 1885 Gordon fell—and should probably have fallen with him. Though possibly, had I been in the Soudan at the time, Gordon, with his usual kindness of heart and thought for others, would have persuaded me to endeavour to place myself in safety,—when Stewart made his attempt to communicate with Lower Egypt.

CHAPTER VIII

BOMBARDMENT

PERHAPS, after all, the feeling uppermost in my mind was one of keen disappointment at not going to Khartoum ; but the event which meant so much to me was summed up in my official record in the pages of Sir Edward Hertslet's cold-blooded but most excellent publication, *The Foreign Office List*, by the terse statement, "did not proceed." Indeed it was all that could be said ; it was as useless to feel regret as to chuckle over the happy escape ; it was as futile to weep for lost opportunities as to rejoice over a happy deliverance ; as stupid to feel egotistically sure that success would have attended my efforts and the slave trade been suppressed, as to prophesy that the whole Soudan would in a few short years be abandoned by the Egyptian Government and given over to the Dervish host, and anarchy.

From May-day in 1882 I was told to work in the Foreign Office under kindly genial William Owen, and a capital time I had. The outside public has an idea that a Foreign Office clerk does not know hard work. In most of the departments not only does he work hard, but he labours like a slave, yet the men being all thoroughbreds, there is no whimpering.

But this pleasant Foreign Office life with such capital comrades was not to last long.

Events were marching very rapidly in Egypt, and an entirely new chapter in the history of that land of tragedies seemed about to open.

In April 1882 an alleged conspiracy among Circassian officers, for the purpose of assassinating Arabi Pasha, the self-constituted leader of the Native Egyptian army officers, was discovered in Cairo. Forty-eight arrests were made, including that of an ex-Minister of War ; and forty out of the forty-eight officers were sentenced to exile for life to the furthest limits of the Soudan, a sentence practically equivalent to death, as few prisoners ever return from the White Nile. The evidence on which the officers were convicted certainly did not prove any design to assassinate, and in order to prevent the carrying out of the crime of condemning innocent men, Great Britain and other Powers advised the Khedive not to confirm the sentences passed by the court-martial. The Ministry, in presence of the Khedive's firm attitude, actually threatened both himself and his family, and without his sanction convened the Chamber of Deputies. Europe became alarmed at the grave turn things had taken, and in the month of May Great Britain and France sent ships-of-war to Alexandria. Then, on the 11th of June, occurred the organized attacks on Europeans in the towns of Alexandria and Tantah, since known as "the Massacres," and there followed very naturally an exodus of the well-to-do, who no longer cared to risk their lives in a country where further bloodshed might take place at any moment. On the fatal 11th of June, Mr. Cookson, H.B.M.'s Consul, was seriously wounded, and his duties were taken over by Mr. Vice-Consul Calvert, who however was unable to bear the strain of responsibility, and was placed on the sick-list, and allowed to proceed to Europe.

At the end of June 1882, I received an official letter which made my heart beat. It ran as follows—

"I am directed by Earl Granville to state to you that, owing to the illness of Consul Cookson and Vice-Consul Calvert, it has become necessary to take steps for at once sending some one conversant with the nature of the duties of her Majesty's Consulate-General at Alexandria to assist in their discharge. Your previous experience of the consular work at the above-mentioned place appears to Lord Granville to render you a fit person for the duty in question, and I am, accordingly, to instruct you to proceed to Alexandria by next Friday's mail."

I well remember that Wednesday. The news reached me whilst I was watching a cricket match at Lord's. Therefore "next Friday's mail" meant starting in about fifty hours' time!

Being in love with prompt action, I did not particularly object to being hustled off—though it was but three months since I had "married a wife," and I felt it hard lines to have to leave her. But I knew that times were stormy in Egypt, and that stormy times often meant a chance of promotion, so I drove at once to Downing Street, expressed my readiness to obey orders, and inquired if there were any further instructions. No, that was all; "proceed to Alexandria as quickly as possible." Yet the next day one of the gentlemen in the Foreign Office had an afterthought which changed the whole tenor of my life; and as the outcome of this afterthought I received the following further despatch—

"You are aware that Mr. Calvert, whose functions at Alexandria you will temporarily discharge, occupied the post of British Delegate to the International Maritime and Quarantine Board of Health, and was the medium of communications between the Board and this Office. I have now to inform you that you are hereby appointed to act for him until further arrangements in that post, and have to instruct you to take the necessary steps, after communication with her Majesty's representative in Egypt, for entering upon the duties which will thus devolve upon you."

Now, though I was aware that Mr. Calvert occupied the post of British Delegate, as a matter of fact I had only the faintest idea what were the duties which thus were to devolve on me. Least of all did I think that this additional and somewhat subordinate appointment was to prove the all-important turning-point in my career.

*   *   *   *   *   *   *

I left London on the evening of the last day of June, after a farewell dinner at the Grosvenor Hotel, travelled night and day (*without* any stoppages, but *with* a courier's passport, which saved me all bother at the frontiers), and arrived at Alexandria soon after daybreak on the 6th of July.

Two of my fellow-passengers were Melton Prior, an artist on *The Illustrated London News*, and Professor E. H. Palmer, a record of whose splendid life and sad death has been handed down to posterity by Sir Walter Besant's able pen. Poor Palmer, who was like myself but newly married, mentioned me in a letter to his young wife as "the new Consul at Alexandria, a very pleasant young fellow," and added, "we are great friends, and get on very well: the Consul had no longer notice to get ready than I had." A few weeks later he was foully murdered in the desert.

In connection with the appointment of Palmer to the delicate mission with which he was entrusted by the British Cabinet—namely, the task of detaching the desert tribes in the Sinai Peninsula from Arabi Pasha, and of persuading them to prevent injury to the Suez Canal—a somewhat curious incident occurred to me. As I was, at the time the matter was under consideration, employed in the Foreign Office, and but lately returned from Suez, it was probably thought that my local knowledge might possibly be useful, so the War Office authorities asked me to look at a series of maps, on which, as far as I recollect, the various Bedouin tribes dwelling in the desert between Suez and Gaza were indicated and located. The names of the authors of each map were either hidden from me purposely, or had not been written on the face of the charts. I looked rapidly through them and explained that though I was "not, an authority on the matter, yet, as my opinion was asked, I frankly did not think that any of the maps were worth much, except this one" (indicating the very map which, as I was informed later, was the one prepared by Professor Palmer). In thus choosing the chart sketched by the Professor, I was in luck's way, for at that date Lord Northbrook had already made up his mind to ask Palmer to go out, and it must have appeared to his lordship that I really knew the ins and outs of the matter.

I landed at Alexandria early on the 6th July, and at once secured rooms at the old Hôtel d'Europe, in Mohamed Ali Square, which at that time stood on the site now occupied by the new law courts, known as the Mixed Tribunals. I have by me the letters I wrote home at the time, and to avoid the tricks which memory so often plays, I will let quotations from the letters in question tell the story of the next few days.

"*Hôtel d'Europe, Alexandria, Sunday, 9th July*, 1882. —I have been here for three days only, yet it seems more like three weeks; each day being so full of dreadful anxiety and worry. On Friday there was fresh fear of massacres, and hundreds upon hundreds of Europeans, chiefly Greeks, French, and Italians, poured out of the town. The *Peluse*, one of the steamers belonging to the Messageries Maritimes line, and now being used as a sort of floating hotel or refuge, has steamed outside the mole, as it was no longer considered safe to lie near the Arsenal. The

P. and O. *Tanjore*, the same steamer in which I arrived on Thursday last from Brindisi, has also moved to a berth outside the inner mole.

"In the afternoon we (the Consulate) began advising all British subjects to go afloat *at once*, as it might be more difficult to do so later on. All British subjects have likewise been told to leave Cairo. Things are indeed so bad that berths have been reserved on the *Tanjore* for all the consular officials, and the archives (important papers, etc.), together with most of our personal baggage, were sent on board during Friday and yesterday. I am only second in command here. I am keeping well, though I feel the heat dreadfully, and the mosquitoes treat me just as badly as if I were an ordinary globe-trotter, and not an old Egyptian. Evidently the new generation of mosquitoes 'know not Joseph.' The town is scarcely recognizable, only two or three (so to speak) solitary shops remain open, and pickets of Arabi's soldiers are all over the town. *All* the private houses are closed. On the faces of the few Europeans one sees there rests a general expression of anxiety and jadedness; in the eyes of the Arabs hatred and exultation; and among all classes, native and alien, one hears of nothing but the one never-ending topic, the 'strained situation'— 'When will the end come?'—'What will be the solution?' It would be quite refreshing to hear some one speak of something wholly unconnected with the Egyptian question. The P. and O. steamers are to cease calling here, and the mails will go *via* the Suez Canal. I shall send this letter to Port Said by a gun-boat told off for the purpose. We have two telephones at the Consulate, one direct to the Admiral, and the other in connection with subscribers through the Central Office."

"*On board s.s. Tanjore, 10th July, evening.*—Last night we all left shore and came afloat (I in a dinghy rowed by the Admiral's secretary and one sailor). I felt most uncomfortable walking down from the hotel to the harbour, being afraid that the pickets might recognize and stop me. A Consul as a hostage would have suited Arabi. I am dog-tired and worried to death. The bombardment of the forts will probably begin to-morrow morning."

*   *   *   *   *   *   *

I have always held, and still firmly believe, that the financiers of Europe were the real instigators of the bombardment of the forts of Alexandria. European capital, to the extent of possibly over a hundred millions sterling, had been sunk or invested in Egypt; commerce and navigation would have suffered to a most serious extent had Arabi not been checked in his determined attempt to introduce a reign of anarchy; Great Britain's trade, both direct and transit, would have been wrecked for months if not for years to come, and England's £4,000,000, which went to pay for the Khedive Ismaïl's Suez Canal shares, would have been jeopardized. So I feel convinced that capitalists played the part of wire-pullers in the events of 1882.

Early in that year Gladstone and Gambetta, as representing the two monied nations of Europe, joined forces and practically guaranteed the Khedive Tewfik against the machinations of the so-called Egyptian National Party, and so it happened that when the Khedive, in the month of May, quarrelled with the Arabi-Sami Ministry, England and France were thus constrained to support his Highness as against his Ministers, by sending fleets with an ultimatum calling on Arabi to resign. The Egyptian National Ministry at once gave way, but the partisan demonstration which followed their resignation forced the Khedive's hand, and he was obliged to appoint Arabi Minister of War, which practically meant that the latter remained the virtual Dictator of Egypt. Then occurred the riots and massacre of the 11th of June, and, aghast at the bloodshed, and realizing the growing insecurity to life and property, Europeans began to leave the country, and the Egyptian funds fell to 52. Now, even granting for the sake of argument that the Rothschilds of the world had not up till that moment influenced the action of the British and French Governments, it seems almost certain that at this acute period financial pressure was brought to bear on them, and the direct and immediate result was armed intervention.

Towards the end of June, and at the beginning of July, Arabi Pasha, notwithstanding repeated representations from the British and French Admirals, displayed great activity in arming and strengthening the forts which commanded the harbour of Alexandria and its approaches, and Admiral Sir Beauchamp Seymour (afterwards Lord Alcester) regarding these hostile preparations as a menace to the fleet under his command, informed Arabi that if the arming of the forts was not forthwith discontinued, the ships would open fire and destroy them.

Arabi, with characteristic obstinacy, persisted in his ill-advised course of action; the French fleet, which so far had acted in concert with the English, appeared dismayed and sailed away, leaving the British fleet to grapple single-handed with the difficulty.

On Tuesday, the 11th of July, we bombarded Alexandria. The principal ships engaged, besides gun-boats, were the *Inflexible*, *Téméraire*, *Superb*, *Sultan*, *Alexandra*, *Monarch*, *Invincible*, and *Penelope*, with an armament consisting of four 81-ton guns, twelve of 25 tons, twenty-four of 18 tons, and twenty-six of $12\frac{1}{2}$ tons, to say nothing of the Gatlings and Nordenfeldts stationed in the tops. The ships fired in all 1731 shot and shell, say an average of twenty-five rounds for each heavy gun. It was fortunate indeed for us that the bombardment did not continue longer than one day, for I believe the ordnance supplies had by the evening of the 11th reached a very low ebb. During the bombardment the sky rapidly became overcast, the discharge of the heavy guns seeming to cause clouds to gather from all quarters, but when the firing ceased they gradually melted away, and the next day the heavens were again beautifully clear and blue.

The British lost five killed and twenty-seven wounded, and a good deal of damage was done to the fleet by Arabi's guns; H.M.S. *Alexandra* being hit about sixty times, the *Sultan* twenty-seven times, and the *Superb*, *Invincible*, *Penelope*, and *Inflexible* some fourteen, eleven, eight, and six times respectively. Arabi's "War News" in a native newspaper published in Cairo, stated that four English men-of-war had been sunk! The incident during the bombardment which perhaps best showed British pluck, was when Harding, a gunner, quietly took up a live shell which had entered H.M.S. *Alexandra*, and which lay spitting and fizzing on the deck, and handling it without flinching, dropped the dread and highly dangerous visitor into a bucket of water.

The guns in the rebel forts consisted of thirty-seven heavy Armstrongs—varying from 18 tons to $6\frac{1}{2}$ tons—four 40-pounder Armstrong breechloaders, some two hundred smooth-bores, and about forty mortars. And from what I saw, when some forty-eight hours later I visited the forts, there is no doubt whatever in my mind that Arabi's gunners were assisted by European mercenaries.

The loss of life in the forts was very heavy; being variously estimated at from 1000 to 2000. In Fort Adda, when the magazine was blown up by a shell from H.M.S. *Inflexible*, a whole battalion of Arabi's soldiers met their death. And the damage to the forts themselves and to their armaments was so great that they were practically in ruins when abandoned; though it must be admitted that very many of the British projectiles either exploded prematurely or failed to explode at all. And this taught our naval authorities at home a lesson by which happily they took an early opportunity of profiting. The fort at Ras-el-Teen was utterly wrecked, and when it was visited by a burying party, which I accompanied, a couple of heavy guns were found reared up on end. Fort Adda was completely demolished by the *Inflexible's* guns, and Pharos suffered greatly also, the minaret of the soldiers' mosque within the fort being blown away, and two turrets reduced to ruins. I believe that the forts in the construction of which masonry had been extensively used, suffered more damage than those in which sand and earthworks had been but roughly thrown up. Possibly this was due to the shell not finding enough resistance to cause them to burst where the casemates were not solidly faced with stone, for in such cases the shell, instead of exploding, simply burrowed into the soft earth and there lay harmlessly imbedded.

The westerly forts of Marabout, Marsa el Khanat, and Mex were silenced by a flotilla of gun-boats, headed by H.M.S. *Condor*, and fairly warm work the gun-boats had, though, curiously enough, I believe that none of them were hit. This must have been owing chiefly to the fact that they, drawing but little water, were able to approach close enough under the forts to render the latter's guns ineffective by reason of their not being able to be depressed on to the attacking flotilla.

*   *   *   *   *   *   *

I will now once again quote from my old letters—
" *S.S. Tanjore*, 12*th July*, 7 *a.m.*—All day yester-

day the bombardment went on, a grand sight, but as full accounts have been cabled home, it is useless my enlarging on it. The town was probably dreadfully knocked about, though not intentionally, as the fire was all directed to the silencing of the forts. Three more explosions have taken place this morning."

"*S.S. Tanjore*, 13*th July*, 5 *p.m., six miles off Alexandria.*—Last night it was very dreadful to see the whole European quarter of the town burning (due entirely to the rebel incendiaries), but the fatal mistake made by our Government has been to bombard the forts before the landing force for the protection of the city had arrived. I know not whether, when we do get ashore, Consuls will be wanted, or any decent house remain standing in the town, or whether water and provisions will be obtainable; I am sick of the whole muddle. Arabi and his troops are reported to be leaving Alexandria for a camp some ten miles outside the city."

"*S.S. Tanjore, in Alexandria Harbour, Sunday Morning, July* 16*th*, 1882.—Yesterday I was dreadfully home-sick. I could not keep quiet; action, I knew, was the only thing to restore me, so, having armed myself, I went ashore as guide to a sort of ambulance party. The town is ruined: Frank Street and the Square unrecognizable. Dead bodies of Arab soldiers lying about everywhere, and the Consulate utterly demolished; all my things lost for ever: such is the fortune of war. I did not, however, uselessly 'waste' time in gazing about me, but hurried to a house (having first borrowed a stretcher) where I had been informed there was a sick woman, bed-ridden and unable to move. Our party passed down the old Bourse Street, and at last found the lady. She was afraid, and obstinately refused to budge, saying that she would rather be burned in her bed than suffer the pain of being moved. Needless to say that, regardless of her screams, I had her (as tenderly as possible) put on the stretcher, and then eight of us, by relays of four, carried her through the burning streets to the hospital. I will not dwell on all the horrors we saw, the daily papers will, I doubt not, be full of dreadful details, and Melton Prior has, I know, sent many sketches.

"I forgot to tell you last week that Mr. Consul Jago, who, I believe, was told by the Foreign Office to come out at the same time that I was, only arrived *two days after the bombardment*, so I decidedly scored by packing up quickly, and obeying orders without the loss of an hour. By the bye, to-morrow is my twenty-seventh birthday."

"*17th July*.—Yesterday afternoon the French steamer *Peluse*, with the Simonds among her passengers, came into harbour, and I went up to town with them. We were present at the execution of an Arab incendiary on the great Square. The man had been caught red-handed setting fire to houses, had been summarily tried, and with scant delay tied up against a tree near the Tribunals, shot, and then and there buried. We had a somewhat narrow escape from a falling house in the Ramleh Boulevard, just past the ruined Consulate. We were a party of seven ; I saw the walls of a burnt-out house tottering, and I cried out that the house was falling in, and (with three of the others) ran *back* in double-quick time. The rest of the party ran *forward*, and only just escaped being buried beneath the ruins, Jemmy Simond being slightly bruised, and all three of them being smothered in the dust. Provisions are horridly dear owing to their scarcity."

"*S.S. Tanjore, off Ras-el-Teen Palace, Alexandria Harbour, 20th July,* 1882.—We have started a temporary Consulate in a part of the Ottoman Bank's premises, but I continue to eat and sleep on board for the present, the town being dreadfully hot, what with the sun and the smouldering fires. The good Sisters at the hospital did not leave during the bombardment, but, I believe, hid themselves in the cellars. Mr. Cornish (of the Water Works) stayed bravely at his post throughout the whole business, and deserves to be well rewarded by his Company and by our Government. The English church is not injured in any way; there is to be Service there next Sunday. The Khedive is now at Ras-el-Teen. Arabi is at Kafr Dawar, fourteen miles away. The mail leaves shortly; I am sending this in the Foreign Office bag."

"*Alexandria, 29th July,* 1882.—Many of the reports one hears are very disquieting. The English are now fairly strong here as regards troops, but the vacillating policy which the Government, contrary to all the advice they have received, is now pursuing, may prove not only disastrous to the whole campaign, but also dangerous to the Europeans, now fast returning to Alexandria. Personally, though I entertain no hopes of a decided move being made for at least three weeks, if not longer, I believe that the situation will have materially altered for the better in ten days or a fortnight.   And I base this hope on the facts that Sir Garnet Wolseley should arrive on the 10th August, and Sir Edward Malet on the 15th or 16th ; that our Indian troops—as well as reinforcements from England—may have arrived by then ; and that the moot point as to whether Turkey, as Suzerain Power, will or will not actually send troops to join us in quelling the rebellion and setting the Khedive once more upon his throne, will by then very probably be finally settled.

"The correspondents now here are Bell (assisted by Cresswell), for *The Times;* J. Drew Gay, for *The Daily Telegraph;* Cameron, for *The Standard;* Skinner (with Chapman), for *The Daily News;* Charles Fitzgerald, for *The Manchester Guardian;* Burleigh, for *The Central News;* Melton Prior, artist, for *The Illustrated London News;* and Villiers, artist, for *The Graphic.* I dare say there are others, but all the above-mentioned gentlemen I know personally.

"I have seen Sister Barbara of the Deaconesses' Hospital, several times, also our friend Dr. Schweinfurth, who seems to think it a great blessing that we did not have to go to Khartoum."

"*2nd August.*—I have been pretty busy this week, and rather seedy. Sir E. Malet is coming out at once, and will be here on the 10th inst.   This is good news.   I am sorry to say that I have to come on shore for good on Sunday, as the Government contract

for the s.s. *Tanjore* expires on the 6th.   I like being
afloat, for the sake of the cool air in the evening.

" Arabi may attack the town this afternoon."

From this date my letters cease.

And now to return to my work.   To me the month
of August was one of great anxiety and worry ; the
threatened water famine gave the several Consulates
much trouble ; claims from persons injured in the
Alexandria riots of June 11th, and from those whose
property had been destroyed by fire after July 11th,
or whose houses had been looted by the rebels during
July 12th and 13th, began to pour in ; and to add to
official troubles, the heat was tremendous, and the
city under martial law.   This meant for one thing
that one could not venture out in the town after
sunset, without possessing the password (or passwords
if one had many quarters of the town to go through).
The military authorities gave the password to the
Consulate, and we communicated it to such British
subjects as we knew to be trustworthy.

At that time I messed, as did most men, at Abbat's
Hotel, and I slept at a house in the Ramleh Boulevard.
Nightly on my way from my hotel to my rooms, I
was challenged by sentries at certain fixed points,
but as I knew the countersigns I got on all right.
Not so the stray foreigner who ventured out.

One of the sentries was posted almost opposite our
house in Cherif Pasha Street near the old Tribunals
(now the Khedivial Club).   We used to watch from
our balcony, and several times witnessed ridiculous
difficulties with the sentry.   Some new arrival—

generally a poor Greek ignorant of the regulations and innocent of English—would come strolling down Cherif Pasha Street after sunset. On nearing the passage which divides the Credit-Lyonnais block from the present Bourse buildings (then the Mixed Tribunals), a sentry, as often as not a raw Irishman, would pop out on the unwary wayfarer, and presenting a nasty steely bayonet on the end of a rifle at him, would call out his "Halt! Who goes there?" The poor Greek, thinking his end was come, in fear and trembling would approach the sentry and volubly try and explain in Greek that he was not an incendiary or a thief, but an honest man. Then Paddy irate—"You dhirty spalpeen, oi'll taych you the fayl of cowld shteel if you don't be afther comin' wid me at once-st." And off the Hellenic subject would be marched to the guard-room.

Then perhaps a higher-class European would pass by, and when the "Halt! Who goes there?" rang out, he would reply, "Friend." When the sentry gave his "Advance one, and give the countersign"—the foreigner, knowing the word, and being anxious at once to satisfy the soldier, often gave the countersign too audibly. "Yis," Pat would answer, "that's roight, but ye naydn't till the whole worruld," and then he would add, "Pass, friend, all's well."

The strain of work, worry, and heat, and the very constant scares at night about the enemy (reported almost every other night during the last half of July as being just outside the Rosetta Gate), had told on my nervous system, and one morning (I think on the morning of 23rd August), I woke about dawn and found myself quite unstrung, and sobbing like a child.

I dressed and went out, but could not pull myself together ; I felt better after meeting fellow-creatures at breakfast. Yet I was wretched, and as Sir Edward Malet's carriage (I think he had that morning arrived in Alexandria) passed through the Square, I stopped it then and there in order to beg to be relieved of my duties.

Later I had some conversation with him in private, and he kindly persuaded me not to act hastily because I was unstrung ; in other words, not to make a fool of myself by leaving my post when the worst was over ; and he further comforted me by agreeing that the outlook seemed promising enough to warrant my telegraphing for my wife. This I did without delay, and she arrived just before Tel-el-Kebir was fought, for I well remember her asking me when I returned home on the morning when the news of the great victory came through, to explain the enthusiasm shown by Arabs and Europeans alike—for when the result of the battle became known, every one in the streets and on the Square (which could be seen from our house) had indiscriminately fallen on one another's necks and embraced for joy. Ah! if England had only declared a protectorate over Egypt that very day ! What years of up-hill fighting it would have saved. Even the French would have *welcomed* the announcement, and all the bad blood since created would never have been engendered. And the dream of so many great men, namely, a firm Anglo-French alliance and friendship, would to-day have been an accomplished fact. But the Cabinet of that day cannot be accused of being of a courageous disposition ; it was composed practically of the same Ministers who later on left Gordon to his fate.

CHAPTER IX

AS BRITISH DELEGATE

IT was at about this period that I first met a now
dear and valued friend, who, in a short sketch which
he entitled "In the Consulate," drew of me as I then
appeared to him the picture which is here given. I,
of course, do wear eye-glasses.

"The gold pince-nez was in its usual place. You
know the look of it yourselves very well ; but you
can scarcely know how valuable such an adjunct to
the natural capabilities may prove in the midst of an
Eastern population ; especially when that population
is no longer simple and natural. In Alexandria, of
all places in the world, the population is least simple
and least natural.

"There the native has had to deal with the Jew
trader. The Jew trader has cheated him, and
naturally the object of the native now is to try and
cheat in turn the Jew trader. The Greek shopkeeper
has led him into bad bargains, and his object now is
to lead the Greek shopkeeper into a bad bargain.
He has been defrauded by his Syrian kinsman, and
his object now is to defraud the Syrian. The Turk

—to whom compassion is unknown—has dealt hardly with him ; his object now is to know no compassion, and to deal hardly, if Allah will but grant him the opportunity, with the Turk.

"Therefore instead of looking for 'peace and truth' through the pince-nez, the eye has to be looking for (and that not merely in the Egyptian proper, but in nearly every denizen of the broad city) every form of deception, the most subtle and crafty of designs, veiled under an appearance and a manner that are the result of long practice and an acumen sharpened to a degree that it would be difficult to exceed.

"We have said that the pince-nez was in its usual place. Amidst what sort of surroundings are we to picture to ourselves the owner of the said pince-nez for the moment? Well, the scene is one of the ordinary official chambers belonging to the Consulate at Alexandria. Such a 'habitation of the soul' will not require elaborate description. It is not the chamber, but the occupant of it that we seek. Extreme simplicity of furniture and decoration is its leading characteristic. The high double windows are thrown wide open towards the sea, the splash of the waters of which is just enough to stir the small 'beach currency' into an audible murmur. There is a porous water-bottle standing on the sill, to catch the cooling draught. The walls self-coloured in a light tint are high, and scarcely relieved by anything that can pass for embellishment. Even the ceiling goes un-ornamented, while nothing more elaborate than a matting covers the floor. Remove the two or three chairs, and there would be really nothing to appeal to the eye in any way, except always—always excepted—the official table and the occupant of the official seat.

"That brings us back to the pince-nez, and to the eyes behind the pince-nez.

"To look above, to look straight through, to look underneath, to look in methods that fill the half-way stations between those various points; and with the minor shades of meaning that hover about the slighter intermediate distances. Looks like these are each and all of them weapons of defence and of attack, sharpened to a keen edge by diplomatic practice. But in this case there is nothing supposititious about the pince-nez. The ornament is not pure ornament. It is the legitimate offspring of a physical need, and being that, has grown into its place and power with a perfectly natural growth.

"There is a certain _dégagé_ solemnity in the look of consummate at-home-ness that strikes you with all the force of a first impression as you first meet the actual glance. You correct your first impression a moment later by admitting to yourself that there is inextricably blended with it an air of being quite ready for business, whether business come in the form of the muzzle of a revolver or of that of the whining petition of one of the poorest of the denizens of the back streets.

"The dress worn is light and to the purpose, but admirably made—always admirably made.

"You may be unconscious of the fact, but you have really stepped within a certain magic ring.

Whether the magician is of common blood, and can unbend as common mortals do, is rather for future experience. Given the occasion, and you may find, as others have found, that the unbending goes to the limit of the extremest ease—but here—and officially, No! Not till the crack of—— Hark! What is that? A noise in the street. The sound of some quarrel, where words run high, and blows with the knife may speedily follow. In a moment the hand is on the bell. In less than half a minute Mustapha has appeared, received his orders, and rushed off down-stairs to the scene of the disturbance. No such element of 'trouble' has any business near the sacred precincts of the Consulate. The Consulate broom will sweep it out of existence, if it is in the power of man to annihilate it. In fact, as we are speaking, 'order is restored.'"

*　　*　　*　　*　　*　　*　　*

And now let me take up the thread of my narrative.

My usual consular duties were varied—and they were multiplied that winter by work in connection with the Indemnity Commission, which deserves at least a passing word. The burning and pillage of Alexandria, the murders committed there, and the losses of all kinds suffered both by Europeans and Egyptians, had given rise to claims amounting to some millions of pounds.

Judicial suits were commenced before both the tribunals of the reform and the native courts. It was not thought expedient, however, to leave to the ordinary tribunals the valuation of the damages of the war, the more especially as the two jurisdictions engaged would not have the same rules of jurisprudence. It was decided therefore to create a special International Commission, with exclusive jurisdiction to receive and examine the claims of the victims of the 1882 insurrection, and to decide, without appeal, on each one of these claims by rejecting them or confirming them by fixing an indemnity.

The commission was composed of eleven members, and I assisted the member nominated by Great Britain, Consul-General Cookson.

But the work which interested me most, and into which I threw myself earnestly and vigorously, was the work which devolved upon me in connection with the Egyptian Maritime and Quarantine Council of Health, on which, it will be remembered, I had as an afterthought been appointed to act as Great Britain's representative when I left the Foreign Office at the end of June.

On studying the powers and duties of the Quarantine Board, I found that it had been only quite recently constituted in its existing form. The Khedivial Decree, dated 3rd January, 1881, stated that the Board was empowered to draw up and enforce regulations for preventing the introduction into Egypt, and the transmission to other countries, of epidemic or epizootic diseases.

In plainer terms, the Board was apparently instituted with a view to making Egypt a dumping-ground, or halfway-house between the East and West ; and its regulations were principally directed against cholera and plague, which always exist in a sporadic or epidemic form either in India or in some portion of the Far East.

I found that the Board, having the power to make its own regulations, had practically relieved the Khedive's Government of all responsibility in quarantine matters, without taking any upon itself. It seemed under no sort of control, its decisions were often arbitrary and capricious, sanitary questions being treated not exclusively on their own merits, but with reference to the political bias of some of its members. The whole vast trade between the East and West was in fact at the mercy of this irresponsible body, which was composed of twenty-three members—nine representatives of Egypt, and fourteen consular delegates representing respectively Austria, Belgium, Denmark, France, Germany, Great Britain, Greece, Holland, Italy, Norway and Sweden, Portugal, Russia, Spain, and Turkey.

I must say that it seemed to me iniquitous that England with her vast commerce should only have the same voting power as Belgium, Denmark, Norway, or Portugal.

The room in which the Board held its meetings was a large one, and the members sat at a long oblong table, the President's chair being in the centre of one side, with the secretary, who took full notes of the proceedings, facing him ; while the delegates of the fourteen foreign Powers and representatives of the Egyptian Government had each his allotted place. The President was provided with a hand-bell, which he gently tinkled on opening and closing the sittings, and rang more loudly on occasions when disorder threatened.

I entered on my duties as British Delegate in July 1882, and naturally found plenty of scope for energy. I was aghast at the injustice done to British commerce and navigation by the inconsequent decisions of the Board, but though I fought many a skirmish in defence of England's interests, I did not absolutely show my teeth or throw down an open defiance to my quarantinist colleagues until May-day in the following year. At the meeting of the Board held on that day I did put my foot down—happily to some purpose, as events proved. A proposal was made to add to the rules already adopted, and to go beyond the Board's previous decisions. I protested, and declared that as the Board persisted in its intention to frame rules that would further fetter British commerce, I had no other course open to me but to retire from the discussion. Inasmuch as Great Britain alone furnished at that time 80 per cent. of the entire Suez Canal traffic, my withdrawal caused some stir, and two or three other members retiring also, the sitting came to an abrupt ending—a *quorum* no longer existing.

A Paris paper published the following grotesquely partisan and mendacious account of the incident—

"Mr. Miéville, who had some time back got himself admitted, in virtue of his being attached to the Consulate, to a seat in the Areopagus which decides quarantine matters in Egypt, has shown himself wild (*féroce*) against every proposal in favour of 'observation,' or quarantine, and—I say this without exaggeration

—has acted like an ill-bred and irascible youth in every discussion in which he has taken part, and in which the question of preservative measures was on the Order of the Day.

"On this occasion (1st May) he suddenly, in the midst of the debate, got up from his seat, and squashing his hat down on his head, left the council chamber crying out, ' I protest, and I leave the meeting so that I may no longer listen to such nonsense.' "

But I could afford to smile at this ridiculous abuse, for my immediate Chiefs in Egypt and the Foreign Office approved my attitude, and at a subsequent meeting, when the question was again brought forward, I was allowed to repeat in Lord Granville's name what I had previously said on my own responsibility, and to again retire from the discussion as a protest against the proposed unnecessary departure from the regulations.

Eventually the threatened dead-lock was avoided, and an arrangement arrived at ; but the incident was not forgotten, and my fellow-delegates, who had already a wholesome respect for me, saw that it was more than ever needful to reckon with me now that, as it seemed, the British Government had determined to support me.

In order to make quite clear how unfounded were certain charges of having been the means of allowing cholera to invade Egypt, brought against me at a later date, I must here, even at the risk of seeming tedious, relate fully one further incident. The Quarantine Council held that ships, *though perfectly clean when arriving in Egyptian ports*, must nevertheless undergo detention if they came from a port considered by the Board to be infected with cholera. To declare Bombay to be infected was the favourite failing of this enlightened Council, and it was so declared on the slightest provocation. For instance, on May 14, 1883, the Council imposed quarantine against all ships arriving from Bombay, because in the past week there had occurred in that city twenty-eight deaths from cholera. I called the Board's attention at the time to the affirmation of the Bombay medical officers, that the cholera was not epidemic, and I urged that surely twenty-eight deaths from cholera in a week could scarcely be considered alarming, when it was remembered that we were treating of India, where cholera is ever present ; and this especially when the population of Bombay (at least 750,000) was borne in mind. My protests, however, were unavailing ; and I only mention this instance, because it will explain how natural it was that I, as guardian of British interests, should on the first available occasion press for the removal of the restriction. In this instance I had not long to wait : on 2nd June I was able to report officially that on the afternoon of the 31st May, I had received the usual weekly health report from Bombay, showing that only nine deaths had occurred during the week ending 29th May ; that I had then and there written to his Excellency the President to submit to the members of the Council a proposal to remove the existing quarantine against Bombay ; that the proposal had been duly submitted and accepted by twelve votes against four ; and that as a result all vessels *leaving* Bombay *after* the 13th June would be received at Suez in free *pratique*, if in the meantime there was no fresh increase in the mortality from cholera in Bombay.

This action on my part—my simple request to the President to submit a proposal to the Board tending to free *clean* vessels from Bombay from a vexatious and uncalled-for restriction—was in the following year made the basis of scurrilous attacks on me, of which I shall have to speak later on.   Now even had the decision to remove quarantine against arrivals from Bombay been either premature or ill-advised—which I maintain most stoutly was not the case, for it did not apply to vessels which might arrive with disease on board, or having had sickness during the voyage, but solely referred to healthy ships—surely any responsibility or blame attaching to such decision would rest, not with the delegate who *proposed* the raising of the quarantine, but with the twelve members of the Board who by their votes *decreed* it.

Happily I received continued and cordial support from my Chiefs, as witness Sir Edward Malet, who, writing to Lord Granville on the Quarantine question, was good enough to speak of me as follows—" Mr. Miéville has, since his appointment as Delegate to the Board, done exceedingly good work.   He has been successful in carrying points which have been of essential benefit to British interests, and I am inclined to attach great value to his opinion. . . .

" The considerable improvement in the conduct of

the Board which has been noticeable since Mr. Miéville has been on it, inclines me to think that a great deal depends upon the activity and judgment of our Delegate, and I would strongly urge that, on Mr. Miéville's departure, a gentleman should be nominated in his place who should have no other functions. The additional expense would be amply justified by the importance of the interests which depend upon the action of the Board, for shipping-masters complain that vast sums have been lost through its vexatious regulations. It must be remembered that the work of the Board is continuous, that it is not sufficient for our Delegate to present himself at the meetings and to urge there a particular point upon his colleagues. . . .

"The British Delegate should have a salary of not less than £600 a year. Hitherto he has been expected to discharge the onerous duties connected with the office for £50 a year . . . and it requires a person with the exceptional earnestness and intelligence of Mr. Miéville to fulfil the duties with zeal for such a sum."

The feeling of gratitude which I, in common with very many others who have served under him, entertain towards that loyal, genial, and sympathetic Chief, Sir Edward Malet, will always remain present with me.

But before proceeding with the narrative of my work as British Quarantine Delegate, I must show how it came to pass that in June 1883 I found myself still in Egypt, when originally (a year before) I had been sent out only to temporarily replace Mr. Vice-

Consul Calvert.   In the first place, my dear old friend, Mr. Calvert, whose health had towards the end of June 1882 broken down under the unusual stress of responsibility, had passed peacefully away two months later, and his successor was not immediately designated. Ultimately, Mr. John F. Russell was appointed Vice-Consul at Alexandria, but he did not relieve me until the spring of 1883.   In the meantime, in April 1883, Lord Granville offered me the Consulship of Rio Grande do Sul ; and, in passing, I had better make a clean breast of it, and frankly admit that when I got the telegram from the Foreign Office, I had *only* the very haziest idea of where this place with the high-sounding name really was ; but with the help of a map the hazy idea soon developed into proud geographical knowledge ; and so when friends, who had not had the advantage of ten minutes' search on a map, ignorantly said, "Where is your new post ? " I was able to reply with scorn for their short-comings, "My dear friends, your education has been sadly neglected."

The same telegram which offered me this South American Consulate, added that I should not be required to leave Alexandria at present, and it thus happened that although the post of Vice-Consul at Alexandria, which I had been originally sent out to occupy, had been filled up by the appointment of Mr. Russell (son of Sir William Howard Russell, the father of war correspondents), yet owing to my work on the Quarantine Council, and on the In-demnity Commission, I was still in Egypt when the cholera appeared at Damietta on the 23rd of June, 1883.

This outbreak of cholera increased my work to a very great extent. In the first place, the meetings of the Quarantine Council were held with inconvenient frequency, and were unduly lengthy. Then (on the 3rd of July) I received instructions from Lord Granville to report on the origin of the outbreak. I well remember my stupefaction and sense of helplessness on receiving the telegram. I was not a medical man, nor had I ever seen a case of cholera, but I could not tell my Chief that the task of making the required report was beyond my powers ; though when I began to write it, I bit my pen considerably. However, there was no time to lose, and the instructions were peremptory, so calling common-sense to my aid, and bearing in mind that two and two put carefully together *must* make four, whether the question was one of facts or figures, I buckled to, and gradually warming to my subject, wrote (and sent off the following day) the Memorandum on the origin of the outbreak of cholera at Damietta, which I cannot do better than quote in full—

"The news from Damietta did not assume definite shape, or at least was not fully confirmed, until Sunday, the 24th June, on which day committees of medical men left both Alexandria and Cairo in order to ascertain on the spot the origin and exact nature of the outbreak. The two delegations joined at Damietta, and after a stay in the town of less than eighteen hours they came away, and reported that the disease was epidemic cholera, but that they were unable to say whether it had been imported or not.

"To show how the disease originated seems in these circumstances very difficult, but, after careful consideration, I submit that it is sufficiently clear that the outbreak is due entirely to local causes, and that it could not have been imported.

"The broad facts which lead me to this conclusion are, that for months past reports from the districts of Damietta and Mansourah have pointed plainly to the inference that, should sanitary measures not be promptly taken, some dire calamity must sooner or later befall the population. Bovine typhus was devastating the district, though the natives denied all knowledge of it, and endeavoured to hide its very existence by having the animals slaughtered as soon as attacked; the tainted meat being sold for food, and the skins disposed of only too readily to clandestine dealers, who store them until favourable opportunity offers for their export.

"Animals dying before they could be killed were thrown by scores into the nearest canals, sometimes literally blocking the water-way, and these canals have all a common outlet—the Nile; and at Damietta, situated as it is on a semi-circular bend of the river, many of the carcases were caught in the reeds near the banks and left to putrefy in the sun, and send off poisonous exhalations.

"The town itself, also, inhabited by some 34,000 souls, is poorly built, almost totally un-Europeanized, and always in a wretchedly bad sanitary condition.

"Again, at the time of the outbreak there was a great fair being held in the town, called the Fair of Sidi Shattar, and with a population already poisoned by living to a great extent during the previous three months on diseased meat, and having only tainted water to drink, I hold that it needed but this unusual agglomeration of persons to cause the calamitous sickness.

"On the other hand, we have strong presumptive evidence that the disease could not possibly have been imported.

"The nearest place known to be infected with cholera was Bombay, and we are assured on high medical authority that there it was not of an epidemic character. The weekly mortality from cholera in that city rose, it is true, in the beginning of May, somewhat suddenly from five to twenty-eight, but quarantine (fourteen days, inclusive of time at sea) was at once imposed in Egyptian ports, and this quarantine was not taken off at Suez until the 27th June, five days after the commencement of the outbreak at Damietta, though the weekly number of deaths in Bombay from cholera had by 5th June once more receded to four.

"Since July 6th, 1882, I have had the honour to hold the position of British Delegate on the Sanitary Council, whose responsible duty it is to protect Egypt from the importation of disease. Before I became a member of this body, general and specific rules of action had been framed by a committee of its members. These rules were duly adopted by the

Board in the autumn of 1882, and have since that time formed the basis of its decisions.

"My voting power on the Board is very small, as I have only one voice among its twenty-two other members; but, acting in accordance, as I believe, with the spirit and letter of the instructions conveyed to me from her Majesty's Government, I have uniformly endeavoured to secure that the Board should not capriciously set aside its own rules, or, by imposing absurd or vexatious quarantines, go beyond them.

" Her Majesty's Government, while approving my course of action, have, it is true, sent me from time to time fresh instructions in this same sense, but I have never received instructions to interfere with, or in any way to endeavour to over-ride, the quarantine regulations framed by the Board itself for the preservation of Egypt, nor have such regulations in any single instance been relaxed in consequence of representations, direct or indirect, from England. True, I have fought many a battle with my colleagues in the interests of British shipowners and of the vast British commerce with the East, but I emphatically assert (and I might appeal to the official records to substantiate my assertion), that I have never for a moment allowed the interests of commerce to in any way take the first place to the danger of the public health.

" I have doubtless protested strongly and repeatedly against sudden and arbitrary changes in the regulations, but I have always held the preservation of Egypt to be my first duty, and have only, as a secondary though very important consideration, striven to secure that, in affording to Egypt protection, undue and vexatious restraints should not be placed on trade and navigation.

"If I have travelled somewhat beyond the immediate question at issue, I have done so in order to show that no relaxation of precautions has at any time taken place in consequence of British interference."

CHAPTER X

CHOLERA

THOSE who have never been in a cholera-stricken city can scarcely realize the awesome sensation as of an unseen messenger flitting through the streets, who wilfully and without reason signs to the Angel of Death to strike down this one or that one or a whole household. The scourge smites in one's own house, flits up the street, misses a dozen others, and smites again without justice, fitness, or cause.

The presence of cholera overshadows each trivial action of daily life. On rising in the morning the thought *will* protrude itself, " Which of us will be taken to-day ? " At meal-times one cannot help dwelling on the divergent views expressed by the medical authorities as to what to eat and drink, and what to avoid. Funeral processions move silently down the streets. The solemn roll of the drums and the dignified pomp of the " Dead March " tell of a military *cortège* paying the last honours to their dead. At night and all night long the funeral processions of the dead pass silently and mournfully, lit up weirdly by the unsteady glare from the huge bonfires which are kindled on open spaces in different quarters of the town, that the flames may purify the air. And the air in a stricken city is at such times close, thick, and oppressive. Indeed the natives of Egypt call cholera "El howa el asfar" (the yellow wind), doubtless from the curious atmospheric conditions—muggy, foggy, calm, and a yellowness in the air—which so often herald the disease or prevail during the time the epidemic is at its height. That there is something in this I am convinced, for though our dull senses may not always perceive anything out of the common, the birds of the air almost invariably desert a cholera-smitten area.

But apart from the fact that the scourge makes its presence felt, in a greater or lesser degree, to the ordinary dweller in a stricken city, I, personally, could not avoid constantly thinking of it. For at the meetings I had to attend as British Sanitary Delegate, cholera was the one subject discussed ; my official despatches treated for the most part of cholera statistics, and my duty further called me to the bedside of many a poor cholera patient. During these visits to the sick and dying, disinfectants were sprayed upon my clothes, and so when in the evening I returned home, my garments generally reeked of evil-smelling solutions, and my wife could not but know from what errand I had come.

On the 14th of July Lord Granville informed Sir Edward Malet that Surgeon-General Hunter, a medical officer of great Indian experience, was being sent to Egypt, the object of his mission being to report as to the character of the disease prevalent there, and to advise whether the Egyptian Government should be urged to take any additional measures for its repression.

Dr. Hunter left London on the 20th of July, and was informed by Lord Granville that, "so far as their other duties permit, Mr. Consul Miéville, temporarily acting as British Delegate to the International Quarantine Board in Egypt, and Dr. Mackie (second British Delegate at that Board) are attached to your mission."

The Egyptian Gazette then made the following announcement—

"We understand that Mr. Consul Miéville having completed his labours in connection with the Indemnity Commission, offered to continue his services on the International Sanitary Council until the termination of the present outbreak of cholera in the country. Mr. Miéville's offer has been accepted by her Majesty's Government, who have given him permission to remain in Egypt until further orders, and have instructed him to place his services at the disposal of Surgeon-General Hunter.

"We trust that the gallant devotion to his duties thus displayed by Mr. Miéville will meet with suitable recognition, for, as our readers are aware, this gentleman was gazetted some time ago her Majesty's Consul at Rio Grande do Sul, and on the conclusion of his work in connection with the indemnity claims was, in the ordinary course, entitled to proceed to take up his appointment, and would thus have avoided the trouble and anxiety inseparable from the duties which he has now voluntarily undertaken to perform *at a time when so many persons are endeavouring to place themselves in safety.*"

As the matter strikes me it would appear that the only plausible excuse the *Gazette* had for according me such a meed of praise lay in the fact, and I am sorry to say it, that the last fourteen words—the which I have italicized—*were but too true.* Panic among a large body of Europeans reigned supreme ; every one who could get clear of the country did so ; those who had intended going to Europe for change hastened their departure, those who had no such intention suddenly altered their minds and said they would take their holiday this year instead of the next, or the one after. Not one of them owned to being afraid, or to being guilty of bolting, but to those that remained the many sudden flittings looked remarkably like panic induced by sheer funk.

At the same time let me honestly confess that I do not wonder at the exodus, or blame those who could get away for so doing. Several times during the epidemic I myself half repented of having stayed on, and very likely had my plucky wife not stopped also to bear me company and share the danger, and had I not been almost too busy to think much of myself, I should have often felt inclined to follow their example and to scuttle. The most exorbitant prices were asked and paid for berths on some of the steamers : the queerest stories gained currency as to fabulous sums given by rich men to charter outside vessels to take them and their families and friends to the other side of the Mediterranean. Indeed there is little use in the non-official remaining during an epidemic: business is practically at a standstill; acquaintances and friends die daily around one, and so suddenly are they taken, that one is constantly reminded of the wise old words—" In the midst of life, we are in death."

I must not forget to add that we in the Queen's service could not have done otherwise than stick to our posts, for we had before our eyes the encouraging example of our great Chief, Sir Edward Malet. I here venture to give two extracts from private letters written by him to me at that time, the first having reference to the pluck of the Khedive Tewfik in contrast to the cowardice of a section of native doctors, and the second showing how very near Death often came to us, stepping even into our very houses.

" *Cairo, July* 25, 1883.—I am delighted that the Khedive should set so good an example as he has done this morning, by visiting, entirely on his own initiative, the cholera hospitals, and showing that he at least was prepared to do his duty whatever might be the consequences."

And again—

" *Cairo, July* 27.—I am sorry to say that my boab, a Berberine, was taken ill with cholera in the night, and when I went to the hospital at Kasr Ain this afternoon to see after him he was already dead : my European servants have taken alarm and wish to be off, so I am beginning to feel the small inconveniences of the epidemic, in addition to the quantity of work it has thrown upon me."

Up to this date the total number of reported deaths from cholera throughout Egypt was close on 10,000, and by the end of July the average *daily* mortality had increased to from 800 to 900. Yet Alexandria itself had suffered little, and the general health of the town continued excellent, though there had been some few deaths daily from the prevailing scourge. I was much struck with this fact, for Alexandria could not in those days be called a very clean city. In the course of my investigations I stumbled across curious food for thought, and I came to the conclusion *that the burning of the city in July* 1882 *had much to do with its comparative immunity from cholera during July* 1883.

I then endeavoured to place on record (officially) certain considerations to which, when the epidemic should happily have terminated, and the whole history thereof come under review, I ventured to think some interest might attach. My memorandum (dated the 4th of August) runs as follows—

"Whether the city of Alexandria will happily be spared altogether from cholera in an epidemic form we cannot presume to foretell, and even whether, should it thus declare itself, the city will escape lightly, is a question where prediction might be at fault. Yet I venture to think that, whatever happens, some interest may attach to the following reasons, which occur to me as explaining in some degree why, since the first appearance of the cholera in Egypt six weeks ago, Alexandria has enjoyed almost entire immunity from the disease. There can be little doubt, I take it, that this is due in the main to the following causes: a plentiful supply of good water, and a sufficiency of pure air.

"The water is taken from the Mahmoudieh Canal, which in turn receives its supply from the Rosetta branch of the Nile at Atfeh. On an average 21,000 tons are daily pumped into the Alexandria pipes, and considering the population of the town does not exceed 210,000, the supply therefore is abundant. As to the quality, I have only to mention that since the month of May last a patent composition, 'alumino-feric,' has been continuously mixed with the water to cause a deposit of part of the earthy matter contained therein ; and this before the water has been allowed to enter the filter-bed, whence it passes through sand into the pipes. In addition, permangan-ate of soda has, during the last few anxious weeks, been daily used, with a view to destroying to some extent the organic matter, and the result has been capital water.

" The second point, viz. a sufficiency of pure air, may be considered as affording a curious and striking instance of how unexpected good may arise out of events which appear at the time of their occurrence calamitous in the extreme. Little more than a year ago a great portion of the European quarter of Alexandria was wantonly destroyed by incendiaries, the great Square and some of the principal streets being after the fire simply heaps of charred ruins.

The walls, it is true, were in many cases left standing, bearing gaunt witness to the past, but these have since either fallen or have been removed, and the total area once occupied by the buildings thus destroyed is now open space, some 115,000 square yards in extent, and serves to-day as lungs to the city, whereas had the fire not occurred, it would be covered, as aforetime, with unhealthy, wretchedly-drained buildings, most of them many-storeyed, and by their great height shutting out light and air from the houses behind them.

"It seems probable that the action of the fire itself must also have done vast good in purifying Alexandria, but however this may be, the fact still remains that the burning of the European quarter gave the city new lungs, covering nearly twenty-four acres of ground, situated, moreover, so advantageously, that the fresh sea-breezes from the north can now reach those squalid quarters where light and air are most wanted, yet hitherto have been least known.

"Prominently, however, as the above points may present themselves to the mind as having contributed to the escape of the city hitherto from a heavy visitation of the scourge now passing over Egypt, it would be unjust not to mention other causes, to which undoubtedly much is due.

"An organization, *ad hoc*, known as the Alexandrian Extraordinary Sanitary Commission, which owes its primary existence to the initiative of Mr. Consul Cookson, has done good work, in cleansing, not the streets only, but the hovels and huts of the poorer

classes, and also by inducing those in a better station
of life to carry out in their own houses such ordinary
sanitary precautions as are so often overlooked or
neglected. The commission has also been instrumental in causing the removal of vast accumulations
of filthy refuse; has exercised supervision over the
food supply of the city, and has prevented an undue
agglomeration of refugees from congregating in Alexandria.

"Thanks also to the exertions of Mr. Cornish, the
resident engineer and manager of the Alexandria
Water Company, the sewage of the town has, since the
9th of July, been pumped out into the bay into six
feet six inches depth of water. At two points engines and pumps, with pipes to the summit levels of
some of the sewers, have been placed to pump up
sea-water for flushing them, and at three other points
water has been laid on from the Water Company's
mains. Boilers also have been placed for melting a
strong solution of sulphate of iron, which is mixed
with the water at the points where it is run into the
sewers, and gangs of men are employed in putting
temporary dams into the sewers to divert the course
of the water in different directions, the dam being
suddenly drawn when the sewer becomes full, thus
causing a rapid flush.

"It must unfortunately be admitted that the sanitary condition of certain quarters of the town is,
nevertheless, still bad enough to, of itself, breed pesti-
lence; yet almost all that could have been done since
the epidemic declared itself at Damietta in June last

has been accomplished, and though it would be rash to predict confidently as to the future, yet we may at least reasonably hope that the scourge, should it ultimately gain some hold here, will not commit such ravages as during the visitation of 1865."

By an unfortunate coincidence, the mortality in Alexandria began to increase two days after the date of the foregoing memorandum. On the 6th of August there were nine deaths—the next day there were 17, on the 11th the number was 32, on the 13th, 44, and on the 17th, 50 (the highest recorded). By the end of the month the daily mortality had happily dwindled down to twelve.

Yet even a maximum of fifty deaths daily in a town of over 200,000 inhabitants certainly justified my prediction that Alexandria would enjoy comparative immunity. Cairo, with *not quite double* the population of Alexandria, lost *nine times as many* (463) in one day.

But to any one unaccustomed to cholera—with its attendant horrors and the constant shocks inseparable therefrom—fifty deaths a day (including personal friends and acquaintances as often as not) are quite enough to have a most dangerously depressing effect. But thanks to my wife's constant cheerful companionship and to the high animal spirits with which Dame Nature has endowed me, I managed to keep a light heart. And in this connection—and also because the epistle is itself good-humouredly clever and genial—I will give a short quotation from a letter addressed to me at the time by Mr. William Andrews, an old and valued Suez friend, now, alas! gathered to his fathers.

"*Suez*, 22 *August*, 1883.—MY DEAR MIÉVILLE," he wrote, "It is refreshing to hear from you, your cherrup is so cheery. You don't seem to be suffering under the 'prevailing epidemic,' and are open for a dose of invigorating 'mixture.' And yet you are what? I have heard of a pasha of many tales (or tails), but you are a Consul holding nominations all over the world, and in the most inaccessible regions ; even my geography is at fault. And the strange thing is, you yourself don't seem to know the way to the appointments : you will require an American axe to pioneer a path and to 'blaze' your course. The trouble then would be when and how would you turn up on 'pay-day' to draw your salary. No, you are wise, stick to the present diggings hot as they are. Bills are discountable and there is a 'market': let remote regions perish while withal you may exist. How would this notice read in the *Gazette*? I mean the *London Gazette*.

" LOST.

" ' Lost in the mahogany forests on the banks of the Rio Grande do Sul, supposed to have been eaten by alligators, a British Consul, may be recognized by his buttons (which are indigestible)—leaves a sorrowing wife and no family. Any alligator returning his remains for cremation will be suitably rewarded by the gift of a spare Egyptian official.'

"As to myself, I am threatening every day to give

Egypt up and retire on my modest competence, where ships do not trouble, and where consuls and burial-grounds are unknown. There, in peace and loving-kindness to all mankind, I would settle accounts with all my friends as well as enemies, returning unto each four-fold of all I ever dispossessed him of. I wish really I could get a good laugh ; ' A sound heart is the life of the flesh,' says a wise man, and a good laugh is as marrow to the bones, say I. Words and my imagination fail me in my opinion of the Sanitary Council ; it is the highest tyranny the world ever witnessed since the days of Nero. Oh, that a court of law was open to bring them up individually for damages, and for absence of logic ! The Autocrat of All the Russias is an infant compared with their doings.

" I have now merely the time to scribble these few lines in compliment to your cheeriness."

With the cholera rapidly dying out, the reason for which I had volunteered to stay on in Egypt ceased to exist ; and early in September I was ordered home. I said good-bye to Alexandria with very keen feelings of regret : the nine years I had passed in the land of Egypt had endeared it to me, and I had made many staunch friends. The bidding " Farewell " seemed the more hard, inasmuch as my future home was to be so far away and in quite a new country, but there is a saying in Egypt that " he who once tastes of the waters of the Nile is sure again to return to drink of them," and this saw was destined to be quickly fulfilled in my case.

CHAPTER XI

WE left Alexandria on board a Khedivial mail steamer bound for Port Said, and there transferred ourselves to the P. and O. s.s. *Kaiser-i-Hind*. We travelled in the company of our good friends the Goussios, and when we boarded the *Kaiser-i-Hind* we found that because we had come from Alexandria, where, though the epidemic was rapidly dying out, daily cases of cholera were still occurring, our little party were looked on, more or less, as unclean, and were at first most severely left alone. This circumstance, together with the fact of Mr. Goussio being a Greek, and our own name having both a foreign sound and look, led to curious little misunderstandings. Quite happy in our own society, and seeing that our Indian and Australian fellow-passengers regarded us somewhat as lepers, we kept much to ourselves, taking up (and making it our own) a pleasant position near the after wheel; and the first evening (the Goussios being accomplished musicians) we sang old choruses. Gradually the songs—for Mr. Goussio had a lovely voice—attracted the attention of a group of young officers from Cairo, who had joined the ship at Ismailia. At first they contented themselves with listening, and then they tried, I fancy, to make out in what language we were singing (we were then humming what they considered a pretty Greek ballad more widely known as " Good-night, Mother "). As soon as we perceived that we had an audience, we thought we would mystify them with " The old stable-jacket." Some of the faces were a study.

The next day some one ventured to speak to my wife, and later the same individual accosted me with the remark, " Madame Miéville knows English wonderfully well!" " Oh, *pretty* well!" said I. Ultimately they found that we *were* English; they felt abashed and were profuse in their apologies.

What a pleasant voyage we had! Many of the Black Watch were on board with brother officers from other regiments—gunners, sappers, and the rest—and a fine festive night they made of it on the evening of the anniversary of the battle of Tel-el-Kebir. There was " Sandy " with his capital violin-playing and his wonderful card-tricks, and " Smiler " (of the same clan) who won the prize, adjudged by the ladies, for the worst-dressed man on board—both they and their comrades on board were " of the very best." Ah me! the merry party is scattered and will never meet again. Some have met soldiers' deaths—for there have been troublous days since then in the blood-soaked Soudan; others have left the service; others again have received well-merited promotion—

one gunner is now Governor of the Royal Military
Academy at Woolwich, young " Smiler " is now, I believe, a colonel, and in command of one of the finest
regiments in the world, and George Goussio, the brave
patriot, is no more, though in his own country, Greece,
which he loved so well, his memory lives and will long
remain a living thing. And Madame Goussio, his
disconsolate widow, who so nobly stayed by her
husband's side when he elected to stick to his post on
shore at Alexandria' during the bombardment, lives
only to carry on his good works, and to mourn his
irreparable loss. . .

Soon after landing in England, I reported myself
in Downing Street, and instead of being told to proceed to my distant South American Consulate, I
was once more temporarily attached to the Foreign
Office, and was instructed to work in the Consular
department under the late Sir H. Percy Anderson
and Mr. (now Sir Clement) Hill. I was again quite
happy in the Foreign Office and made many staunch
friends.

But this pleasant state of things early threatened
to end rather abruptly, for after a couple of months a
friendly, but, as I then thought, officious Under-Secretary of State began one afternoon to ask questions.
" Have you not got a consulate, Miéville ? " asked he.
" Certainly," said I. " In America ? " queried he.
" Yes," replied I. " South America ? " persisted he.
" I believe so," I answered. " Well," said he, " you
cannot stay on working here for ever, so you must
either proceed to your post, or you will be placed on

half-pay." I pleaded for a week's delay, which was accorded me, and the conversation terminated. At the end of the week I went to the great Under-Secretary and informed him that *I would take the half-pay*. This was by no means what he had intended, but he distinctly remembered having suggested this alternative course, so could not back out of it, and thus it came to pass that once more against my name appeared in the official record the statement, " Did not proceed." For, before I had completed my four months on half-salary, propitious fates intervened, a brilliant chance was offered me, and the provinces of Rio Grande do Sul and Santa Catarina were provided with another Consul. And if the notice "LOST, a British Consul," evolved out of the fertile brain of my dear old Suez friend, is ever really wanted, the reward will be offered for the remains of some more worthy official than the author of these every-day reminiscences.

But I am anticipating. I must here record an example of the stupidity of Red Tape. One of my first acts after my arrival in London had been to inquire how it was that I had never received the Egyptian war medals—the Queen's silver medal and the Khedive's bronze star—to which I was undoubtedly entitled, my subordinates in the Alexandria Consulate at the time of the bombardment having already received them. I was informed that my name had not been included in the list of officials sent home at the time, and that now my application was too late. I pointed out that the cause of the omission of my name from the original list was not far to seek. The gentleman who for some occult reason had been allowed, or requested, to send in the names of civilians after the bombardment, was a non-official (in fact a contractor to her Majesty's ships in Egyptian waters): he had known, and been friendly with me for years, and he came to me at the time and asked to be permitted to include my name in his list : I demurred to this course, telling him that my name would doubtless be sent home through some more official channel. There the matter for the time ended. Kindly Everard Wylde of the Foreign Office, who had been good enough to explain matters at the Admiralty, advised me not to worry any more about it. However, I am not easily beaten by routine and red tape, so I set to work with a will, and pestered both Admiralty and Horse Guards, until the end of it was that it was officially placed on record that I had been present at the bombardment in a responsible position, that my life had been many times in danger, that my intimate knowledge of both fortifications and town of Alexandria had been of service, and that I had landed, fully armed, and had accompanied, if not conducted, burial parties sent into the ruined Adda and Pharos forts. And I worked with such fixed determination, that in February 1884 I was officially informed that the Egyptian medal and bronze star would be sent to me. And from Brussels, where he had on leaving Egypt been appointed Minister Plenipotentiary, Sir Edward Malet wrote—

"MY DEAR MIÉVILLE,

"I am very glad that the hearts of our officials have been softened. It was absurd that I should have the medals and you not.

"Yours sincerely,
"E. B. MALET."

It is exactly such ill-advised and shabby acts by the departments at home that cause irritation to men who have borne the burden and heat of the day, and it is all the more culpable since nobody gains by it.

And now I come to another, perhaps THE turning-point in my career. I was quietly working in the Foreign Office one afternoon in the middle of February 1884, when a senior clerk came in and said to me, "You know all these ancient and modern Egyptian dignitaries, can you help me to make out this name?" He then told me that a cipher telegram had arrived from Cairo stating in substance that the native President of the Quarantine Board in Egypt had been transferred to another post, and that the best man to fill the vacant presidentship would appear to be a certain . . . if his services could be secured. By an extraordinary coincidence the name, I found, was *my own!* Sensation!

I left the Foreign Office purposely early that afternoon, and, being careful to leave my address, betook myself to Folkestone for pleasant meditation and a whiff of the sea. And there I received a note from a secretary telling me that Lord Granville had just heard that the office of President of the Alexandria Board of Health was vacant, and would be glad to know if I would wish for the appointment in case he had an opportunity of recommending me for it. I lost no time in telegraphing in the affirmative, and the next day went up to Downing Street, where I thought it only just and right to point out that the appointment, if made, would be a most unpopular one at first, and be sure to meet with much antagonism. "For," said I, "when British representative on the Board, I was obliged many times and oft to rub up my fellow-delegates the wrong way, and to constantly oppose their pet theories, and even apart from this objection I fancy the Board will not exactly relish having its debates presided over by a non-medical man." I further added that most of the members were old enough "to be my father"; indeed the disparity in our ages was really very marked, for later on I ascertained that, while my own age was under twenty-nine, the average age of the other members was forty-six.

But though I thought it fair to make Lord Granville aware of these drawbacks to the nomination, I did not by any manner of means intend to convey the impression that I feared the possible opposition.

Two days passed, but I received no further tidings, at least none of a definite nature; but the third day on opening my *Times* I was pleasantly surprised to read under "Latest Intelligence" the cablegram—

"*Cairo, February* 24.—Mr. Walter Miéville, formerly British Consul at Alexandria, has been named President of the Alexandria Quarantine Board."

Congratulations poured in, but the curious part of it was that all the Foreign Office congratulations were accompanied by the remark (varying only in form), "You seem to have got the right side of Baring and Clifford Lloyd." Baring was Sir Evelyn Baring (now Viscount Cromer), who had in October 1883 succeeded Sir Edward Malet as British Agent and Consul-General in Egypt, and Clifford Lloyd was the lately appointed English Under-Secretary at the Egyptian Home Office. I am afraid my Foreign Office friends only smiled when I said I knew neither Sir Evelyn Baring nor Mr. Clifford Lloyd. Yet, oddly enough, it so happened that I had never set eyes on or communicated with either one or the other, though, from all I could glean, it was owing to their strong representations that I had been selected for the presidentship.

My own impression is that conscientiously casting about for a man to fill the vacancy, and not content to put a square peg into a round hole, these two had tumbled across some record—probably Sir Edward Malet's despatches—testifying to my work as the former British Delegate, and had come to the conclusion that my struggles, single-handed against twenty colleagues, on behalf of navigation, were likely to prove of more avail were I President of the Board with consequently increased power.

Within a week from the date of reading in *The Times* the news of my appointment, my wife and I were on our way once more to the land of Egypt, but this time in the service of a new master, the Khedive Mehemet Tewfik.

Meanwhile all was not running quite smoothly for

me in Cairo. I never could quite fathom the true
secret history connected with the appointment, but
there is no doubt that a hitch occurred somewhere.
In after years I on two or three occasions attempted
to induce the Khedive to tell me all about the
difficulty, but his Highness always laughingly turned
the conversation.

A party evidently existed about the court in Cairo
—an anti-English, anti-reform, and therefore anti-
Clifford Lloyd party—who when they heard the
presidentship was vacant set up a candidate of their
own ; and so well did they push their man (a pasha
of Austrian nationality, it was said) that the ministers
were inclined to look favourably on the nomination,
and I think even went so far as to encourage him to
hope that he would be appointed President. The
story commonly current alleged that they even congratulated the pasha. Be this how it may, the
opposition party were jubilant, and an inkling of
their cause for rejoicing was apparently conveyed to
Clifford Lloyd. Now Mr. Clifford Lloyd was, as
Irish history amply testifies, a man of prompt, as well
as strong, decisive action ; so when he heard of
possible opposition to the nomination which he himself had decided would be the best, he took up his pen
and without more ado he wrote the following highly
characteristic announcement, which duly appeared
on the 26th of February in the Egyptian official
organ—

"Il a plu au Gouvernement Egyptien de nommer

M. Walter Frederick Miéville, Président du Conseil Sanitaire Maritime et Quarantenaire.

"Pour le Ministre de l'Intérieur,

"Le Sous-Secrétaire d'État,

"CLIFFORD LLOYD."

The words *Il a plu* must have appeared very quaint to foreigners in general, and Frenchmen in particular ; but, being so evidently a literal translation of the English formula "it has pleased," they proved unmistakably that the announcement had been made directly by Clifford Lloyd himself, though he had signed it "For the Minister of the Interior." At all events this paragraph, published in the *Official Gazette*, cut the ground from under the feet of the opposition, for the Egyptian Government could not well repudiate the deliberate act of their English Under-Secretary. Possibly some little annoyance was felt in certain quarters, possibly also some mild remonstrance was addressed by the Minister to his over-zealous colleague, but his action was final, and in the next day's issue of the *Official Journal*, I was gazetted by a decree drawn up in proper legal form, signed by his Highness the Khedive and counter-signed by their Excellencies Nubar Pasha, as Prime Minister, and Sabet Pasha, as Minister of the Interior. This decree was evidently in substitution of the somewhat irregular announcement, "It has pleased the Egyptian Government to appoint . . ."

The good ship *Gwalior* steamed into Alexandria harbour on Thursday, the 6th of March, 1884, and

" Monsieur le Président " and " Madame la Présidente " found themselves once more in the hospitable land of Egypt, with a difference only in title and emoluments, and owing allegiance to his Highness the Khedive as well as to their own Sovereign Lady.

I had been lazy on board ship for three days, but on touching shore idleness and I would be strangers for some time to come. So, without the loss of an hour, I dressed for the part I had to play—a black broadcloth suit (the coat being cut very like a clergyman's) and a close-fitting red cap with a black tassel hanging from the top. The clerical coat is locally known as a " Stambouline," and the red head-gear as a " tarboosh " or " fez," and together they constitute the official garb or uniform of civilians in the Egyptian Government service. Thus attired I took train to the capital, and the next morning presented myself at the Palace of Ismailiah, where I had been informed the Khedive was in residence. The master of ceremonies on duty that day, Tonino Pasha (or Bey as he then was), an agreeable official, an Italian by birth, received me at once, but rather damped my ardour by saying that his Highness could not see me, it being Friday, which to a Mohammedan is the equivalent of the Christian Sunday or the Hebrew Sabbath. The excuse for not receiving me—if excuse it was—seemed so plausible and reasonable that I almost turned on my heel, but I thought of the work waiting for me at Alexandria and chafed at the delay, so decided to try again. " I quite understand the reason, my dear Bey," said I, " but under the circumstances I must ask you to tell the Khedive I am here. His Highness is probably anxious to see me, and might not be pleased to hear you had sent me away." But Tonino was not inclined to give way, and it was only after the most dogged insistence that I persuaded him to disturb the Khedive. Happily, his Highness was in a very good humour (for the matter of that I rarely saw him otherwise), and said he would see me, so my importunity had its reward, and I was ushered into my new master's presence.

As I entered the audience-chamber, a good-sized room gorgeous with its Louis XV. furniture, thick silk curtains, and costly upholstery, the Khedive rose, and taking a step forward, put out his hand to welcome me, for I had previously been known to him when in Egypt as British Consul. Mehemet Tewfik was about thirty years of age, of average height but somewhat inclined to stoutness. His kindly pleasant face, with its regular features and neatly-trimmed brown beard, cut all round to follow the natural lines of the chin and not terminating in a point, may fitly be described as handsome. But however opinions might differ as to his looks, no one who saw him often could fail to like his pleasant, genial expression.

On the threshold I "salaamed" his Highness, that is I bent low, and with the right hand nearly touched the ground, then straightening myself, lightly and rapidly placed the hand on the heart, lips, and forehead, the significance of which graceful gesture being, that by touching the ground one promises obedience and humility, and by touching heart, lips, and forehead that one will render loyal, truthful, and intelligent service. Then advancing to where he stood, I took the Khedive's outstretched hand and made my little speech.

"Monseigneur," said I, "as I have loyally served my Queen, so will I serve your Highness so long as I wear your uniform. More than this no one can promise, though they may use more flowery language."

The Khedive replied, "I know I can trust you, doctor, and you may always rely on me to help you."

I thanked him and explained that I was *not* a doctor; but his Highness often in after years repeated the mistake and addressed me as "doctor," finding it somewhat difficult, I suppose, to realize that a civilian could preside over the deliberations of a medical body, and have, besides, many doctors working under him. We then chatted on indifferent subjects, the only remark that I recall being, "You will like my service better than a consulate in Brazil." This was said laughingly, and I replied "Mahloom," which is the Arabic equivalent for "why, certainly." The rest of that day, and all the next, was taken up in paying official visits to Egyptian Cabinet Ministers, and to European diplomatic agents, and then I went back to Alexandria to begin my new work in earnest.

My first official act was to say to the Head Office Staff a few words in reply to their address of welcome and congratulation.

CHAPTER XII

ABUSE

I CANNOT better give an idea of the constant difficulties which were thrust upon us by the French, and which beset all our administrative acts in Egypt during these years, than by giving their attitude in the cholera year ; and I therefore let them speak as much as possible in the next few chapters out of their own mouths.

When I let it be clearly understood at the Foreign Office, that my appointment was bound to be unpopular and to meet with much antagonism, I meant what I said, and I gave what seemed to me full and sufficient reasons. But I frankly admit that I was quite unprepared for the frequency, scurrility, and virulence of the attacks which were made in the anti-English Press in France and in Egypt against my nomination. And, as showing *what many an Anglo-Egyptian official besides myself* had in these early days of the occupation to put up with in return for their endeavours to introduce reforms, I translate from the original French a few specimens of the articles and paragraphs in which I was held up, almost daily, to public contumely, scorn, and contempt.

Le Bosphore Egyptien of the 29th February, 1884, wrote thus—

"It is self-evident! the English want to avenge themselves for the firm and constant opposition to the establishment of their pretended reforms which they encounter at every step and at every minute. To-day we see them trying to organize the introduction of cholera into Europe. Do not believe, however, that the eminent reformers to whom we owe this serious step have been influenced, in doing what they have done, by any consideration for the general weal. They have simply obeyed orders issued from the City by manufacturers of underwear and by cinnamon merchants whose watchword, as is well known, is 'No delays, on any pretext whatever, must be allowed to interfere with British homeward-bound merchant vessels from India.' And Great Britain has been pleased to parade her noble sentiments towards humanity by placing at the head of the Maritime and Quarantine Council a loyal servant of her Gracious Majesty the Queen.

"Ever happy in her choice, England has designated to fill this important position Consul Miéville, who, during the cholera epidemic which has lately devastated Egypt, acted in the way we all remember, and to whom we must in all justice attribute the responsibility for introducing cholera in 1883 into the Nile Valley. We may perhaps be told that England, by the fact of the appointment of one of her sons to the

Presidentship of the Maritime and Quarantine Council, only secures in reality one more vote on a Board composed of representatives of foreign Powers and of Egyptian Government officials, and that we are wrong to give to a simple and unimportant incident a gravity which it does not possess.

"We shall reply by saying that Egypto-English officials increase at such a rate that we may very likely find, in but a short time, nothing but Englishmen in the Egyptian Government Departments. As a matter of fact, if we examine the actual composition of the Maritime and Quarantine Council, we shall discover that, setting aside the delegates of the Powers, the Egyptian members are for the most part Britishers.

"The President, Mr. Miéville, is English; the Director-General of Customs is English; the Comptroller-General of Ports and Lights is English; the Harbour-Master at Alexandria is English; and as for the natives on the Board, such as the doctor of the Alexandria Hospital, the Sanitary Inspector, and others, shall we be taxed with exaggeration or bad faith if we affirm that these functionaries will be expected to servilely obey all orders emanating from the English President under penalty of losing their posts on showing the slightest inclination to independence? We hardly think so. The nomination of Mr. Miéville to the presidentship cannot be otherwise thought of by us than as a culpable act; and the public already call it 'The Triumph of Cholera.'"

Then *Le Courrier de France*, a Paris paper, printed the following effusions—

" Our Letters from Egypt, No. I.

" Thanks to Mr. Clifford Lloyd, and to Sabet Pasha, Minister of the Interior, who, as is well known, is but a regular signing machine, the Quarantine Board has been given to an Englishman, and what an Englishman! You shall know all about him immediately, but first for the history of his appointment.

" The Cabinet had been called together especially to nominate the famous President of the Maritime and Quarantine Council. The candidates put forward were a Frenchman, Ardouin Bey, Inspector-General of the Quarantine Service; an Austrian, Federigo Pasha, holding the Egyptian rank of Vice-Admiral; and a Greek doctor, Neroutsos Bey, an ex-official of the Sanitary Administration. After a somewhat lengthy verbal interchange of ideas, Ardouin Bey was set aside *because he was French*, Neroutsos Bey for other reasons, and the suffrages of the Ministers were thus in favour of Federigo Pasha. Federigo is a good man, grown grey in the Egyptian service, and also well enough liked in the country. The thought that guided the voters was thus an eminently reasonable one; being unable to give the post to a Frenchman by reason of his nationality, the Ministers gave it to an Austrian, almost an Egyptian, incapable of not giving due weight to the opinions of the European delegates when expressed at the Quarantine meetings.

"His appointment was thus secured, when Mr. Clifford Lloyd received a telegram from London, a telegram sent to him through Sir Evelyn Baring, who accompanied it by a few lines. It was simply an order given by London to the Egyptian Ministry to appoint to the post of President of the Council in question a fourth candidate designated by the English Cabinet ; a candidate whose name was given in full in Lord Granville's telegram. The Egyptian Ministry, all Anglophil as it was, was astonished both at the process employed and at the choice made. This surprise found expression, and it was further observed that probably Europe would receive badly the nomination of an Englishman as head of the Quarantine Board, and that France especially, which had consented to retire her candidate in favour of either an Austrian, an Italian, or a Greek, or above all in favour of an Egyptian, would not accept an Englishman who had very often expressed opinions . . . against quarantine. Mr. Clifford Lloyd listened to these observations, shrugged his shoulders, and limited himself to saying, 'In Egypt what pleases England must be carried out. As to France and Europe, we have not here to consider what they may think ; if they address complaints to us, we will send them on to London.'

"In spite of this haughty declaration, a proposal was made to adjourn the matter of the Presidency for a few days. But on this Mr. Clifford Lloyd, without deigning to reply, left the Ministers, and in order to put an end to this hesitation, which he evidently considered as a want of respect to the Queen's Cabine he drew up and signed the following note, of which the insolent and imperious wording closed the door to all negotiations whatsoever—

"'It has pleased the Egyptian Government to appoint Walter Frederick Miéville, Esquire, President of the Maritime and Quarantine Council.'

" It is not necessary to say that this brutal manner of obliging the Nubar Ministry to give way was severely criticized here. The proceeding was characterized as indecent, and one asked oneself if benevolent Europe and placid France would put up, without complaint, with what may be said to be a most rude scoff at them. For it must be, after all, one of two things ; either Europe means that quarantine shall be imposed in Egypt during the cholera season in India, or she does not. If she does not, then let her recall her delegates on the Quarantine Council, for to-morrow they will assuredly be made game of by the new President. If she does, then let her insist on the appointment of Mr. Miéville, so insulting for her, being cancelled, and let her insist on the independent and international character of the Quarantine Board being preserved.

"And now let me present to you his Excellency Walter Frederick Miéville, President of the Quarantine Board—

"Mr. Miéville is a young man thirty or thirty-two years of age at most. He came to Alexandria a dozen years ago from the Foreign Office, where, like a lot of other young fellows, he was without position other than that of an unpaid *attaché*.

" Being in poor health, he was sent to Egypt to gain

strength, and to find some sort of a billet. At first there was an idea of getting him into the English Telegraph Company at Alexandria. He had discovered in this city a distant relation, who was none other than Mr. Cookson, the Consul and Judge. This sickly young Englishman was treated like a spoilt child by the British colony, who forgave him all his irritability; and this was a pity, as ever since it has formed an integral part of his character. His relation, Mr. Cookson, in spite of, or perhaps because of this, continued to show him great affection. Thanks to him, Walter Miéville was, by a knowing move, appointed Consul at Khartoum; a hard post, and therefore paid at the rate of £600 a year. It was certainly never intended to send him there, but simply to give him a position and salary, for salaries in England run on until the holder of a post sends in his resignation. A little later on he was medically examined, and the doctors pronounced the young Consul to be unfit to proceed to his post. Another gentleman was appointed, and Mr. Miéville has nearly ever since been employed in the Alexandria Consulate, except for four months, when he was sent to act at Suez. And now it is still near to Mr. Cookson, and under his wing, that the President of the Quarantine Council has found a good billet. No wonder then that the appointment of such a President is considered astounding, and augurs ill for the future administration of the Quarantine service.

"Mr. Miéville, having married here, went off to London to complain of his nomination to a Consulship in Brazil which, like a gutter-tile, had just fallen on his head. Mr. Cookson, it would appear, has succeeded in staving off the necessity of Mr. Miéville's going to Brazil, to the great detriment, we may be sure, of the preservation of public health in Egypt and in Europe."

"*Our Letters from Egypt, No. V.*

"All the preservative measures against cholera—which nevertheless rages with intensity in Bombay and Calcutta—are suspended ever since the nomination of an English President named Miéville, an astounding choice if ever there was one. I knew little Walter, in the days when quite inoffensively he made us merry on our donkey-riding parties by galloping along with his back turned to his donkey's head. Who would have ventured then to prophesy that, much less inoffensive, he would be called on by his country to put his foot against the door of Egypt to prevent it shutting and keeping out Indian cholera?

"The appointment is a mad one."

And again *Le Bosphore Egyptien*, on the 20th of April in the same year, wrote—

"Mr. Miéville has not rested on his laurels; after having presented Egypt in 1883 with an epidemic of cholera, here he is making ready to introduce the terrible scourge into Europe. A telegram came to hand yesterday afternoon after we had gone to press, announcing that a case of cholera had occurred on board a vessel from India during its passage through the Suez Canal. This news has produced both in Alexandria and Cairo considerable stir. The exact facts are that the English transport, H.M.S. *Crocodile*, from Bombay, a city in which numerous cases of cholera occur daily, arrived at Port Said on the 15th instant at half-past six in the evening. The vessel entered the port flying the quarantine flag, and did not let down her accommodation-ladders. The Canal pilot, who had been taken on board at Ismailia, was at once isolated in quarantine. Before her arrival at Suez the *Crocodile* had buried at sea a man whom the ship's surgeon declared had died of liver complaint. It was only between Ismailia and Port Said that a case of cholera occurred.

"It is evident that Europe is threatened by the excessive facilities granted by Mr. Miéville, who is the commercial, rather than the sanitary, agent of Great Britain in Egypt, and we are led to hope that, in consequence of what has just happened, Mr. Miéville will be relegated to the sweets of private life."

Then *Le Moustique*, a weekly humorous paper printed in Cairo, thought fit to notice me.

"(1) CHIT-CHAT.

"Last Monday, on the occasion of the general holiday of Cham-el-Nessin (the sniffing of the Zephyr), there was a great show of policemen, both English and native, in our streets. Why? For whose special benefit were these warlike preparations? Mystery. Some say that it was to stop the cholera, which had escaped from Suez, and was on its way to Cairo in order to personally thank the Honourable Mr. Clifford Lloyd for his goodness in appointing Mr. Walter Miéville President of the Quarantine Council. However this may be, the day has passed quietly, the evening likewise."

"(II) LATEST NEWS.

" The cholera, now in the port of Suez with a load of microbes, has approached Mr. Miéville with a view to obtaining permission to traverse the Canal in order to sell its goods in Europe. We trust that Mr. Miéville will grant the request if he does not wish to be accused of monopolizing the whole of this merchandise for Egypt's use."

"(III) TELEGRAMS.

By travelling Mosquitoes.
(Special service of the ' Mosquito.')

"*Suez, 25th April*, 1884.

"Mr. Miéville has bought an immense plot of ground on which to install an establishment for the acclimatization of microbes.

"Bravo! Very practical, Mr. Miéville."

And once again *Le Bosphore Egyptien,* on the 1st of May, 1884, eased its mind by the following—

"The English transport, the *Crocodile,* has reached England, having had on board six cases of cholera, three of which were fatal, since leaving Suez. Our readers will remember the profound emotion caused among us by the news that a case of cholera had occurred on board an English vessel transiting the isthmus; this ship was the *Crocodile*, to which Mr. Miéville, the English President of the Quarantine Council, had granted permission to pass, although she had come from an infected country, and although cases of cholera had occurred on board before her entry into the Canal. Thus it is clear to what dreadful consequences the British authorities in general and Mr. Miéville in particular expose the public health of the Asiatic provinces bordering the Canal, and of the whole of Europe. Thanks to the presence of Mr. Miéville at the head of the Council, thanks to the complicity of the English agents of every kind and sort who have invaded official positions in Egypt, Europe cannot have any confidence in the observance by English vessels coming from India of the international regulations. This evil ought to be rooted up, and that with the briefest delay. But Mr. Miéville is decidedly much stronger than all the European Powers clubbed together."

CHAPTER XIII

CONFUTATION AND ENCOURAGEMENT

I. Confutation.

FOR a very long time this stream of abuse continued; I will now confine myself to a few glimpses of the real truth.

During the years the abuse flowed on I never gave the reptile Press the satisfaction of eliciting from me any sort of an answer, direct or indirect. I only put pen to paper when my Minister transmitted to me (officially or semi-officially) complaints or accusations brought against me by some foreign representative. The more vicious and mendacious articles *did* sometimes make me desire to refute, by a strong wholesome dose of the true facts, the fallacious arguments employed, but I kept cool, and steadily declined to be drawn into a newspaper controversy. Once only did I ever communicate in any way with the editor of *Le Bosphore Egyptien*, and it was when the abusive paragraphs about me at last ceased. Then I sent through a mutual friend an invitation to the whole staff *to dine with me*, where and when they liked, provided only that their scurrilous sheet should continue, as before, to attack and abuse me. The actual message I sent (verbally, of course) was couched in familiar French — "Tell *Le Bosphore* fellows," said I, "that the abuse they have showered upon me for so long has, by constantly calling attention to me and my work, done me great good both in Downing Street and with Baring; that I am accordingly grateful, but that I am now disconsolate at the cessation of the attacks; that I will therefore stand the lot a jolly good dinner, if the editor will promise to take me up again in the good old strain."

Le Bosphore Egyptien declined my invitation, having evidently received a fresh cue; indeed as a matter of fact many medical luminaries in France were by that time fast coming round to sounder views on quarantine questions.

I shall not be far wrong in summing up the accusations brought against me thus—

1. That I introduced cholera into Egypt in 1883.

2. That I influenced the Egyptian members of the Quarantine Board to vote against their consciences, and was thus enabled to ride roughshod over the delegates of the foreign Powers.

3. That I accorded undue facilities to British shipping in general; and in the particular case of H.M.S. *Crocodile*, wrongfully allowed her to pass through the Suez Canal.

I will deal in turn with the three points of this indictment.

To pretend that I introduced cholera into Egypt in 1883 is childish mendacity. It is true that at the time of the visitation I was British Delegate on the Quarantine Board, but I had but one vote out of twenty-two. Had I therefore personally voted in the most criminal way, I could have done no harm. It is true that on the 31st May, 1883, I *proposed* that the quarantine then existing against Bombay should, in respect of *clean* vessels, be raised. It is true that my proposal was accepted, but it did not come into force till June 27, *i. e.* (it will be remembered) some days after cholera had broken out at Damietta. And even had the quarantine been raised *before* the outbreak, it would still be necessary to clearly trace the origin of the disease to direct importation from Bombay before imputing blame to any one. Then again, such blame could under no possible circumstances be laid at my door, for the decision of the Council to raise the quarantine (setting aside the actual fact that it could not have had any connection with the outbreak of cholera) had been taken by a majority of three to one. Seven representatives of the Powers and five Egyptian members voted in favour of the motion, while only the delegates of Austria, France, Italy, and Portugal voted against it. The accusation was in all probability brought forward with a view to annoy, and, if possible, dishearten me. Or it may even have been hoped that I should, if the attacks were virulent enough, be forced or induced to resign. It was one of the last efforts of the obstinate partisans of the antiquated and unsound theory that a vessel should be treated with sole reference to the state of health existing in the port of departure. Indeed in a few more years this misguided and behind-the-age group tardily acknowledged their stupidity, and in a body adopted the only sound principle to work on in quarantine matters: namely, that of treating vessels according to the state of health prevailing on board during the voyage, and at the actual time of arrival.

It is alleged that by reason of the large Egyptian voting power, of the undue influence exercised by me over the *Anglo*-Egyptian members, and of the threats used by me towards the *Native* Egyptian delegates, I managed to control the decisions of the Council, and to practically swamp the representatives of the fourteen foreign Powers. In 1885 this accusation was made officially by the Austrian Delegate, and I had no difficulty whatever in confounding my accuser, by simply presenting an analysis of the voting in fifty-three important cases affecting the public health. This analysis showed that in only nine cases out of the fifty-three had the Egyptian votes influenced in any way the decisions arrived at; that is to say, if the votes of the Egyptian members—native and English—are in the forty-four remaining cases eliminated altogether, the result of the voting in each case remains the same. In other words, the delegates of the European Powers had matters absolutely their own way forty-four times out of fifty-three.

The above answer to the second count in the indictment is to a certain extent applicable to the third count also. Being but the executive officer, I, as President, could not, even if I had so wished, have granted undue facilities to British shipping. When I say "could not," of course I mean without incurring needless personal risk, for had I done so in defiance of the Council's regulations or special decisions, I should have laid myself open to severe rebuke, if not actual dismissal, for it must be obvious that I was surrounded by most watchful enemies, who would have been overjoyed to catch me tripping. Moreover, I consider that a vaguely general accusation of showing favouritism need only be met, unless specific cases are cited, by a general denial. That denial I emphatically give. In all the long years I was President, I never wittingly did for a British vessel what I would not have done, and did do, when occasion offered, for vessels flying any other flag. When, however, a specific case is brought forward, a categorical answer should be given. I must therefore, though with much reluctance, deal fully with the case of H.M.S. *Crocodile*. I do this here, for it is a very marked example of the great danger and discredit to the country, to say nothing of international complication, which may arise from the evasion in Egypt by even under officials of rules approved by those in authority over them.

I am accused of having wrongfully allowed this transport to pass through the Suez Canal. As a matter of fact, I heard nothing whatever about her *until she had traversed the Canal*, and the case of cholera was reported to me by the Quarantine doctor at Port Said. But I did not at the time (nor do I wish to now) try to make my subordinate officer at the southern end of the Canal the scapegoat. He acted according to his lights, and in my opinion he acted rightly, *and as I should have done had I been in his place.* I at once assumed the entire responsibility. What happened was this. On the arrival of H.M.S. *Crocodile* at Suez, the usual interrogatories were administered to the medical officer in charge, and in reply to the question, " Have any of the passengers or crew died in any port of call, on board or on shore, or during the voyage ? " the doctor replied, "Yes, two children and three soldiers (invalids); all five from ordinary diseases." This was in writing, and was duly signed. And, in addition, the same medical official gave the Quarantine doctor the following certificate—

"Crocodile, at Suez, 14th April, 1884.

" I hereby certify that five deaths (two of children, three of men) have occurred on board during the passage from Bombay. The deaths were not owing to epidemic or contagious disease."

In the face of this declaration, my subordinate at Suez could not do otherwise than allow the *Crocodile* to proceed on her voyage. When, however, I heard of the death from cholera which had occurred on board while the *Crocodile* was still in the Canal, I thought there was something wrong somewhere, and I kept myself informed concerning the health of the vessel between Port Said and England. I learned that five further cases of cholera occurred between Port Said and Malta—three of which proved fatal. Then when the London *Times* of the 1st of May reached Egypt, I found to my disgust that the same doctor who had certified that there had been no epidemic or contagious disease between Bombay and Suez had, according to the *Times*, admitted, on arrival in England, that there had been at least one death from cholera *four days out* from Bombay. I was much annoyed, and sat down and wrote to the British Delegate, pointing out that, according to *The Times*, it would seem that from the tenor of the declarations made by the medical officers of H.M.S. *Crocodile* on her arrival in England, choleraic symptoms were noticed among her passengers almost immediately after the vessel's departure from Bombay, and that when the transport had been but four days at sea, a soldier named Sullivan had succumbed to a violent attack of Asiatic cholera, being carried off *in two hours*. I added that I was quite willing to admit that this account might not be correct ; but on the other hand considered, if the facts were as related in *The Times*, that a shameful and criminal act had been committed ; for the doctor who signed the Interrogatory and Certificate of Health at Suez had affirmed that during the passage from Bombay to Suez there had been no deaths on board the *Crocodile*, except five from ordinary diseases. I then begged the delegate, most urgently, to be good enough to request his Government to institute searching inquiries, in order that the truth might be ascertained and the guilty punished, if the facts as stated in my letter were found to be exact.

I believe that in transmitting my complaint to the proper quarter, the British Delegate stated that if the information on which my letter was founded was correct, the injury done to British interests and to the influence of the British Delegate at the Board, by the non-declaration at Suez of cases of cholera which happened on board the *Crocodile* before arriving at that port, could hardly be exaggerated.

And I much fear that the information *was* substantially correct, for *no answer was ever vouchsafed*.

Under the circumstances I think it will be allowed that, whoever else may have acted wrongly, no possible blame could attach to the Quarantine officials for having allowed the *Crocodile* to transit the Suez Canal.

II. *Encouragement.*

It seems to me that on the principle of hearing both sides (and since I have, as courtesy demanded, given the first fire to the opposition), I may now let counsel for the defence briefly reply.

The Daily News. London, 3rd March, 1884.

" Mr. Miéville, who has had considerable experience of official life in Egypt, has been appointed President of the International Quarantine Board. The efforts lately made to stop British ships from passing through the Suez Canal, on the pretext of the existence of cholera in India, renders this appointment one of great importance."

The Times. London, 5th March, 1884.

" Mr. Clifford Lloyd, writing on the last day of last year, describes the reforms introduced into Egypt in relation to prisons, police, sanitation, and so forth. It is to be noted, however, that even these beginnings of reform have only been possible to Englishmen of exceptional energy, setting aside the fiction of independent Egyptian administrators. The appointment of an Englishman, Mr. Miéville, as President of the Quarantine Board, is a step in the right direction, of importance enough to call for notice. The Quarantine Board has been a centre of anti-English intrigue, which has done considerable injury to our commerce with India. Mr. Miéville's appointment will curtail its powers for mischief, and secure fair play for English interests."

The Egyptian Gazette. Alexandria, 2nd April, 1884.

" As our readers are aware, all vessels in times when quarantine is imposed by the Egyptian Quarantine Board against arrivals from India are obliged, even though in the most perfect sanitary condition, to complete on their arrival at Suez the term of fourteen days, counting the time occupied on the voyage, before being admitted to free *pratique.*

" This regulation has fallen with peculiar and undue severity on the vessels belonging to the large French, Italian, and British Mail Companies, inasmuch as, owing to their superior steam-power, they reach Suez in much less time than ordinary merchant vessels, these latter generally taking from thirteen to fourteen days for the voyage.

" We are indeed glad to see that the Quarantine Board have given this matter their serious consideration, and to learn that at a meeting held yesterday, it was decided unanimously to reduce the period of quarantine for the future from fourteen to eleven days in the case of ships-of-war, and in the case of vessels engaged in a regular mail service, and having a duly qualified medical officer permanently on the ship's articles. The modification thus provisionally introduced is of great importance."

The Times. London, 3rd April, 1884.
(By Eastern Company's Cables.)

"*Alexandria, 2nd April.*

"The period which must elapse after the departure from Bombay before vessels are allowed *pratique* at Suez has been reduced from fourteen to eleven days. This result has been achieved by the tact of Mr. Miéville, the new President of the Quarantine Board, who succeeded in procuring the voluntary proposal of the change by the French and Italian delegates, and instead of snatching a bare majority, carried the proposal with no dissentient, there being only one abstainer among eighteen members."

The Times. London, 11th June, 1884.

"At the eighty-seventh half-yearly meeting of the Peninsular and Oriental Company, held yesterday, the Chairman, Sir T. Sutherland, in speaking of the difficulties caused by the re-imposition upon travellers of quarantine in Egypt and in Italy, said that, with regard to the quarantine in Egypt, the vexatious delays had been greatly lessened since the appointment as President of the International Board of an Englishman."

* * * * * * *

Though by so doing I am anticipating events by a few months, I give the following brief extract from a private letter written by me to a relative—

> "*Alexandria, 11th November* 1884.

"I am less busy and pushed for time just now, having, happily, despatched my Budget for 1885 to Cairo for submission to the Cabinet, which, by the bye, is in this country called 'the Council of Ministers.' It is a very good Budget, and *even my enemies* on the Quarantine Board made pretty speeches about the success of my administration during the last six months, *and voted me thanks.* They also voted me *an increase of salary.*

"Shortly, the facts are these. The Budget for the year that ended on the 30th September last was a poor one, and it was thought when the Budget was framed that there would be a balance of but £220—instead of which I handed over on 30th September, 1884, more than nine thousand pounds! And in addition I had met extraordinary expenses, to the extent of some £1700—the which had not been provided for in the Budget. These are rather dry details, but I know you will be interested, as in a way they represent the result of my seven months' anxious efforts to place the service on such a sound basis that peculation and *backsheesh* should henceforward be unknown and practically impossible."

CHAPTER XIV

THRUST AND PARRY

THE Parisian paper, *Le Courrier de France*, of the 2nd of May, 1884, gave prominence to the following—

"*Letter from Egypt.*

"I have always told the truth as to what passes in Egypt, and as to the consequences to be feared. Unhappily my voice has ever been *vox clamantis in deserto.* I do not feel discouraged, but I have, however, the right to point out that a certain big newspaper, which in its greatness disdains to quote me as its authority, does not scruple to adopt my views, and after the lapse of a month for examination and verification, to appropriate them as its own. Thus the *Temps*, and I do not even bear it any grudge for its conduct, has at last decided to speak of Miéville and of the calamitous character of his appointment as President of the Quarantine Council. And what *Le Courrier de France* was unable to accomplish the *Temps* has effected; it has disturbed, troubled, and interrupted the autocratic British governors in Egypt, and led Miéville to amend his ways. I should feel no bitterness if the triumph of the *Temps* was a solid victory, but, as you will soon perceive, it is not so.

"President Miéville, being momentarily obliged to give way before the cries of alarm so persistently raised, yielded by deciding on the re-establishment of quarantine against Indian arrivals, from Calcutta right round to Bassein, that is to beyond Bombay, thus including that port in the edict.   But no one who knows anything of the working or mechanism of the Quarantine service will feel secure solely by reason of this decision.

" Here, when it is a question of quarantine carried on under the English, the Quarantine staff has no choice but to follow its President's lead, for I do not fear contradiction when I affirm that it, more than the staff of any other Egyptian department, is absolutely in the power of the man who commands it.   From the highest functionary down to the humblest office boy, Mr. Miéville has only slaves whose sole preoccupation, and all-absorbing care, is to humour in all things and by all means their temporary master, who by a word, and without ceding the right of complaint or explanation, can remove them from their posts and cast them into the direst misery.   What a lot of Abd-el-Kader Pashas have I met with here, not only among military men but among civilians ; not only among the ranks of native officials, but also, alas ! among the ranks of European functionaries!   How many times have I heard this lamentable answer : ' I am of your opinion, certainly ! a thousand times of your opinion ; but do not suppose I shall say so, for if I did I should undoubtedly be sent about my business.   It is, I admit, a fine thing to be able to tell the truth and take the consequences, but it is a luxury not to be indulged in when, like myself, a man has brought his family abroad with him, and when that family relies on him alone for daily bread. Wait till I get out of this Egyptian prison and I will speak out.'

" Now given this state of things, can any one suppose that Mr. Miéville, the enemy of quarantine, who because of this enmity, and solely because of it, was appointed by England President of the Quarantine Council; can any one suppose, I say, that Mr. Miéville, after being constrained by the *bawlings* of Europe to reimpose quarantine against vessels from British India, will display much zeal in seeing that his staff seriously carries out a measure which has been wrung from, not to say imposed on, him? And can any one suppose that the staff, knowing the secret wishes of the master, will show more zeal than he does, or zeal independent of his? It would indeed be too silly to delude oneself with any such illusion. Thus we have quarantine on paper, free *pratique* in reality."

The accusations contained in the above " Letter from Egypt " are somewhat hard to meet, for they are based on an invention of the writer's fertile brain ; and further, it seems pretty obvious that he started the invention in order to have a peg on which to hang general abuse. He says that in consequence of the outcry in Europe *I* decided to re-establish quarantine against India. As a matter of fact I had little to do with the decision, further than presiding at the meeting of the Board at which it was taken. Again, it was a decision *unanimously* come to ; it *was* to this extent due to me that it was unanimous, in so far that before the meeting I begged the British Delegate not to oppose the motion. I had pointed out to him that inasmuch as the Quarantinist members had been reasonable when canvassed with a view to reducing by three days the scale of quarantine for men-of-war and postal steamers, and had carried the reduction without a single dissentient, so ought the Anti-Quarantinist delegates to refrain from active opposition when cholera was declared epidemic in India. I then explained that there really were no Anti-Quarantinists (nor could there be any on a Quarantine Board), except in the sense of certain members being desirous of substituting sound for obsolete theories. For I always held that patience and loyalty would wear down the opposition of the so-called Quarantinist party, and that gradually it must dawn on their prejudiced minds that a system of quarantine based on the common-sense view of treating vessels as foul *when found foul at the port of arrival*, must be a greater safeguard to the country than treating ships as clean or unclean according to their port of departure. This scarcely tallies with the charge that I had yielded to pressure and clamour, and that the measure had been *imposed on me*.

As to the second count in the indictment, that the staff, at my instigation, or to curry favour with me, applied the decisions of the Board carelessly, all I need say is, that had they done so it would have been against my express instructions and wishes, given repeatedly, both officially and privately.

That the members of the staff were at the President's mercy is a stupid fabrication, for my powers in regard to both doctors and clerks were ridiculously small : as a matter of fact, the Board's constitution laid down that all complaints against, or cases of misconduct on the part of members of the staff, were to be brought before a Disciplinary Board for inquiry. And even this Committee of Discipline could but inflict on the culpable a fine not exceeding a month's salary; for if it was thought that the offence merited heavier punishment, then the Committee were required to draw up a report and submit it to the Plenary Council to pronounce upon at its next sitting. Greater guarantees than these for ensuring both the independence and just treatment of the staff would appear almost impossible.

The same paper, *Le Courrier de France*, again attacked me on the 2nd of May, 1884.

"*Letter from Egypt.*

"The incident of the case of cholera that occurred on an English transport in the Suez Canal has produced a great sensation. Dame Europe, my friend, what does this emotion mean? The incident which so upsets you is not abnormal, or even isolated ; it will be followed by many others of the same description, and when cholera shows its sinister face in Mediterranean ports, you will scream out with alarm, an alarm quite as unjustifiable as your emotion is to-day, for you have willed it so, dear lady.   In order to protect the interests of British commerce, the English have thrown down the barriers which had been erected against the horrible scourge.   Cholera profits thereby ; it is but natural, it fulfils its destiny, I had nearly said its duty.

"Everything has its use here below : cholera decimates peoples, the English annex them.   Therefore it is for peoples to beware of both cholera and the English, the one bringing the other.   The person named Miéville, the English agent, who dragged his poverty through the streets of Alexandria, was appointed, no one knew how, Sanitary Delegate on the Quarantine Council.   In the place of talent, this man has a keen perception of what is required of him, and at once undertook to prove that quarantine is to cholera what a skimmer is to a shower, that is to say, a ridiculous preservative.

" The Miéville hit the right nail on the head.

" Sir E. Baring congratulated him, Sir Clifford Lloyd beamed on him, and her Gracious Majesty testified her satisfaction by placing him at the head of that very institution whose express mission it is to ward off the invading scourge by means of quarantine.   Did the Powers breathe a word on learning of this astounding nomination ?   No.   Catch the statesmen of Europe paying attention to the appointment of any ' John Bull ' whatsoever to the presidency of the Egyptian Maritime Council.   They have, indeed, other fish to fry—very well, let us say no more about it, and leave *Messire Choléra* to speak !   Alas, how many other

Miévilles swarm in the different administrations, gnawing away and destroying under the auspices of their worthy master, Mr. Clifford Lloyd ; and, sad to have to relate, the demolishing Irishman has known how to make the Minister himself bow the knee ; nay, better still, he has made him his most faithful agent ! Yes, Abd-el-Kader Pasha, the valiant General who would have tranquillized the Soudan had the repression of the revolt there been included in the British programme, Abd-el-Kader Pasha, whom the English have treated like a drummer-boy, has become the most humble and most devoted servant of Clifford Lloyd."

I should have only treated this scurrilous (but amusing) article with silent contempt, but the writer unwittingly stumbled on a truth which has doubtless been for some time patent to the reader, namely, that Europe would have herself alone to blame if cholera should unhappily invade her. For when the news of the outbreak of cholera in June 1883 reached Europe, the first and self-evident duty of the Sanitary authorities of the several countries north of the Mediterranean, was to set their houses in order, and to prescribe and enforce such measures as might seem best to them, with a view to warding off the imminent danger of the cholera being conveyed from Egypt across what is, after all, but an inland lake. Instead, therefore, of wasting ink in clamouring in *1884* against a harmless individual like myself, the wiser course for the French Press to have taken, would have been to press on the Government in *1883* the urgency of

cleansing the insanitary city of Marseilles, of ordering
a thorough medical inspection of all vessels arriving
via Egypt at Marseilles or Toulon, and the isolation
of all persons suffering, or suspected to be suffering,
from diseases of a choleraic nature.   It has, I believe,
never been for one moment alleged that the Egyptian
Quarantine Board was instituted as a *substitute* for the
Quarantine Services of the whole of Europe ; indeed,
such a pretension would have been *too* absurd.   The
Egyptian Board was entrusted with the task of pro-
tecting Egypt, and, by so doing, of endeavouring at
the same time to prevent cholera and plague from
being transmitted to Europe ; it was, in fact, intended
to serve as an outpost.

Once this line of defence had been unfortunately
broken, as in 1883, common-sense dictated increased
vigilance in the ports all along the northern littoral of
the Mediterranean.   Yet the Powers seemingly did
practically nothing, and when, nearly *a year* afterwards,
they awoke to the danger, it was then so late in the day
that they cast about for a scapegoat, and my appointment coming opportunely, the French reptile Press,
possibly inspired, began to cry out that the new
President of the Egyptian Board would undoubtedly
soon manage to infect Europe with cholera.   The
stupidity of the contention is apparent, unless I had
sinister and inhuman designs on Europe's well-being,
and unless all the sanitary officers in the Mediterranean
ports of Europe were bribed by me, to declare foul
ships free from disease.   The writer of this abuse was
indeed perfectly right then, when he said that Dame

Europe would have no just reason to cry out, even should cholera reach her shores.

Next month my old friend *Le Bosphore Egyptien* comes again into action.

"The cholera has broken out at Toulon; several fatal cases have already occurred. Eight thousand persons have left the town, flying from the epidemic. It was certain, it was inevitable. Our readers have not forgotten the note of alarm we sounded when the incident of the *Crocodile* took place. We said if care was not taken, and if the old sanitary system which had worked so well was not reverted to, one day or another the scourge would manage to find its way through the Suez Canal and reach Europe. To-day the cholera is at Toulon, to-morrow it may be at Paris, Vienna, Berlin, etc. Who will stop it?

"*But let Europe perish rather than the trade of the Liverpool and Manchester merchants.*

"As there remained no other evil to work in Egypt, is it surprising that the English should try their hand elsewhere? Bombardments, cholera, insurrections, disasters of all sorts have they bestowed upon us with unequalled generosity: there was nothing else to do here. But Europe was untouched, and it was very necessary that she also should come under the ill-omened influence of a brutal egotism."

As I have already exploded the theory that the Egyptian Quarantine Council as a whole, or myself as its President, could (even had we so willed) have endowed Europe with cholera, I will only mention that as soon as I was officially informed of the existence of cholera at Toulon, I summoned the Council together, and it was decided to apply the same regulations to ships from the French littoral as had been applied to those from British India.

These rules, as a matter of course, fell heavier on vessels from France than on arrivals from India, as the duration of the voyage from Marseilles being so very considerably less, the detention in Egyptian waters under the scale of quarantine was consequently much greater.

This turned the French Press in Egypt perfectly rabid, and in their anger they exposed to the public gaze how little logic there was in their desire for more stringent quarantine ; for this, so please you, was made to constitute a fresh grievance, and was as usual put down to me, though the Council itself, and not I, had framed and passed the original law. I had, it is true, been instrumental in inducing the Board to *reduce the scale by three days* for certain ships, but this was all in *favour* of the French mail steamers.

Enter *Le Bosphore Egyptien* (Cairo, the 27th of June, 1884), smiling airily—

"Mr. Miéville is triumphant, Miéville is happy. Henceforth the President of the Quarantine Council does not mean to hear himself taxed with impartiality, or to allow it to be said that he does not most rigorously apply the sanitary regulations.

"Plague on it ! Seven days' quarantine on French vessels coming from Marseilles—there's a radical measure if you like !

"But the very next day the English mail steamer from Brindisi is allowed free *pratique*, and President Miéville never reflects that possibly among her passengers may be included persons who have fled from France and joined the British steamer either at Venice or Brindisi.

"This time no one can say that Mr. Miéville has two weights and two measures. He has only one rule: all English vessels to receive *pratique*, all French vessels to be quarantined."

The answer is simple. On the one hand, Brindisi being an *Italian* port, I had no power whatever to stop the vessel, as the Board had only decided on quarantining ships from the *French* Mediterranean littoral ; and on the other hand, even had there been refugees from France on board, it is evident that they would have to be considered by Egypt as clean, as they must have journeyed from France to Italy either by land or by sea. If by land, the authorities would have detained and subjected them to fumigation on the frontier ; if by sea they would have performed their quarantine in some Italian lazaretto.

Instead of my own comments I cannot do better than quote a paragraph from *The Egyptian Gazette* of the 30th of June, 1884.

"Some of our contemporaries, who are noted for being ardent supporters of quarantine measures when British shipowners are to be the sufferers, are very virulent in their attacks on Mr. W. F. Miéville, the President of the Quarantine Board, although they are perfectly well aware that he is the executive officer of the Board, and merely carries out its decisions. Fairness and impartiality are unfortunately qualities which are lacking in the conductors of the journals to which we refer.

"We have no mission to defend the Quarantine Board, and, besides, we believe in more scientific means being used to prevent the spread of disease than having recourse to quarantine, sanitary cordons, and other similar measures, which are relics of barbarism unworthy of the nineteenth century.

"Justification for the action of the Quarantine Board is, however, to be found in the fact that precisely similar precautions have been taken by the International Board at Constantinople, and by the Hellenic Sanitary authorities in respect of vessels arriving from French ports on the Mediterranean littoral, and that it has not been deemed necessary to adopt similar measures in respect of vessels arriving from Italian ports."

This called forth from *L'Union Egyptienne* (a French paper published in Alexandria) a leading article in large type, headed—

"MR. MIÉVILLE

AND

THE EGYPTIAN GAZETTE,"

in which the same old assertions are repeated, and which I need not give at length.

Then the dear, faithful old *Bosphore*, fearing that

I may not find the abuse of *L'Union Egyptienne* sufficiently strong, chimes in, in its pleasant, down-right, knock-me-down style—"Let us hope that one of the first things Europe will do, will be to re-organize the Council and rid the presidential *fauteuil* of this personage, whose presence is a permanent source of danger both to Egypt and to Europe. Mr. Miéville may have all the qualifications that go to make a good father of a family, and a militiaman, even a vice-president of a Temperance or Prevention of Cruelty to Animals Society; but as to the position he now fills, he has superabundantly proved himself a nobody, and partial at that. When complaints are made against Mr. Miéville for making use of two weights and two measures, he does but turn his eyes towards England, saying—'Oh, my country, I sacrifice for thee both my conscience and my gods, but thy commercial interests and those of the Peninsular and Oriental are secure!'"

And in token that I bear no ill-will to *Le Bosphore Egyptien* for its persistency and consistency in attacking me, I will be generous and leave to it the last word.

CHAPTER XV

SMUGGLERS AND THE POST OFFICE

WHEN I first went to Egypt, five-and-twenty years
ago, a most curious state of things prevailed, for not
only had every foreign Power jurisdiction over its own
subjects—a jurisdiction exercised by consular judges
—but most of the European Powers had even their
own post offices. As years went on this extraordinary
condition of things had to be greatly modified. The
consular courts renounced jurisdiction over the members of their several colonies except in " unmixed " or
criminal cases (by unmixed I mean cases where Greek
was against Greek, Frenchman against Frenchman,
Italian against Italian, and so forth), and, by agree-
ment, the jurisdiction was vested in the international
mixed tribunals. This arrangement relieved the consular judges of much of their former work. And so
with the post offices. When the Egyptian post office
(which is now under the excellent guidance of Yusef
Saba Pasha and Charteris Bey) began, by the regularity of its system, to inspire confidence, the foreign
Powers one by one gave up their post offices ; but the
French, always jealous of such privileges, would not

abandon their rights : thus at last it came about that the French was the only foreign post office left in Alexandria.

For some considerable time previous to July 1884, the Customs authorities had noticed that certain jewellers imported hundreds upon hundreds of *empty jewel-cases :* this perplexed the minds of the officials whose business it was to prevent smuggling. The explanation might possibly be that the jewellers themselves fashioned their own jewellery, yet though frequent visits were, I believe, privately made to the shops under suspicion, no home-made articles were ever offered for sale. The Customs officials were fairly puzzled, but they were convinced that jewellery *was* being smuggled into the country ; only how the contraband goods were passed in remained a mystery.

This was the position of affairs when cholera broke out in France, and the Quarantine Council took measures against arrivals from that country. Now, as President and executive officer, it became my duty to instruct my subordinates at the various ports to disinfect everything that came into Egypt from France. Before the quarantine had been long in force the doctor or clerk in charge of the disinfection of the Parcels Post at Alexandria informed me that many parcels when opened for disinfecting purposes were found to contain jewellery. Thereupon I firmly refused to give up the packages of jewellery to the French post office until shown the Custom-house receipt, stating that the jewels in question had paid duty.

The jewel-cases being valueless and bulky were

sent to Alexandria empty, and the small duty paid on them at the Alexandria Custom-house; the valuable jewels wherewith to fill them were posted in *France*, so that they should come straight to, and be delivered *direct* by, the French postal authorities. The packages were registered, and judging by the post-marks were usually posted in a small village near the Franco-Swiss frontier. The mystery of the empty cases being solved, the Customs authorities were jubilant. But if the Customs and myself were contented, others *were not so satisfied.*

Leaving aside the smugglers themselves (who I admit had *solid* financial reasons for being annoyed), my action in temporarily detaining the jewellery gave great umbrage to the French diplomatic and postal authorities, and consequently to my abusive friends of the French local Press. The French postmaster even went so far as to threaten me in my own office, saying that if I did not immediately give him delivery of the Parcels Post he should cable to Paris demanding my instant dismissal.

"Monsieur le Receveur," I replied, "I really think it is the wisest thing you *can* do: it cannot possibly affect me, and it will show your Government that you are a zealous official, and will likewise cover your responsibility."

In laying the matter before the French diplomatic representative, Monsieur le Receveur des Postes Françaises à Alexandrie stated, I believe, that on presenting himself to withdraw from the Quarantine Office the registered packets brought over by the mail steamer *La Seyne*, on the 25th of June, after the expiration of the period of quarantine prescribed by the regulations, the Port Sanitary Officer had refused to give him delivery of four registered letters addressed to certain jewellers of Alexandria, alleging that the Customs had seized the four letters because they contained articles on which duty was leviable.

"He had," he said, "addressed himself in vain to the President of the Quarantine Council, pointing out to that functionary that the giving up of the mails to the lazaretto, in the interests of health, constituted an actual trust which the Quarantine administration had not the right to make over to a third party, and certainly not to the Customs, who had no right of control over postal matter, which should be treated with the most absolute secrecy."

Then the irate French diplomatic agent complained to the Egyptian Government, ending somewhat in the following strain—

"The conduct both of the Director of the Customs and the President of the International Sanitary Council should be severely blamed, and the necessity thus obviated of having to bring to the notice of the French Government this regrettable incident."

I refrain from comment other than simply saying that French diplomacy would have done better, in my humble opinion, by sending to the Customs and myself letters of thanks for having exposed a fraud which, all unwittingly, the French local post office had rendered possible.

For the next two months the *Bosphore* published

occasional and desultory attacks on me for continuing to refuse to let jewellery be smuggled into the country; but the line I had adopted seemed to me, if not technically right, to be at least straightforward and honest, so I would not give way. It was not until the following October that an understanding was come to. I forget the exact terms, but I do not doubt that the following account taken from the *Bosphore* is substantially correct—

"The conflict between the Egyptian Customs administration and the French Postal authorities on the subject of the letters and parcels which Mr. Miéville, in his capacity of grand disinfector, thought fit to hand over to the local Custom-house, has been at last arranged.

"The letters and parcels are to be delivered to the consignees in the presence of the French authorities, who will proceed to open them before the parties interested; if the parcels contain articles on which duty is leviable, that duty must forthwith be paid or the articles will be returned to the sender.

"This is an excellent solution of the difficulty, for it is strictly in accordance with law."

CHAPTER XVI

UNDER THE YELLOW FLAG

WHEN writing about the cholera epidemic which visited Egypt in 1883, I made some mention of the extraordinary exodus of all those European residents of Alexandria who could possibly get away; things were now reversed. Egypt was clean, Europe was infected; and no sooner did it become known that cholera was at Toulon than with one accord the Alexandrians, and for the matter of that Cairenes also, who were in Europe on pleasure bent, made up their minds to return to Egypt before the infection should spread to other and more frequented parts of France.

Perhaps this was the wisest thing my fellow-citizens could have done, but simple as the fact sounds when thus baldly stated, it was anything but simple to me. It meant that arrangements had to be at once made by the already much-worried and hard-worked President for the accommodation in quarantine of hundreds of passengers each week. And when it is remembered that no passenger, however easy-tempered and good-natured he or she may be, exactly relishes being forcibly detained for a week in a lazaretto, and is therefore quite prepared, even as a pastime, and for want of something better to do, to find fault with everything, it will easily be credited that I did not anticipate a very joyous time that summer.

Happily I was not taken altogether unawares, as at the suggestion of Nubar Pasha I had myself inspected, a couple of months before, the building which served as a lazaretto at Alexandria. I had found it rather dilapidated (it was situated outside the suburb known as Gabarri): it seemed, however, admirably suited to its present purpose, though, not having been used for many years, it was certainly not in a fit state for the reception of Europeans, fastidious or otherwise. No time was lost, and by July the lazaretto was in a fair state of repair, but I wanted a further sum of £500 to complete it. So I sent in an official application, but did not at once obtain the credit. This was annoying, so I wrote privately to Nubar Pasha, begging him to wake up the Office of Works, and for answer I received a telegram asking me to send in an estimate, with plans, etc. This request seemed to me to savour a great deal too much of red-tapeism and dilatoriness, for obviously it would take time to make plans and estimates, and more time to get them approved by the Public Works.

Meanwhile, steamer after steamer chock-full of returning Europeans and Egyptians would be arriving in Alexandria harbour, flying the yellow flag of quarantine. So I took up my best quill pen and wrote to the Prime Minister a private note which may somewhat have astonished him, but which had the desired effect ; it ran as follows—

"MON CHER MINISTRE,

"I have just received your telegram asking me to send to Cairo an estimate with plans of the work still to be done at the Gabarri lazaretto.

"I beg to point out, and your Excellency will easily understand the reasons, that it would be difficult to prepare an exact estimate. I believe, however, that £500 will cover the cost.

"Inasmuch as precious time will be lost if the matter is referred to the Ministry of Public Works, I propose to go on with the work to-morrow, and, as it is a question of humanity, *I take upon myself the responsibility of the disbursements.*

"I trust, mon cher Ministre, that you will approve this way of regarding the matter, and I beg you to accept *l'expression de mes sentiments très dévoués.*

"W. F. MIÉVILLE."

An astute statesman like Nubar Pasha could not fail to see that it would never do for it to be said that I had paid out of my own pocket for the repairs of a Government building, and the next morning I received the following telegram—

"Your note received. You can have the £500 you mention.

"NUBAR."

This essential point satisfactorily settled, I plunged into the details of house-furnishing and housekeeping.

I personally saw that the beds were comfortable, and the linen clean and wholesome; had little tents rigged up in the various sections to serve as bath-rooms for the men; engaged a small army of servants, and last, but not least, made a contract with a restaurant-keeper to cater *well* (and fairly reason-ably) for the relays of quarantine prisoners.

I have used the word "sections." To each vessel were allotted three or more "sections"—for the passengers of the three different classes—and each vessel's passengers, as well as each of the sections allotted to such vessel, were kept isolated the one from the other. Thus if a case of cholera occurred in the lazaretto among the passengers of "ship A," it did not affect the term of detention being under-gone by the passengers of "ship B," and if the pas-senger attacked was in Section I. of "ship A," only the persons in that particular section re-commenced their seven days' quarantine (from the date of the patient being removed to the cholera hospital), while Sections II. and III., though belonging to the same "ship A," were not required to do so.

But to return to the caterer: I particularly im-pressed upon him the great importance of wholesome, well-cooked food—my only *real* hope of keeping the forcibly-detained passengers in fairly good humour during their seven days' imprisonment was *through their internal economies.* I had heard it said "of old time" that the way even to a man's heart lies in that direction, so I hoped that to try so to secure his good-will would be sound policy. And my hope was justi-

fied, as will be seen from the following newspaper
cuttings.

Now my old friend *Le Bosphore* found itself rather
in a quandary; it did not, on the one hand, wish not
to mention a subject very generally talked of, for
many high diplomatic and other dignitaries, as well as
the majority of the Alexandria and Cairo residents
who go to make up "society," had passed through
Gabarri and spoken kindly of their treatment at the
lazaretto; nor did the journal desire on the other
hand to give any credit to that very Mr. Miéville
whom it so scurrilously, in season and out of season,
abused. But the editor's fertile brain was equal to
the occasion; he decided to praise the Gabarri lazaretto, but to say that my second in command—the
Inspector-General of the Quarantine Service, Dr.
Ardouin Bey—was responsible for the excellence of
the arrangements.

Le Bosphore Egyptien.

"For once in a way the authorities merit congratulation in a matter of organization; to tell the truth,
the installation for passengers who have to purge
quarantine is almost perfect. It was at Gabarri,
where the passengers of the *Alphée*, each one healthier
than the other, had been landed, that I discovered
this surprising fact.

"The rooms have been fitted up with remarkable
care and attention to detail; moreover the meals and
attendance leave nothing to be desired, and everywhere
the greatest cleanliness prevails. From nine a.m. the

gates of the lazaretto are open to visitors, who are permitted to talk and laugh with the *détenus* across barriers divided by a somewhat wide space ; and if need be, visitors can by means of a contrivance on rails send in books, newspapers, and other articles.

"We congratulate most sincerely Dr. Ardouin Bey, the Director of the Service."

And later—

Le Bosphore Egyptien.

"I have just made a fresh and very careful visit to the lazaretto, and have minutely inspected the bed-chambers, the dining-rooms, linen, kitchens, and the service generally. I am glad to acknowledge that all was of the best. The passengers of every class, and they are numerous since the simultaneous arrival of the *Said* and the Italian steamer, express themselves as very satisfied with the way in which they are cared for, I was going to say petted. Only . . . they would prefer to be free. Their freedom, that is what they ask for with a unanimity easy to understand."

*   *   *   *   *   *   *

And in conclusion let one of those most nearly concerned be heard, viz. one of the unfortunate passengers themselves. The account appeared in a magazine for December 1884, and was written by the late Mr. Herbert G. Fuller, for many years a well-known tutor at Cambridge—

"SEVEN DAYS' QUARANTINE AT ALEXANDRIA.

"Arriving on November 13th at the harbour of Alexandria on a P. and O. steamer from Brindisi, we were doomed to pass seven days in quarantine. With many misgivings as to the nature of the experiences we were to undergo, we were conveyed in a lighter to the Quarantine Wharf, directed to disembark and place ourselves in the special train awaiting us. We might have been electric batteries, to judge from the excessive caution taken by every one to avoid any direct meddling with us : undoubtedly, unseen by ourselves, we wore labels, marked *dangerous*. Before long we were drawing near to a circular building surrounded by a high wall, and our approach was the signal for a veritable babel of excited jeers, proceeding from the apparent lunatics of different nations who were seen clambering at the barred windows.

"The train at a standstill, and emptied of its passengers, we passed through a gate with sentinels on either side into a large circular enclosure two hundred and fifty yards in diameter. We were within the Lazaretto Gabarri, and looked round to see to what we had been brought. The one-storeyed buildings which we had seen from the outside encircled the whole enclosure, and were fronted by a colonnade. At a distance of twenty yards from this, and with an interval of five yards, a double paling seven feet high had been erected ; the rooms and space thus cut off from the centre are divided into sections separated from each other by a similar double paling. Boards variously inscribed distinguished the sections, the whole appearance reminding one forcibly of a cattle show or well-arranged Zoological Garden. Every section includes one room set apart for dining purposes, and from three to seven rooms with three beds in each. The only two first-class passengers by our steamer, we were conducted by ourselves into one of these sections, and the gates padlocked after us. We now felt prisoners indeed. However, we were not to be quite alone, for two Arab servants were sent into quarantine to attend upon us, and like ourselves were to be considered for a week impure to the rest of the world. By the system of double palings a neutral ground, five yards in width, separated us even from our neighbours in misfortune, and a sentinel on the outside of every section was prepared to enforce the order of "thus far but no farther." In the centre of the enclosure two rectangular dilapidated buildings —once a residence of a former Khedive—are now devoted to the kitchen, and to the use of the managers and some of the employees. But to return to the part allotted to ourselves; it was by no means void of the picturesque; the drooping branches of two acacia trees lent a kindly shade, and, close beside the one, a small tent by the water-tap formed a retreat for our morning plunge. On two wooden rails connecting two openings in the front palings, and worked from each end by a chain, was a small truck which conveys to the imprisoned their food, and anything else that may be desired. Two meals a day are served from the kitchen—lunch at eleven o'clock, and dinner at five o'clock. Coffee and tea are prepared by the Arab servants in attendance. A description how each day passed would no doubt be tedious, but a few words about our Arab servants and the devices by which captives contrive to while away their imprisonment may not be uninteresting.

"We had not been prisoners many minutes before we observed one of the Arabs busy with pencil and paper; the latter he handed to us, and on it was written, 'Moustafa, that my name, thank you, sir!' Well, Moustafa turned out generally useless and often in the way; he knew a little English which he ventilated in writing, he would spend hours writing out short stories, mixing up cats and cows and good fathers in a manner that had not even the merit of being amusing, while the usual refrain of every composition was a request to be taken into our service, or a petition for *backsheesh*. Needless to say we wearied of Moustafa. The other fellow could neither read nor write, but had a frank, open countenance with a pleasing grin. This was Mohammed. He knew no English, but had picked up sufficient Italian for all practical purposes.

"We were fortunate in having a box of books with us, and consequently, being a small party, spent most of our time either reading or writing; in the evening, when wearied of these, we either whiled away the time with dominoes, at which Mohammed considered himself an authority, or were engaged in avoiding the attacks of mosquitoes, which some nights literally swarmed upon us.

"For our exercise we had recourse to pastimes of earlier days, to practising balancing feats, and to the charms of leap-frog, into the mysteries of which our Arabs were duly initiated. In the section on our left was a large party of eight or ten Italians, whose ages apparently ranged from twenty to sixty. We quite envied their mirth. After each meal, for about an hour, there were shouts of hearty laughter springing from evident enjoyment of their athletics in quarantine. On looking to ascertain the source of so much sport, I discovered it was the familiar nursery game of puss-in-the-corner.

"In one of the third-class divisions there were some members of a French operatic company who enlivened our evenings with songs. Their time was up on the Monday morning, and it was amusing to see them in the distance on Sunday night, each with a lighted candle, tramping in single file round and round their enclosure as they sang the 'Marseillaise,' evidently marching to freedom on the morrow. We had various other diversions ; one day a native juggler, another the trial of an Arab steed, a young and spirited animal which gave us a good exhibition of speed as well as of Arab horsemanship. On our last day all our baggage was fumigated, and we received a visit from the Customs officials. The *cuisine* was good, and the officials and attendants were civil and obliging. Through the kindness of the President of the Quarantine and Sanitary Board—no other than my old

schoolfellow Miéville—through whose kind offices
no doubt we were the objects of much extra attention
—we were supplied with all the copies of *The Times*
most recently to hand. After all we did not have
such a bad time of it, and though we were very glad
to be at liberty again, every one will confess there are
worse places in which to be imprisoned than the
Lazaretto Gabarri."

CHAPTER XVII

TWO BATTLES ROYAL

I HAVE had occasion to refer to the assertion made by the Austrian representative on the Quarantine Council, that the preponderance of Egyptian votes converted the decisions of the Board from international into purely Egyptian decisions. I now have to revert to the subject, but let me first give brief extracts from the refreshingly breezy, though of course incorrect and exaggerated accounts, published in the local anti-English Press.

Le Phare d'Alexandrie of the 3rd of March, 1885, in an article headed " A Serious Conflict," wrote—

" The Powers have decided to send instructions to the Consuls-General to submit to the Egyptian Government on the one hand, and to the Board itself on the other, a project for the reconstruction of the Quarantine Council. This very morning the discussion on the subject was entered upon at a meeting of the Council.

" The Austro-Hungarian Delegate started the hare, and at the opening of the sitting expressed the opinion —which is ours also—that the Quarantine Board, constituted as it now is, and acting as it has done for the past two years, no longer offers a guarantee for the sufficient protection of the States situated on the shores of the Mediterranean. He then put forward certain proposals, notably one for the reorganization of the Board, by the reduction of the number of Egyptian votes.

"After the setting forth of these proposals, Mr. Walter Miéville, President of the Council, got up from the *fauteuil présidentiel* to reply.

"He seemed strangely moved, and in a voice trembling and restrained by a feeling which resembled nothing less than joy, he declared that his position as President of the Council and as representative of the Egyptian Government would not permit of his allowing such proposals to be discussed and put to the vote.

"These words, according to our information, were the signal for a general and extremely lively debate.

"The delegates of the Powers, copies of the regulations in hand, and strong in the knowledge of their rights, demonstrated by convincing argument that no article of the rules forbad the discussion of the Austro-Hungarian proposals.

"After this discussion, which was more stormy than profitable, had lasted some time, the President, who would listen to nothing, perceiving that on this occasion all the delegates of the Powers were of one mind, and that in all probability he would not get a majority—the President set himself to ring his bell despairingly, and declared the sitting at an end. A convenient way of getting rid of a difficulty.

" Immediately afterwards a collective protest was drawn up for insertion in the minutes of proceedings, and signed by the delegates of Austria, Germany, Spain, France, Greece, Italy, Portugal, Russia, and Turkey."

Le Courrier de France followed the lead with a history of the joint protest, and the article, which extends to four columns, thus closes—

" That is where the question now is.   Sir E. Baring is at the present time causing a search to be made in the archives of the several Egyptian Ministries, in the hope that some old document may be discovered, conferring on the President of the Quarantine Board the privilege of insolence of which Mr. Miéville has just so largely availed himself towards his colleagues."

I took no heed of the newspaper abuse, but as a reply to the protest of the delegates of certain foreign Powers, I thought it expedient to draw up the following official Note—

" The Sanitary Delegate of Austro-Hungary, at the meeting of the 3rd of March, stated *inter alia*—

" 1. (*a*) That the decisions of the Council betrayed both hesitations and contradictions.

"(*b*) That the consequence of this conduct on the part of the Council had been most deplorable. Cholera in Egypt in 1883, and in Europe in 1884.

"(*c*) That the public accused the Council of, and held it responsible for, these disasters, believing that the decisions of the Council were the expression of the views and will of all Europe.

" 2. That by reason of the predominance of the Egyptian votes, the decisions of the Council, which pass for international, are in reality simply Egyptian decisions.

" Without in any way going into the merits of the questions raised by sub-sections (*a*), (*b*), and (*c*) of the first statement, let us for a moment admit their correctness. Let us then substitute for the second statement, ' that the decisions are in reality Egyptian,' the *facts* as they result from official documents, namely—that out of fifty-three decisions taken by the Council since its creation (January 1881) until the present time for the imposition or raising of quarantine against foreign countries, in nine times only did the Egyptian votes influence the decisions arrived at, that is to say, that if the Egyptian votes are eliminated from the forty-four ballots, the result in each case would have been the same.

" And it follows that, admitting the exactitude of the facts mentioned in (*a*), (*b*), (*c*), *the responsibility would fall, at least in the proportion of forty-four times out of fifty-three, on the delegates of the foreign Powers.*

"W. F. MIÉVILLE,

" President."

This Note, a copy of which was sent to each member of the Board, so effectually destroyed the Austrian Delegate's arguments, and so turned the tables on the foreign delegates, that for a season discretion and circumspection were the order of the day, and the President enjoyed comparative peace.

I will only add, in conclusion, two points—

First, that both the Egyptian Prime Minister and Minister of the Interior approved and upheld my action, and wrote to me saying that "the Government of his Highness considers that you were right in not permitting the discussion of a question that went beyond the powers conferred on the members of the Council by the decree of the 3rd of January, 1884."

Secondly, that I was not at all opposed in principle to the Austrian proposals (indeed I afterwards did my best to have three of them embodied in the rules); I only objected to the tactless and irregular way of bringing them forward. And when some years later the famous proposal for the re-organization of the Council by the reduction of the number of the Egyptian votes came once more on the *tapis*, and became the subject of diplomatic negotiations, I agreed to that also.

I pointed out to the Government that the Egyptian votes were scarcely ever of use, and that I had without their aid been able to bring about many useful reforms favourable to commerce and navigation.

At the same time, I was fully aware that the European Powers still thought I did in some extraordinary way manage to conjure with the Egyptian votes, so I advised the Government to encourage this illusion while the negotiations were pending, and instead of abandoning the Egyptian votes simply as a graceful act, to stipulate for some *quid pro quo*, which in my opinion *should be nothing less than the consent of the*

Powers to the substitution of an enlightened, for the present antiquated, system of protection against epidemic diseases.

The strain of the past harassing year had begun to tell on my health, for though I had treated all attacks on me in the foreign Press with silence, though I had done what seemed to me to be my duty, and had let no outside influences disturb the even tenor of my way, yet I had had many worries and annoyances to contend with, and the whole service to reorganize and put on a sound basis. My administration was a large one, the outlying offices being very numerous, as my jurisdiction extended not only the whole length of Egypt's Mediterranean littoral, but along the desert frontier from El-Arish (near Gaza) in the north, to Akaba in the south, and then again round the Sinai Peninsula, and all down the Gulf of Suez and the western shore of the Red Sea. Then the staff of doctors, employees, and sanitary guards (some sailors, some soldiers) was consequently very large, often troublesome, and sadly requiring to be weeded out.

At first I thought little of feeling out-of-sorts, but when the feeling became the rule rather than the exception, I asked Dr. Mackie to professionally examine and prescribe for me. As many hundreds of all nationalities in Egypt will gratefully acknowledge, the late Sir James Mackie knew his work (and the country in which his labours lay) thoroughly, and I had in common with others perfect confidence in his opinion. Having overhauled me he sat down and wrote a certificate, which he handed to me, saying—

"My dear Miéville, the sooner you get away for a few months of rest the better."

In the face of his clear language there was but one thing to be done. So I applied for, and was granted three months' leave, and by the end of the month was on the high seas on board the P. and O. steamer *Parramatta*.

My wife and I found most cheery passengers—and sports, games, dances, and amusements of all kinds in full swing. And shaking off the remembrance of official worries and the depression induced by the knowledge that my heart was affected, in a day or two after leaving Port Said we felt fit for anything, "from pitch-and-toss to manslaughter."

We found also a most excellent newspaper on board, and as most of the passengers (for of course the passengers were the sole contributors) had already in the course of the long voyage from Australia been pumped pretty dry by the enterprising editors, these gentlemen seized on me and said I must do my duty and furnish a column of "copy" twice a week, in return for which *I should be allowed to peruse all the back numbers !*

The *Parramatta* duly arrived in the Royal Albert Docks. Then came a pleasant period of rest—lazing at Lord's watching my beloved cricket ; lazing at Sandown in the Isle of Wight playing with children, and being initiated by them into the mysteries of "paddling" and the building of castles on the sands ; and lazing finally in the charmingly picturesque valley of the Wye, visiting the old home and the old friends of my dear mother ; and being addressed as " *Master* Walter " by the faithful old retainers and wrinkled, weather-beaten old villagers was music sweeter far to me than " Excellence " or " Monsieur le Président."

Then the holiday came to an end, and only the memory of it and of the voyage on the *Parramatta* remained.

The voyage back to Egypt in the P. and O. *Rome* was not eventful.

On landing at Alexandria I had a fairly busy time officially, but it was not owing to opposition on the part of the delegates, who, as the French saying has it, had " put much water in their wine, and quieted down."

So Quarantine matters went smoothly for some months, yet it soon became clear that the respite from petty worries was only a temporary one, for, in the month of December, Nubar Pasha, the Home Minister, communicated with me officially, for any remarks I might desire to offer, a protest signed by seven foreign delegates to the Board.

I need not give the text of the protest, nor of my reply. Both documents, though lengthy, can be summed up in a few sentences.

The delegates' protest set forth that five vessels had been authorized by the Quarantine Board to transit the Suez Canal in defiance of the general regulations ; and that this had been brought about by the votes of a majority of members of the Board *over a united minority represented by the seven signatories of the protest.*

On carefully studying the minutes of the meetings at which the cases of the five vessels in question had been discussed and decided, I ascertained that at not one of the five meetings did more than four of these complaining delegates vote together, and I further discovered that *two* of the seven signatories of the protest were only present at one of the five meetings, *and that, even on that solitary occasion, they had voted with the MAJORITY*.

This disclosure, when officially brought to the Minister's notice, put the two delegates completely out of court, and doubtless their powers of invention were taxed to the uttermost when endeavouring to explain to their respective Governments how it was they had signed the protest *as members of the minority*.

Once again had my opponents chosen their ground badly, and I heard that the diplomates in Cairo, seeing how by the clear marshalling of hard facts I had destroyed the arguments put forward by the delegates, instructed their representatives on the Quarantine Board to confine themselves in future to voting as they were directed, and to reporting the decisions arrived at. And this *was* in substance the result of the incident which I always think of as " the battle of the five ships."

CHAPTER XVIII

THE YEAR OF JUBILEE

THE results obtained in the first two years of my occupancy of the Presidentship were made the subject of a special review by *The Times*, and the article concluded in the following strain—

"Considerable benefit had been conferred by Mr. Miéville* upon British commerce, amounting to 80 per cent. of the entire traffic.

"But the President of the Quarantine Board is an Egyptian official, and it is necessary to show that these advantages to the foreign public have not been obtained at any expense to the Government. On this account it is satisfactory to note that the ordinary receipts (exclusive of those for exceptional quarantines against Europe) have increased 31 per cent., a result obtained by constant care and by the institution of a system of rigid control. This increase has permitted the raising of the salaries of the formerly underpaid employees, the abolition of dues on fishing vessels, and important modifications in the rules regarding the importation of cattle, with a consequent redistribution of these charges, in many cases amount-

ing to a reduction of 38 per cent. as compared with
the former tariff. It is hoped, also, that the exceeding
heavy dues now charged for the disinfection of merchandise in quarantine may be very shortly abolished,
and that other improvements in the service, hitherto
neglected for want of money, will likewise become
practicable, as the cash balance, which on March 1,
1884, was only £2500, stands to-day at nearly
£25,000."

In the month of May 1887 I was sent by the
Government of Egypt on a special mission to the
capitals of Austria, France, Germany, and Great
Britain, but as it was of a confidential character, I
cannot in these pages divulge its nature.

> "There are cases when the simple truth is difficult to tell,
> When 'tis better that the truth should not be known,
> So we'd better leave her lying at the bottom of the well,
> And agree to let both truth and well alone."

Suffice it to say that I finally succeeded in what it
was hoped I might bring about, though, oddly enough,
not in the manner indicated by the Khedive's Prime
Minister.

I decided to proceed first to Vienna, as I feared
that I might there have a rather difficult *rôle* to play,
and I desired to grapple with the hardest part of my
task without delay; otherwise I knew I should feel
like the man who hesitates on the cold river's bank
before bathing, less and less inclined to take the
plunge. Vienna was, besides, the capital which was
geographically indicated as the most natural to begin
at, as I could take it on my way to the others.

The Austrian Foreign Office must have been somewhat puzzled to know what manner of man to expect, for of course they had been advised of my approaching visit. On the one hand, they were in possession of such accounts of me as the Austro-Hungarian Delegate in Alexandria may have been pleased from time to time to send to his Government—accounts, I take it, which can only have been of a rather unfavourable nature, considering the many acute differences of opinion I had constantly had with him. On the other hand, the Vienna Foreign Office had very probably read a most flattering description of me, and of my supposed wheedling ways of carrying on negotiations, which had appeared about that period in a book written in German by an Austrian doctor; a book which seemed to me to have been penned with the sole and express object of abusing the Egyptian Quarantine Administration, yet which, nevertheless, spoke of me personally in the following terms—

"President Miéville, a good-looking man of middle age, with an intelligent expression, made on me an extremely pleasing, I may say sympathetic, impression.

"In his bearing, manner, and conversation ; in the way he apparently improvised words which he had in reality long considered ; in the way that he understood how to lead the conversation to the topic which *he* desired to discuss, and knew how to unite in his language amiability with the energetic expression of opposing views, he was the prototype of a cautious diplomatist.

"I have never had to do with a man who was so

carefully calculating, and who weighed his words so prudently as the President of the Board."

These two conflicting descriptions must, as I have already said, have sorely puzzled the good diplomates in Vienna, if indeed they had gone to both sources for information.

We (for my wife accompanied me) arrived at the Austrian capital in time, be it said in passing, for the Austrian Derby, and were well received and most hospitably entertained, being given boxes at the Opera, with most gorgeously-attired flunkeys to usher us in and to speed our departure. Of course I called on kindly, courtly Sir Augustus Paget, who at that time was still British Ambassador to the Court of the Dual Monarchy.

My official relations with the Vienna Foreign Office were from the outset most pleasant, and gradually became quite cordial, and the frequent interchange of ideas that took place between us undoubtedly laid the foundations for the good understanding which has since borne much good fruit.

Before I left Cairo I had been furnished with general instructions as to my mission—instructions which left much to my discretion, but which laid down the broad lines on which I was to proceed. Now, very shortly after my arrival in Vienna, the conclusion forced itself on my mind that these broad lines were not the best to follow in the true interests of Egypt, so, without hesitation, I boldly abandoned them, and during the remainder of my mission worked on a totally different basis.

We said good-bye to the Prater and the Ringstrasse, and took train to Berlin, and every now and then during the journey the question would present itself to me, "Have I done right?" For to go a little beyond one's instructions is a not uncommon thing for men of initiative to do, and is susceptible of explanation; but to depart from them altogether savours almost of disobedience or defiance, and is therefore a dangerous proceeding. Yet what else could I have done? It would have been worse than useless to have asked for fresh instructions, and no telegram could have thoroughly explained the situation. Besides, I had no code-book with me. So I acted on my own responsibility, and it is scarcely to be wondered at, when thinking it all over in the train as the express ran smoothly on hour after hour toward Berlin, that the thought should ever and anon occur, "Have I acted rightly?"

The first day in Berlin was a holiday, as all the city was going out to the Tempelhof to see a great review. So in the morning I called on the British Ambassador, who was none other than my old Chief, Sir Edward Malet, who received me most cordially.

He advised me to drive out to the Tempelhof Feld to see the manoeuvres. So back I went to the hotel, and having ordered a comfortable carriage, we drove off to see the review. And now we are very glad that we did go that day, for we saw three generations of Emperors: the old Emperor William I., the late Emperor Frederick, and the present sovereign Wilhelm II. We were pleased at the time also, though the wind was bitterly cold, and seemed to devote a great deal too much of its attention to the poor shivering travellers from sunny Egypt.

That same evening we dined at the Embassy, and a most pleasant dinner it was. We did not stay long in Berlin, but soon betook ourselves to London, leaving our visit to Paris until after the Queen's Jubilee festivities were over.

Now, one reason why I proceeded straight to London without first visiting the Quai D'Orsay, was that the Prime Minister of Egypt, Nubar Pasha, was in the British capital; and I could thus tell him *vivâ voce* about what I had done, and what I had left undone, with regard to the instructions he had given me. He received me as pleasantly and heartily as ever, but he seemed to listen to my narrative with indifference. However, he did not seem to disapprove my action in departing from my instructions, which was the chief point so far as I was personally concerned. The truth of the matter was, that Nubar Pasha was then engaged in a battle royal with Sir Evelyn Baring and Sir Edgar Vincent, a battle in which he suffered defeat, though he kept in office for another twelvemonths.

I then called on Sir Evelyn Baring—who was also in London—but was not fortunate enough to find him at home, and so I left a note in which I told him of the *volte-face* I had made in Vienna. In reply he wrote to me, "*Les beaux esprits se rencontrent.* Curiously enough, I had independently come to the same general conclusions as are stated in your note. I should much like to talk to you on the detail. Let me know when you will be in London, and we will arrange to meet."

Such being the opinion of a soldier-diplomate of such keen intellect and varied experience as Sir Evelyn Baring (now Viscount Cromer), I no longer felt any qualms on the score of the independent action I had taken in venturing to abandon the lines which I had originally been instructed to follow during my mission.

There is one reason why the Queen's Jubilee was for me personally a time of rejoicing independently of the warm feelings of loyalty to the sovereign which that day dwelt in the hearts of all our Queen-Empress's faithful subjects. On June 20, 1887, I was staying near London. We were on the next day to see the procession from an excellent point of view near the Horse Guards. In the afternoon, about tea-time, I happened to be near the outside gate of the house where I was being entertained, when a postman trudged by, and, seeing me, stopped and handed me a letter, which proved to be from Lord Salisbury, the Queen's Prime Minister, and which began with this sentence—" I have great pleasure in informing you that her Majesty has been pleased to confer on you, on this occasion, the honour of Companion of St. Michael and St. George."

Congratulations poured in. Sir Evelyn Baring wrote—" I was very glad that you got your well-earned C.M.G." And Sir Charles Cookson's letter began—" I sincerely congratulate you on the recognition of the services which you have rendered, and hope it is only an earnest of future distinctions and promotion."

My old friends and colleagues in the Consulate-General and Consular Court at Alexandria sent me a collective message, whilst the *Egyptian Gazette* made the following comment—

"Mr. Miéville, President of the Quarantine Board, has displayed such ability in the various positions he has held, that his being included in the list of recipients of honours was almost a matter of course, and his numerous friends in Egypt will heartily congratulate him on the recognition which his services have now received."

CHAPTER XIX

THE MECCA PILGRIMAGE

THE writer of an article in *The Times* of 11th September, 1886, brought to a close his account of the benefits which had been conferred under my administration on commerce and navigation by saying—"It is hoped, also, that the exceedingly heavy dues now charged for disinfection of merchandise in quarantine may be very shortly abolished."

Happily, I was able in 1888 not only to abolish the dues, but to get the Council to abolish the disinfection itself. It may seem absurd that I should have had to hammer away for four solid years before being able to induce the Powers or their represent-atives to consent to condemn a principle which all medical men knew, or at least believed, to be in all cases useless, and in many an iniquitous imposition. From the day I assumed the Presidency, I never ceased to openly declare that the disinfection of non-susceptible goods was a farce, and unworthy of a Council composed for the most part of medical men, and my satisfaction was great indeed when the announcement appeared in the *Journal Officiel* (which in Egypt is what the *London Gazette* is in England), that the Council had decided to abolish the disinfection of merchandise imported into the country.

Of course exception had to be made in the case of certain articles which are known often to be the vehicles for carrying the germs of disease, such as rags, soiled bedding or personal linen, carpets and untanned skins. The measure released the great bulk of merchandise, and tended to develop a large transit trade hitherto diverted from Egyptian ports by the prohibitory quarantine tariff.

The following incident, of no importance in itself, shows clearly the Khedive Tewfik's kindly and observant nature. I very often had long conversations with his Highness, who took a keen interest in my work, and especially in the efforts I made to improve the lot of the many hundreds of natives who served under me at outlying offices, lazarettos, quarantine encampments, cattle stations, etc. Naturally, being so often at the Palace, I heard little things said that it was possible sometimes to turn to account. For instance, one day in the office of the Masters of Ceremonies, I was told that the Khedive felt somewhat vexed at the conduct of a certain official who had called some small vessels belonging to and used by a Government administration by fancy European names, having nothing to do with either the service in which they were employed, or with Egypt as a country. Later on, I had occasion to order in England a powerful launch for our Suez office, and remembering what I had heard, as related above, I ventured to write to a friend at the Palace requesting him, if he thought the Khedive would not mind being troubled, to ask his Highness to choose a name for the new Quarantine steam-launch. The answer came promptly back that the *Khedive desired that the launch for the service of which Mr. Mieville was the head, should be called " El Mounsef."*

When I add that the Arabic words " El Mounsef" mean "The Just," it will be easily understood that I felt honoured.

Ordinary, everyday work occupied me during the next twelve months, the monotony whereof was broken only by a flying visit to England on "urgent private affairs." The errand to London was not of a pleasant nature ; but when six months later my much-beloved and loving mother was taken to her rest, I rejoiced that, through having been summoned to England on other matters, I had thus been enabled to see her again—for what, alas! proved to be the last time.

The following year I had again to proceed to Europe—this time *on sick leave.* Most of my time was spent among the Swiss mountains, and I rapidly picked up strength. This rapid convalescence was fortunate, for the London papers in August published telegrams as to a "conflict having arisen between the Egyptian Government and the Quarantine Board." *The Morning Post's* correspondent cabled, " Riaz Pasha (the Prime Minister) rejects any responsibility in the matter, and the *question has now reached a deadlock.* Another example is thus afforded of the mischievous nature of international meddling with the internal affairs of Egypt."

As soon as I heard of the deadlock I hurried back to my post, arriving in Alexandria at the end of August, and being at once received in private audience by the Khedive.

I found that not only had a serious difference of opinion on a matter of jurisdiction arisen between the Government and the Quarantine Board, but that cholera had manifested itself among the pilgrims at Mecca, and this, when it occurs, constitutes a grave danger to Egypt by reason of the thousands of the faithful who return to the Nile Valley from the infected area at the termination of each pilgrimage.

A few words as to this " Haj " or pilgrimage.

Mecca, from the earliest times, that is to say for many centuries before the birth of Mohammed in 571 A.D., had been a religious centre. The ancient Arab tribes yearly made pilgrimages to Mecca to kiss the Black Stone which, legend has it, fell from heaven in the days of Adam, but which scientists incline to think is only an aërolite. Like the Moham-medans of to-day, these ancient peoples made the seven circuits of the sacred temple known as the Ka'abah, which then contained, besides the Black Stone, three hundred and sixty idols, since destroyed by Mohammed.

Mecca at the present day is yearly thronged with the followers of Islam, who journey thither for the appointed feast-time from the north, the south, the east, and the west. In fact, Moslems from the uttermost parts of the earth, of all nationalities, and speaking in divers tongues, there do annually congregate. But to-day Mecca has to share its reputation for sanctity with the neighbouring town of Medina, rendered holy in the eyes of the faithful in that the Prophet Mohammed, from the time of the Hegira or Flight, lived there. At Medina also Mohammed died and was buried; and it was from Medina that "in the name of Allah, the Compassionate, the Merciful," the religious law as to the pilgrimage was given.

"Proclaim among the people a pilgrimage: let them come to thee on foot, and on every fleet camel, coming by every deep pass, to be present at its benefits to them, and to make mention of Allah's name at the appointed days over the beasts with which He hath provided them; then eat thereof, and feed the poor and needy; then let them end the neglect of their persons, and pay their vows, and make the circuit of the ancient House."

This edict, and kindred passages from the Koran, has led Mohammedans to consider that, to make certain of admittance into heaven, each one *must* at least once in his lifetime perform the pilgrimage to the Hedjaz. And if he is by circumstances absolutely prevented from himself journeying to Medina and Mecca, then he is enjoined to perform the pilgrimage by proxy, by providing a poor co-religionist with the necessary funds. There is a quaintly pretty Moslem saying to the effect that he who in person journeys to Mecca makes the circuit of the Ka'abah, while he who can only make the pilgrimage in his heart is himself encircled by the Ka'abah.

Pilgrims arriving by sea usually land at the Red Sea port of Jeddah, and, after doing homage at the tomb of our common mother Eve, proceed to Mecca by camel or on foot. At Mecca they—reciting many prayers the while—perform the ceremony of " Tawaf " or Circumambulation, making the round of the Ka'abah seven times ; kissing the sacred Black Stone, and drinking of the salt-bitter waters of the holy well called Zem-zem. The pilgrims then bless the Prophet, and ask Allah for that which their souls desire at one or more of the sacred spots (there are in all fifteen stations) *where*, in their belief, *prayers are always granted*. Later on, a visit is made to Mount Arafat, and to the Valley of Moona, where, as of old time, sacrifices of animals are made.

No Christians are allowed to visit either Medina or Mecca.

Happily I soon managed to patch up the difference, or deadlock, between the Government and the Quarantine Board, and then turned the Board's attention to the more serious matter of doing all that was humanly possible to ward off the danger of the pilgrims returning from Mecca and Medina to Egypt, bringing cholera germs with them.

We stopped every homeward-bound pilgrim vessel, and made the pilgrims perform quarantine at an encampment near the little village of Tor, which is situated on the Sinai Peninsula, one hundred and twenty miles south of Suez.

Over ten thousand pilgrims passed that year through the encampment, each batch purging a minimum quarantine of fifteen days. About four per cent. of the total number died at Tor, a remarkably small percentage all things considered (in itself an eloquent testimony to the care and attention bestowed on the poor pilgrims by the Quarantine Medical Staff), and Egypt was saved.

The danger of an invasion of the cholera being now completely at an end, I set to work to efface from Riaz Pasha's mind all remembrance of the unfortunate conflict between the Government and the Council, which had taken place during my absence in the summer. To this end I first suggested that the Council should vote a most friendly Order of the Day: the idea found favour, and on 10th December, 1890, the Council unanimously agreed to it—"The epidemic of cholera which broke out in the Hedjaz during the pilgrimage of 1890 did not spread beyond Djebel Tor; Egypt and Europe have been spared, thanks to the carrying out of the measures decreed by the Egyptian Maritime and Quarantine Council; but the Council does not forget that it would have been powerless to attain such a completely satisfactory result had not his Highness the Khedive placed liberally at the Council's disposal everything that was asked for.

"Now that the campaign has thus happily been brought to a successful issue, the members of the

Council consider it their first duty to beg his Excellency Riaz Pasha to be their intermediary in conveying to his Highness the Khedive the expression of their feelings of profound gratitude. They would likewise beg his Excellency himself to accept their thanks for the great and constant help rendered by the officials of all ranks, and by officers and troops, in the common task of defending and preserving from the scourge both Egypt and Europe."

This I communicated officially the same day to the Prime Minister, and on his vouchsafing a most cordial reply, I considered the incident of the "deadlock" as being finally and satisfactorily terminated.

Success had thus attended our joint efforts, a success in great measure due to the loyal, unflagging service of all my staff at the Tor Encampment and at the Suez Office, no less than to the labours of my two secretaries, Lombardo Bey and Mr. Peter Cavafy, and of that hard-working and intelligent officer Mr. George Zananiri, then chief of the native clerks, and now, I am glad to think, the Secretary-General of the whole Administration.

But in the case of Mr. Cavafy and myself, who had entered on the struggle in but poor health (for it will be remembered that I was on sick leave at the time of the outbreak), the heavy bill which we had drawn on Nature's bank had to be met. Mr. Cavafy, who had been ailing for some considerable time, found the tax on his strength too great, and on the 17th March, 1891, he breathed his last. The next day his relations, friends, and colleagues stood around his grave in the cemetery outside the Rosetta Gate of the city. I was unable to attend the funeral, being myself confined to bed with malarial fever, which so often attacks the run-down and over-worked, and indeed I could not shake off the effects till I had taken a trip to the Engadine for a few weeks.

Twelve days after my return (25th May) I wrote the following private letter to my sister in England; it speaks for itself—

"Alexandria, Monday.

"I only posted my last letter to you on Saturday, but something has since occurred which, I know, will interest you, so I will tell you of it while the circumstances are quite fresh in my mind.

"About half-past nine o'clock this morning, my chief interpreter came to me and said that in one of the Arabic newspapers it was stated that at the request of the new Minister of the Interior the Khedive had sent for me and given me instructions as to the coming Pilgrimage. 'It is news to me,' I replied, 'but of course the paper knows better than I do.' A quarter of an hour later the interpreter came into my room again, saying—'Some one from Ras-el-Teen Palace wants you at the telephone,' so I switched myself on to the main line (for I have a *private* wire also to the port), and after the usual 'Hullo!' and 'Who's there?' a Master of Ceremonies told me that if I was not very busy his Highness wished to speak to me. I replied that I would at once wait on the Khedive.

"Now coming as it did on the heels, as it were, of

the newspaper report, I drew the hasty but natural conclusion that his Highness desired to talk to me about quarantine matters. Hastily donning my best Stambouline coat and tarboosh, I drove off to Ras-el-Teen, was at once admitted to a private audience, and for some ten minutes or so the Pilgrimage and Quarantine questions generally occupied the field. But the Khedive fidgeted, and quite evidently had something else on his mind. At last his Highness said—'I wish to give you something for yourself, Doctor; would you prefer a grade or a decoration?' I thanked him for his kind thought towards me, and intimated that the latter would please me more than an Egyptian title (Pasha or Bey). His Highness at once said—'I quite agree with you, and shall confer on you the dignity of a Grand Officer of the Imperial Order of the Medjidieh.' He then summoned a secretary, gave certain orders in Turkish, and for the next quarter of an hour chatted pleasantly with me. Then the Brevet and Insignia of the Order were brought in, and the Khedive himself handed them to me, with gracious and complimentary words on the work I had done under his Government during the past seven years."

So many Englishmen have had one of the five classes of the Order of the Medjidieh bestowed on them, that I think it may be of some interest if I here give a copy of the Brevet, and a very brief description of the Order.

Translation of Brevet (from the original Turkish).

"ABDUL HAMID KHAN,

The most Distinguished and Most Honourable

SULTAN,

Highly preserved in Glory by

THE ALMIGHTY.

"In consideration of what has been submitted to our Sublime Government by the High Khediviate of Egypt, praying that our Imperial sentiments be extended to Mr. Miéville, President of the Sanitary and Quarantine Council in Alexandria, on account of his accomplishments and administrative knowledge,

"We deliver to him this Our Imperial Berat, conferring on him the dignity of the Second Class of the Medjidi, and forward to him the Insignia of the Order.

"Done on the fourteenth day of the month of Chawal, 1308. Registered in the books of the Protected City."

The Medjidi, or Medjidieh, is a Turkish Order, and was instituted by Sultan Abdul Medjid (the Slave of the Glorious One), in the year 1268 A.H. (corresponding to the end of 1851 or the beginning of 1852 A.D.), as a recompense to be given in recognition of either civil or military services. The name Medjidieh is derived from the Turkish word Medjid— glorious.

The words printed in Turkish on the Star of the
Order round the Thoughra, or Seal of the Sultan, are
Hameeat (Energy), Sadakat (Honesty), and Gheerat
(Zeal). Below the Thoughra is the date 1268.

The Order contains five classes, and as information
on this subject is generally very inaccessible, I append
the following details.[1]

In accordance with the regulations respecting the
acceptance of foreign Orders by British subjects, I in
due course applied for, and was granted, the Queen's
Licence to accept and wear the Insignia of the Order.

And to bring clearly home to the reader the kind
of work that in the case of Englishmen so decorated
has generally preceded the bestowal of such Orders, I
cannot do better than quote from Sir Evelyn Baring's
despatch to Lord Salisbury, dated 29th of March,
1891, not as it applies to me personally, but to the

---

[1] *First Class, or Grand Coraon*, the Insignia of which consists
of a broad red ribbon, with small green edging, to be worn
obliquely over *right* shoulder, and a star or *plaque* of silver,
with gold and red enamelled centre, to be worn on *left* breast.

Second Class, or Grand Officer, the Insignia of which consists
of a star or *plaque* (as for the First Class), to be worn on *right*
breast, and a smaller star to be worn round the neck attached
to a ribbon of the same colours, only narrower, as described
above.

Third Class, or Commander, same Insignia as for Second
Class, but without star or *plaque* on breast.

Fourth Class, or Officer, of which the Insignia consists of a
small star (worn on *left* breast), suspended from a narrow ribbon,
on which is superposed a *rosette* (of same ribbon).

Fifth Class, or Chevalier, Insignia the same as for Fourth
Class, *but without rosette.*

whole body of officials who gave their life work to the betterment of Egypt—

"When allusion is made to the English influence now exerted over the Egyptian Administration, what is really meant, therefore, is that thirty-nine Englishmen, holding superior appointments, at a cost of £E.37,700 a year, are employed. These form, in fact, the backbone of the Egyptian Civil Administration.

"The number appears to me to be exceedingly small when the amount of work to be done is considered. Indeed, it is a constant source of astonishment to me that so much has been already done with such a very inadequate European staff. As to the amount of the salaries, it cannot be doubted that it is well worth the while of the Egyptian tax-payers to secure the services of these thirty-nine officials at a cost of £E.37,700 a year.

"I cannot speak too highly of the services rendered by this small body of English officials. They have all occupied positions of much difficulty. Many of them have had to conduct a large part of their business in a very difficult Oriental language. All have had generally to use French, rather than English, as the medium of communication with those who speak any European language. Their efforts to effect reforms have been but too frequently met with active hostility or passive obstruction. They have had to guide and persuade rather than to command, and they have had to rely far more on their powers of persuasion than on any diplomatic support which, as the representative of her Majesty's Government, I have been able to afford them.   It is, in fact, only on very rare occasions, and generally in a very mild form, that that support has been accorded to them. They have had to display a large amount of tact, judgment, knowledge of the world, elasticity of mind, and resource in adapting themselves to a condition of society and to administrative systems to which they had not been previously accustomed.   That they should have generally displayed these qualities in an eminent degree is all the more remarkable in that a departmental training in England, or in India, which most of them had previously received, necessitates the exercise of these qualities in a far less degree than is required in Egypt."

CHAPTER XX

THE PILGRIMS' WAY

ARABIA in general, and especially the Turkish province of the Hedjaz (in which the holy cities of Islam are situated), is peculiarly subject to invasions of cholera and plague, for if either of these dread diseases is, at the date of the setting out of the pilgrims, raging in the country from whence they journey, it is almost certain that the germs of the disease will be carried, either by land or by sea, into the Hedjaz. Then the terrible overcrowding of the scores of thousands of the faithful in and around the city of Mecca; the dire poverty of many of the pilgrims, the bad food and foul water, to say nothing of the primitive and inadequate sanitary arrangements, together act like fire to tinder—and often, even before the days of sacrifice at Moona have arrived, an awful epidemic is decimating the multitude.

Poor faithful souls! "Who can escape God, who created all things, and to whom all things must one day return?" "Allah, the compassionate, the merciful, knoweth what was before them, and what shall come after them." It is not to be wondered at that the

danger of the returning pilgrims, carrying seeds of
the scourge with them to their homes, is very great.
Now, as I have already stated, one of the duties of
the Egyptian Quarantine Council was to prevent
this importation of disease by pilgrims returning to
countries north of Jeddah—to Egypt, Turkey, Morocco,
Algeria, Tunis.

Towards the end of May 1891, the existence of
cholera at the gates of the Hedjaz was notified to
us by the Turkish authorities, as it had been the
previous year, and, as I was determined there should
be no repetition of the deadlock which had been
brought about, during my absence in the previous
year, simply on a question of conflict of jurisdiction,
I persuaded the Board to leave the entire arrangements for the camp at Tor in my hands. I thought
at the time, and I still believe, that the Council were
glad and relieved at being thus able to rid themselves
temporarily of a part of their responsibility, but that
they considered me rather a simpleton to take it
upon myself. Such considerations were, however, of
little moment to me: I had never shirked responsibility, and I knew that, unfettered, I had a much
better chance of success.

I set to work with a will, and elaborated a set of
rules, the which, if observed, would, I hoped, facilitate
the work of those in authority under me at the Tor
encampment, ensure order in the several divisions,
and promote the comfort and well-being of the
pilgrims ; and I took especial care that the rules were
such as could be easily and thoroughly carried out,

and not regulations excellent on paper yet hopelessly unworkable in practice.

I laid down that the general encampment was to be not less than six hundred and fifty yards from the shore, and also from the village of Tor itself; that the pilgrims from each ship were to be housed in tents pitched in two long lines—no one tent to contain more than eight pilgrims; that each encampment was to be two hundred and seventy yards distant from its neighbour; and that soldiers were to be posted not only round the encampment as a whole, but also between each separate section, to prevent communication between the pilgrims from the several ships. Excellent sanitary arrangements were contrived, which were to be disinfected three times a day, and moved at frequent intervals to fresh ground. Camels were to be employed all day bringing in fresh water in skins from the adjacent wells, and the tanks placed at the ends of each section were to be thus kept constantly filled. As to eatables, shops were to be attached to each camp, and the owners thereof obliged by contract to sell food, etc., to the pilgrims at a certain (very moderate) fixed tariff, and of course to remain prisoners and abide by the regulations until the pilgrims in the section to which they were for the time being attached, should be declared to be no longer unclean. These petty merchants were allowed also to establish at the extremity of the section with which they cast in their lot a restaurant and *café*, where pilgrims in easy circumstances could have their meals, and play such games as dominoes, draughts, and backgammon.

Twice a day each tent was to be thoroughly aired, and rubbish and refuse swept up and burnt. Twice a day also ·a doctor was to visit each individual pilgrim, and those found ailing were to be sent at once to the general, or to the cholera, hospital.

Then a well-provided drug store was established, and a competent officer appointed to superintend the preparation of the huge quantities of disinfectants necessary. A special staff was told off to control the disinfecting apparatus, for each pilgrim, on his or her arrival, was given a temporary change of clothing while their own garments were disinfected. Their baggage also had to be overhauled and disinfected. Each pilgrim was subjected to this ordeal a second time two or three days before his departure. The period of quarantine was fixed at fifteen days, and while the pilgrims were purging their quarantine in camp, a separate staff of men thus had time to thoroughly disinfect the vessel to which they belonged, and which, by law, was forced to wait until her passengers had purged their quarantine.

I may add that the little port of Tor is one hundred and twenty miles south of Suez, and that unfortunately there existed no telegraphic line beween it and Egypt, though, needless to say, I had yearly urged on the Government the necessity of quick communication. As a matter of fact, all my instructions to the Director of the camp were sent to Tor from Suez either by camel-post or by special steamer.

The Khedive took great interest in all the arrangements, and frequently sent for me to discuss even the smallest details, and at last he expressed a desire to

despatch one of his *aides-de-camp* to Tor to draw up
a perfectly independent report; for though I told his
Highness all that I myself heard, yet my news came
from my own doctors and staff, and was naturally
open to the suspicion of being somewhat one-sided,
for such interested persons would be almost sure to
present everything in the most favourable aspect.
When his Highness suggested to me that he should
like to send an *aide-de-camp*, he evidently had doubts
as to how I should regard the proposal, for his kindly
face brightened considerably when I welcomed his
suggestion, thanking him for his interest in the work,
and saying, "And now, Monseigneur, we ought to
hear of the defects and shortcomings, and so be able
to correct and rectify them."

Thus the matter was settled, the special messenger
duly despatched, and on receipt of his first report the
Khedive had parts of it communicated to the local
Press.

I will now give two telegrams which appeared in
The Times, and which speak for themselves.

"*Alexandria, Sept.* 1.—The International Quarantine Board has wisely avoided a repetition of last
year's deadlock, by giving President Miéville a free
hand to draw up Quarantine regulations. These
have worked satisfactorily, and the pilgrims from
Mecca arriving in Egypt are in a thoroughly healthy
condition."

"*Alexandria, Oct.* 8.—Twelve thousand pilgrims,
half of whom were Egyptians, have passed through
the Quarantine encampment at Tor, where ample

provision in all respects was made by the International Board, whose measures, with the Khedive's support, and liberal charity towards the poorest pilgrims, have probably saved Egypt from an invasion of the cholera which prevailed in the Hedjaz during the pilgrim season."

The Tor encampment was finally broken up on the 1st of October. Cholera had been kept out of Egypt, and at Tor itself we had only had 121 deaths (from cholera and other diseases) out of a total of 11,950 pilgrims who had there purged their quarantine. And let me here place once again on record my deep indebtedness to the Tor staff. Their untiring devotion to duty under most trying circumstances was beyond all praise. I had always endeavoured to be a just Chief to them, and by willing and devoted service did they repay me a hundred-fold.

But the strain was great, and, though happily I did not break down, it will be seen by the two following extracts taken from private letters written at the time, that Nature was well-nigh exhausted.

"*9th October*, 1891.—The horror of going off suddenly here in exile is often present to me. I see so many cases of men retiring too late. . . . I know my heart is weak. . . . I admit (joyfully) that I *may* live to a good old age, but not if I do not get more rest and less worry."

"*19th October*, 1891.—The cholera is still in the Hedjaz, and also at Damascus. My Alexandria lazaretto is chock-full of the aristocracy of Syria, flying from the epidemic. My hands also are full.

This year there seems to be no peace (for the wicked). I am doing my best. I can do no more; but another year like this will kill me. I had again another slight seizure in the office last Friday, but only for a few seconds."

I may add that it was with a glow of pleasure that we who worked in distant lands found that our efforts were not wholly lost on the good people at home; for such a statement as this one from the *St. James's Gazette* brings comfort to those who give their best years to the State.

"Egypt has shown us that we are still the members of an Imperial race, fit to rule the earth, to found empires, to raise the fallen, and to crush the proud. It has been pleasant to turn away from the petty squabbles and trumpery quarrels, the paltry intrigues of the domestic party fight, to a land where the leaders of Englishmen are not wire-pullers or platform orators, and where our countrymen do not talk, but work. Leaving the Harcourts and the Laboucheres, the caucuses and the 'federations,' to rave and gabble, some few score of quiet Englishmen, in these half-dozen years, have been fighting the battle of civilization and justice, and winning it. We scarcely know their names; when we meet them over here we regard them only as inconspicuous military men, or as civilians who have got very moderately 'good berths' in Egypt; we have not thought it necessary to confer on even the best of them the titular distinctions which are not hard to earn by a pushing mediocrity who serves his time with sufficient assiduity in the House of Commons. But it is this little knot of men who are doing such work in one of the waste places of the world as no other has done since the better days of the Roman rule. They have pushed back barbarism into its deserts, and kept it there ; they have lightened the taxes of a people ground down for centuries by the infamous Eastern revenue system ; they have abolished the slavery of the *corvée ;* they have made the life and property of the peasant secure ; they irrigated his fields, drained his towns, and fought the cholera-fiend for him."

CHAPTER XXI

DEATH OF THE KHEDIVE TEWFIK

IN October 1891 I wrote in a private letter to a friend—"It is more than possible, nay, it is almost probable, that I shall shortly be relieved of my present functions. Hitherto it has been kept a profound secret, but now it has become known to many that a Conference of the Great Powers is shortly to be held at Venice to consider certain proposals—emanating from Austria—for the re-organization of the Egyptian Quarantine Board. Underlying the official proposals is the ardent desire to get rid of me by hook or crook, as Austria and the other Quarantine Powers feel that so long as I continue to occupy the Presidency their efforts to hamper commerce and navigation will not be attended with the same success as before my appointment in 1884. All the means employed in the past seven years to oust me having proved of no avail, it is now proposed to attain the desired end by passing a resolution to the effect that the President should be a doctor of medicine. I honestly think this proposal reasonable, though I laugh in my sleeve at its transparency as a device for getting rid of poor obnoxious me."

Later in the month I again wrote to the same correspondent—" I have been down to talk to the Khedive, who has kindly promised that if he is consulted in the matter of who should represent Egypt at the Venice International Conference, he should speak in favour of *my* going.   So there seems every chance of my being at Venice to speak up for myself in the unlikely event of an open attack on my administrative acts as President."

It was ultimately decided that I should go to Venice as second Egyptian Delegate, the chief of the misson being an exceedingly clever Copt, Boutros Pasha Ghali, with, as third member, a native doctor, Mahmoud Pasha Sidky, the son-in-law of my friend, Mustapha Pasha Fehmy, the Prime Minister.

A few days after receiving official intimation to hold myself in readiness, I heard a sinister rumour that the extra allowance to the Egyptian delegates during the mission was to be fixed at a rather low figure, so off I went to the Palace, and in a most cheery interview with the Khedive, I pointed out that as President of the very Board whose constitution and organization was to be discussed at Venice, many of the representatives of the European Powers would assuredly wish to consult and negotiate with me privately.   I then drew a comical picture of myself sitting on my bed in a stuffy room in an Italian hotel, with some swell diplomate or medical celebrity occupying the one and only safe chair.   The Khedive laughed, and I said, " Our allowance ought really to be liberal enough to permit of our having a decent sitting-room ; " and his Highness replied, " I will speak to my Ministers."

A few days later a paragraph went the round of the papers saying that at the last Cabinet Council it had been decided to grant to each of the delegates a special allowance, exclusive of travelling expenses.

I at once took train to Cairo, and begged an audience of the Khedive. This was accorded, and I warmly thanked his Highness for his great kindness in securing for us such generous treatment.

On leaving, his Highness accompanied me with his hand on my shoulder to the door of the audience chamber, and on shaking hands said, " Now that you will be able to have a sitting-room at Venice, I shall send you a photograph to place in it."—" To adorn it, Effendina," I replied. And so we parted smilingly and cordially. The Khedive was as good as his word.

I still have the portrait, and greatly prize it, as I was told subsequently that it was one of the last, if not the very last, the Khedive ever signed.

Less than a fortnight later his Highness was suddenly taken ill, and on the 7th January following —nineteen days after I had taken my leave of him— the kindly Khedive Tewfik passed away.

And I venture to think I shall not tax my readers' patience, if I relate two further instances in which I was the recipient of his Highness's favours.

The Khedive's thoughtfulness was displayed towards me in the first case on the sad occasion of my dear mother's death, when, on learning the news, and knowing that on account of pressure of work I had been unable to be present during her last illness, his Highness commanded his Master of Ceremonies to write me a letter of sympathy in my grievous bereavement. It was a kindly, thoughtful act, and touched me deeply.

The second incident, which shows his great sense of justice, requires more telling. My wife had been ill, and was ordered up the Nile for change ; and I wrote privately to Riaz Pasha, the then Prime Minister, asking him to let me accompany the invalid for a few days without my absence counting a regular leave against me. Now Riaz Pasha, in my humble opinion, was not over fond of European functionaries, so the thought struck me that if I wrote to him in his own tongue it would put him in a good humour, and show him at the same time that British officials tried to get in touch with the natives by learning their language. My private letter therefore was despatched in *Arabic*, but the reply, when it came, was written in *French*. As the tenor of the answer was favourable, I pocketed the quasi-affront, but did not forget it, and some months afterwards, when the Khedive, by addressing me in Arabic, gave me a chance of easing my mind, I did so by saying, " Your Highness's Prime Minister does not like European officials to talk Arabic." This provoked the query, " Why do you say that ? " and the whole story came out. The Khedive seemed amused, but said nothing. However, he evidently pondered over it, as a few days later, when receiving some native notabilities, his

Highness repeated the tale, suppressing only my name, and adding (so, at least, an Egyptian who was present told me afterwards)—" If a European in my service were to write to me in Arabic, I should be so pleased that I would reply to him with my own hand." Whether the implied rebuke ever reached the Minister's ear I do not know.

As the correspondent of *The Times* said in telegraphing the sad news of the Khedive's death—" Universal regret will be felt for the ruler who showed the greatest patience and sagacity throughout all troubles, and who, by incessant hard work and consultation with the heads of every department, had obtained a grasp of the entire administration with an intelligent comprehension of the general situation. The Khedive had won the love of the country by his solicitude for his people."

There are few monarchs, I take it, who would not be proud indeed if they could hope that of them it could at their demise be as truly written as in the case of the Khedive Mehemet Tewfik—

" He won the love of the country by his solicitude for his people."

Six weeks later, when I once more visited Cairo, it was for me a sacred duty to at once make a pilgrimage to his still unfinished tomb; and I had none but grateful, affectionate thoughts as I stood near my late master's last resting-place in silent Farewell.

CHAPTER XXII

MINISTERING ANGELS

ON my return to Alexandria from the capital, I was terribly busy, collecting papers to be used at Venice for reference; arranging with my second in command for the carrying on of the current work of the administration during my absence, packing my personal effects, and attending to the thousand and one things that crop up almost miraculously, and most inopportunely, whenever a sudden move has to be made. And time was very short, for I only left Cairo on the evening of the 19th, and three days afterwards the s.s. *Thalia* left Alexandria for Brindisi. Almost immediately after the vessel steamed out of the harbour I went below, feeling feverish and over-wrought. But I felt also a glow of satisfaction that I had at last a chance of appearing on a more European enterprise.

The fever continued, my temperature rose higher and higher, and at last on Christmas Eve the ship's surgeon and two other doctors who were on board entertained little doubt that I was in for a serious attack of small-pox.

At daylight on Christmas morning the ship entered

the port of Brindisi, and the captain and surgeon, at the instance of my friends the other doctors, decided to take me on to Trieste, where the *Thalia* was due to arrive the following day. I think this course was dictated by two considerations—one, the difficulty of getting the Italian authorities to let me land at Brindisi were they to learn that I was suffering from a contagious disease ; and secondly, the knowledge that the vessel flying the Austrian flag would, on the other hand, be sure of favourable treatment in the port of Trieste. Let us charitably trust—though subsequent events make such a trust seem misplaced —that there was also present in some minds the humanitarian consideration of the want of decent hospital accommodation at Brindisi.

The original decision to take me on to Trieste was, however, for some unexplained reason, abandoned, possibly out of consideration for the feelings of the other passengers, and it was decided to smuggle me on shore at Brindisi. I say "smuggle," because I can hardly believe that the local sanitary authorities were informed of the nature of my disease, even if they were told that I was ill at all.

I will not attempt to lay blame on any one for this change of front ; but it seemed to my lay mind little short of criminal to morally force a small-pox patient from his warm berth, land him in a small boat on a raw morning with the thermometer at 52° Fahrenheit, require him to *walk* from the quay to the hospital, and to go through the usual slow Custom-house inspection on the way.

Being myself the sufferer, my judgment in the matter may indeed have been warped ; yet though I quite understood that the few other passengers on the *Thalia* may have felt relieved at being rid of such an unwelcome fellow-passenger as a small-pox patient, it appeared to me at the time a barbarously cruel thing for the captain to do, to turn out of the vessel, neck and crop, a sick man, and a delicately-nurtured lady, his wife, at dawn on a cold day in a strange land—and that on the day of the Christ. Where indeed was the good-will toward men ?

We were landed about 6.30 a.m., and duly arrived at the hospital ; we took possession of an apparently deserted ward, containing some eight or ten beds ; no fire-place — stone flooring — no comforts, and scarcely the bare necessaries for washing purposes, only a basin on a chair, and, for lights, candles stuck in bottles.

But here let me say at once that I do not desire to speak against the hospital arrangements ; the truth was that the dilapidated place had never been intended to accommodate private patients ; but rather to house the poorest of the poor (and they are legion in Italy), to many of whom a bed to lie on and a roof for shelter constitute comfort, if not luxury. And with regard to the candles in bottles, I must place gratefully on record in this place, lest later I forget it, that ultimately the bottles were replaced by silver candlesticks from a little chapel.

I crawled into one of the beds (it had over it No. 12), more dead than alive ; feeling, I think, more miserable than I had before conceived it possible to feel. Here was the Christmas morning which should have been so full of merriment—and I, instead of jubilant, stricken with a foul sickness, in miserable surroundings, and with bitter food for contemplation in the apparent destruction of all my hopes of making my little mark at an International Conference.

At about eight in the morning a doctor put in his appearance. He was not endowed with an undue quantity of tact, for after looking at me from a respectful distance, he expressed a rather decided opinion that I should not be allowed to remain even in my present cold and poorly furnished quarters, but that the authorities would hustle me off to some isolated building miles away, and so tranquillize the official mind on the score of contagion.

But even a worm will turn—even a crushed worm; and I roused myself and stormed at him and rated him in my very best Italian, the which, if not grammatical, is fluent and comprehensive; the poor man incontinently turned tail, and fled, and I am happy to say he never returned. I did not, however, rest on my laurels, but asked my wife to send for the British Consul, and also to telegraph in my name to the Italian Minister for Foreign Affairs at Rome. Next some officials, pompous, important, and fussy, outwardly brave in gaudy uniforms, inwardly shaking with fear of infection, came, and glared at us through a glass door, and then told us from the same vantage-ground that we could not stay where we were. But I refused to budge unless force was used.

In the result I was allowed to stay where I had at first lain me down.

Then, in the midst of our sore trials, came some rays of sunshine. The first ray—a very bright one —was a venerable woman's face.

It seemed to us indeed an angel's face; and it belonged to the Mother Superior—a Sister of the noble Society of St. Vincent of Paul.

Cheering and pleasant indeed did the fearless lady appear to us, as, in the spotless white linen coif and neat uniform of her order, she came forward and greeted my wife with outstretched hand and comforting words. And what a contrast did her courage present to the timid behaviour of the fearsome civic functionaries who had interviewed us from behind the glass door!

The good mother bustled about, giving orders right and left; beaming kindly upon us the while, and assuring and reassuring us that she would never let the authorities turn us out. Then came the second ray in the shape of the new doctor, middle-aged, genial, and cheerful; so we didn't inquire too closely into his cleverness or capacity.

And a third appeared to dispel the gloom—and this third ray took the form of an English gentleman, Mr. Hall, a resident in Brindisi, who, hearing of the plight of his fellow-countryman, had come to offer assistance, counsel, and consolation. "A happy Christmas to you!" said he, and the greeting in his kindly tones did not seem out of place in spite of the sad circumstances, for these rays of sunshine had caused us once more to feel hopeful.

Ah! the difference between the behaviour of those who first had to do with us, and who seemed to shun and avoid us as if we were plague-stricken, and the fearless conduct and bearing of the three sympathetic souls. These last were indeed Samaritans.

There is no gainsaying that at first the big bare ward struck cold and seemed very wretched, but after receiving these little acts of kindness, we were more inclined to try and persuade ourselves that the building was not so *very* desolate, or the stone floor so *bitterly* cold after all. So the day wore on, the shadows lengthened and deepened, darkness set in ; and in a few short hours Christmas 1891 had joined the other eighteen hundred and ninety vanished Christmases.

I spent a troubled, restless night, with a high temperature. The soup administered to me for nourishment was poor ; milk seemed scarce, and the tea was vile. The next day, however, we managed to order a good supply of goat's milk to be brought night and morning. How well I remember the tinkling of the goats' bells as they straggled up the street in the early morning — before even the day broke — and browsed (on paper and refuse chiefly) under the hospital windows, while one of the flock was being milked for our benefit. How anxiously and restlessly I waited hour after hour, night after night, for this, to me, welcome sound, for I knew that the tinkling meant that another awful night was well-nigh over. Then through the kind help of the Consul we obtained a pot of Liebig and a spirit-lamp, and later on we set

the wires to work and telegraphed for all sorts of
things to anxious and willing friends in London,
and a day or two later supplies poured in—tea,
medicines, face - sponges, disinfectants, and the
rest.

Happily we found that outside our window there
was a balcony—some seven yards long—and there
my wife, who was my constant nurse night and day
was able to get a little exercise and fresh air.

In addition to the Mother Superior already mentioned, who was a very help in trouble, another Sister
daily visited us—Sister Marie,—a good brave lady,
who, however, by reason of her youth and lesser
experience, and possibly also from being of a more
timid nature than the Mother Superior, shrank somewhat from actual contact with me. I mention this
solely because it enhances the courage and loving
goodness of her subsequent conduct.

Two servants tended us—both, alas! since dead—
a woman with a past, called Candida, and a man
named Giovanni. Both were very rough, and quite
unused to looking after gentlefolk, but both were
right willing.

Candida was a strong wench, who would nightly,
at about 8 p.m., lift me bodily up in the top mattress
and deposit me on one of the vacant beds, while she
and Giovanni freshened up the straw with which the
under mattress was stuffed. Candida was very devout,
and had a special faith in and leaning towards a
certain shrine to the Virgin in, I believe, the town of
Bari. She confided in me that she would pray to

this Blessed Lady for me, and so I might rest assured that I should speedily recover.

She would, when I was able to bandy a few words of chaff with her, tell me the Brindisi gossip, or, if that failed, she would relate curious episodes, generally serio-comical, of her past experiences. She was a faithful soul, and I doubt not that the good-natured service she rendered us will be counted to her for righteousness.

Giovanni, too, in his own rough way, showed sympathy to the stranded strangers, and was always ready and willing to obey our behests smilingly, and with as much alacrity as his southern nature admitted of.

The two Sisters, the doctor, and the two servants were, as it turned out, to be our sole companions for four weeks. And we were fortunate in having fallen in with such kindly souls!

On Sunday, two days after Christmas, I was bright enough to dictate a few sentences in a letter. It lies before me now—

"There is a desperately comic side to this business. Every official in the place has mixed himself up with my ghastly sickness. This morning we received a formidable document holding us responsible for the spread of the disease (should other cases occur in the town). This was followed up by a visit from the sub-prefect, who, bowing profoundly, said he called because it was his duty, but who in fact did so to satisfy himself that we were really being kept prisoners."

For the next week I was dangerously ill, but

constant attention and good nursing preserved me. On the 7th of January, when there was some slight amelioration in my condition, our spirits once more sank down to zero, for my wife-nurse took the disease. She managed to write to London—

"I am in for the disease : I had to give in at four o'clock, when my temperature was close on 102°. I turned in with a sinking heart. My bed was near Walter's, and the table, with the milk, etc., on it, was put between us. Poor old W., he pulled himself together and wanted to telegraph for a nurse, but I would not hear of it."

And I must now revert to Sister Marie, for notwithstanding her evident horror of the dread scourge, no sooner did she see that my wife had caught the disease than, forgetful of herself, she allowed her woman's heart free play, and straightway *kissed* her !

So it happened that I had my turn at nursing, though, being myself scarcely convalescent, I fear I was not much use. It was a curious predicament to be in—the sick tending the sick.

Then, as if our cup were not even then full to overflowing, came the sad news of the sudden death of Khedive Tewfik. I felt it most keenly, as he had always been most friendly to me, and when I had last seen him, he had appeared to be in robust health. The Mother Superior said on hearing the news—" It has pleased Heaven to take the Prince surrounded in his palace with every luxury, and to spare you nursed in this poor wretched hospital : let us be thankful."

Meanwhile the Conference had been opened at

Venice, and I received frantic telegrams and letters as to this point and that, for—and I say it in no boastful spirit—there is little doubt that my absence was causing much inconvenience, if not dismay, in certain quarters. My advocacy of some reforms, and my reasoned opposition to other proposals, had been reckoned on, and the Brindisi disaster had not been dreamt of, much less provided against. I answered all inquiries as best I could from my sick-bed, and counselled the staving off by adjournments of such questions as required special knowledge of the inner working of the Quarantine Administration for their enlightened solution; and I must say that if fate had been unkind to us in disabling us by sickness, the stars themselves later on seemed to fight for us in their courses.

The sittings of the Conference of the 5th and 7th of January were formal; the sitting of the 8th was adjourned in token of mournful respect for the Khedive, and that of the 15th in consequence of the receipt of the intelligence of the death of the Duke of Clarence. Then followed a very brief meeting on the 16th, which adjourned till the 23rd of January, on which day the Egyptian Delegation appeared for the first time in full force, for I had joined my able colleagues and taken my seat.

But I am somewhat anticipating events, and must hark me back for a little to the hospital at Brindisi.

On the 13th of January things began to be more cheerful, and our delight was great at receiving a visit from a passing friend, Mr. Favarger, who brought me a supply of novels, cigars, and cigarettes, and a long Indian deck-chair.

On the 14th I got up for the first time, and three days later we had a walk. Then we said good-bye to the Halls, and to those in the town who had shown us real kindness, and in the early morning of the 20th we tried with very full hearts to thank the good Sisters before starting for the express train to Venice.

CHAPTER XXIII

VENICE AT LAST

DOUBTLESS every Conference between the Powers
has two histories, the official history or record of the
discussions at the sittings—which record of the Venice
International Sanitary Conference extends to some
350 pages—and the secret history, which, as often as
not, is never written, and never wholly known, even to
many of the members taking part in the Conference.
It sometimes happens that this secret history leaks
out little by little, as the years roll on ; but it has
then but little interest, except to a few.

I arrived at Venice on Thursday, the 21st January,
1892 ; it was, I remember, a beautiful moonlight morning ; and much of the secret history of the Conference
was, I believe, made in the following forty-eight hours.
The weather was bitterly cold (I confess I had never
known what cruel weather was till I visited Venice
that winter) ; many of the delegates were tired of
dilly-dallying, for that is what they had practically been
doing for three weeks, as none of the really thorny
points had up to that time been solved, or even
entered upon. Those delegates who were busy men in
their own countries, chafed at the waste of time ; certain

others, who were remunerated in a lump sum, were desirous of curtailing their stay (and at the same time their expenses); while other delegates honestly wanted to see an understanding arrived at, honourable alike to the two great opposing camps, the quarantinists and the (so-called) anti-quarantinists.

Thus, when I bustled round paying official calls to my co-delegates, I found the ground most favourable for the sowing of the seed of that hardy plant, common-sense.   So I lost no time, and I heard that many of the eminent diplomates and world-renowned physicians were somewhat astonished by my frankness, directness, and manifest sincerity.   Some of these personages had met me before, some already knew me almost intimately, all had been primed as to my presumed and supposed leanings, but none had ever before seen me in quite the same *rôle* as I then assumed.   Yet I was not playing a part; I only judged it opportune at that particular juncture to appear in my true character; to disabuse certain minds of maliciously-instilled prejudices against me ; to show how arduous, difficult, and delicate had been my post for years past ; and to make it as clear as noon-day that the President's position was, in short, far from being a bed of roses.

Confidence begat confidence ; difficulties disappeared ; beating about the bush went out of fashion ; active interchange of ideas was the order of the day ; and I venture to think that more real work was got through at the sittings held on the next two days—at which I spoke some twenty times—than had been accomplished during the previous eight meetings.

I do not lay claim to the credit of this happy state of things, but I have no hesitation in saying that I felt, as I still feel, that to some extent I had been, with the help of the circumstances which I have endeavoured to set forth, instrumental in bringing it about. Many of the diplomates, and others with whom it was my good fortune and privilege to be associated, were men of exceptional capacity and of the highest standing. And I may add that so favourable was the opinion they were indulgent enough to form of the way I had tried to "hold the balance even," for eight long years, that the project to oust me from the Chairmanship of the Quarantine Board was practically and almost tacitly abandoned. On the evening of the second day *The Times* correspondent was able to telegraph to London, that the Conference "*had arrived at the solution of all points except one, in the reconciliation of opposing views presented for consideration*," and to add to his message the, to me, most pregnant and satisfactory phrase—" Mr. Miéville was to-day unanimously re-elected President (of the Egyptian Board), his discharge of the duties of the office eliciting high encomiums from the delegates of the various Powers."

Great Britain was represented at the Conference by Mr. J. W. Lowther, Under-Secretary of State for Foreign Affairs, Dr. Mackie, C.M.G. (delegate to the Alexandria Quarantine Board), and Mr. Harry Farnall, C.M.G. (of the Foreign Office).

On the afternoon of Sunday, 24th January, the wife of Dr. Mackie died. She had arrived in Venice in good health, had contracted a cold which I think went to the lungs, and the sad termination to the illness cast a gloom over all of us. To me it was a personal grief. I did my best to comfort and help Dr. Mackie, and stayed with him until quite late in the evening.

I am tempted here to quote the history of the next few days from old letters kindly lent to me by the relation to whom they were addressed. It is true they were written by my wife, and that they are much too flattering, and to a great degree prejudiced, yet if the commendatory passages are taken with a good modicum of salt, a not unfair estimate should be arrived at.

"Danieli's Hotel, Venice.

"23rd January.—Walter is now at the Conference, making his first speech. We lunched with Count von Leyden, Germany's diplomatic representative at the Conference. From the conversation I gleaned that they have done nothing but talk, talk, talk. France's proposals with regard to the free passage of vessels through the Canal seem the soundest of those propounded. Walter has been two days now going into the question with ——, who told him this morning that he *now* felt that France's proposals were the most reasonable. You see he had become convinced, and it is hoped that all the others will see it too. If this point is settled to-day, they will quickly proceed to other matters of importance, and the Conference will be over in ten days. When they begin to get out of their depths, Walter is able to show them where they are. He has studied the question in all its bearings."

"25th January.—I have been *dreadfully* upset by

Mrs. Mackie's death. Somehow it seems to me that misfortunes will never end. To crown all, Walter took cold yesterday. There was a *big* committee meeting arranged for to-day, and when it was known that the doctors thought it better for Walter not to go out, the whole body of committee men came to our rooms, *and the committee meetings are now held in our sitting-room.* This shows how indispensable Walter is, and really it was paying him a great compliment.

"It had been thought possible to end the Conference to-morrow, but certain further preliminaries must be arranged here. I was told yesterday that Walter was the life and soul of the Conference. I only hope it will not be too great a strain on him. They are hurrying things too much; you see, they have been here twenty days doing nothing, but now they make tremendous way, and as the Austrian representative told me, 'It is at last becoming excessively interesting.' Do not think I am exaggerating. From the attitude of those delegates I personally know, and they are nearly all diplomates, I can see how highly they think of Walter."

"*28th January.*—There is no doubt that W. has a slight attack of pleurisy. There is an idea that the Conference will be over in a day or two. There has just come an invitation for him to dine with the King's brother, the Duke of Genoa, to-morrow, at the Palace, but he certainly will not be one of the guests."

"*29th January.*—Both the doctors advise us to go through to Naples at once with Dr. Mackie, as this place is the worst we could stay in. Dr. Zancarol, who has been extremely kind, says he should not like to leave W. behind in Venice in his present weak state, and that we should be wise to make a move to a warmer climate. The only difficulty is the getting to the station by gondola."

" 30*th January*.—The Conference is over. We go with Dr. Mackie to Rome to-morrow, leaving here at 2.25 p.m. It will be a comfort having Dr. Mackie with us all the way from here to Alexandria, and we may be a comfort in another way to him, as he is restless and unhappy, and must be kept from thinking too much of his bereavement."

"Continental Hotel, Rome.

" 1*st February*.—Here we are in the Eternal City. Walter bore the journey very well, but he has had a narrow escape. Mr. Lowther and Mr. Farnall were so very nice at the end ; they said W. had done good work during the few days he was in harness, and they were half afraid they had driven him too much. What a terribly unfortunate time it has been ! I left Venice in fear and trembling. In my heart of hearts I was *so* anxious. W. looked so weak, and was a complete wreck ; Dr. Zancarol was right, however, the change to a warmer climate has done him good."

And now a few words as to the general and practical results of the Conference. To me, personally, it was a great satisfaction, inasmuch as most of the

important conclusions arrived at were *miles* in advance
of what the Quarantinist Powers had hitherto admitted,
and, as a matter of fact, were practically the very conclusions for advocating and upholding which I had been
so vilified and abused in a certain section of the Continental Press. It would be tedious to go into the
whole Convention in detail; but it may be interesting
if I take one important point—the point on which,
indeed, many others hinge—and give in columns, side
by side, a synopsis of Article I. of the old regulations
in vogue, since May 1884, for the prevention of the
importation into Egypt of cholera, and of Article I.
of regulations against cholera as agreed to by the
Venice Conference.

OLD CHOLERA REGULATIONS.	NEW CHOLERA REGULATIONS.
ARTICLE I.	ARTICLE I.
Vessels arriving from in-fected ports having no suspi-cion of cholera on board, to undergo seven days' quarantine, subject to the following sliding scale—	*All clean vessels* to be at once admitted to free *pratique* without taking into account the tenor of their bills of health (*i. e.* the state of health in the port of departure).

After 8 days' voyage, only 6 days' quarantine.

  ,, 9 ,,   ,,   ,, 5 ,,   ,,
  ,, 10 ,,   ,,   ,, 4 ,,   ,,
  ,, 11 ,,   ,,   ,, 3 ,,   ,,
  ,, 12 ,,   ,,   ,, 2 ,,   ,,
  ,, 13 ,,   or more, 24 hours' quarantine.

This scale to be modified for war-vessels
and postal steamers as follows—

After 8 days' voyage, 3 days' quarantine.

  ,, 9 ,,   ,,   2 ,,   ,,
  ,, 10 ,,   or more, 24 hours' quarantine.

Now it will be seen at a glance that the principle of judging a vessel by the state of health at the port of departure—a principle which I have always held to be absurd and unjust—was frankly abandoned at Venice, and the common-sense principle of treating a vessel according to whether *she herself* had or had not disease on board substituted. This change of front was indeed a great step in advance, and reflects the greatest credit on the Quarantinist party. This may seem a somewhat paradoxical conclusion for me to draw, but I hold that it wanted great moral courage for the Quarantinist Powers of Europe to abandon so completely their ancient theories, and to recognize so thoroughly that their old opponents had all along been in the right.

I do not cite the further Articles of the cholera regulations, dealing with vessels having, or having had during the voyage, disease on board, because I have never been opposed to most stringent measures in such cases, though my inclination has always been in favour of thorough disinfection in preference to undue detention.

A year later his Majesty Umberto I., King of Italy, conferred on me a high honour, by raising me to the dignity of a Grand Officer of the Order of the Crown of Italy, and I was most warmly congratulated by all the newspapers, in Egypt French as well as English.

CHAPTER XXIV

THE NEW KHEDIVE

THE young Khedive, Abbas the Second, is the elder son of the Khedive Tewfik, whom he succeeded. He was born in 1874, was educated in Austria, and, like so many Orientals, quickly mastered languages; and, besides Turkish and Arabic, speaks English, French, and German. He is kindly and bright in disposition; loves horses and dogs, and sports of all kinds; keeps a racing stud, and encourages athletics, cricket, and football in the native colleges. This speaks well for any man, and I shall be greatly surprised if Abbas Hilmi Pasha does not, as years bring experience, develop into a most capable ruler.

One of my first duties after my return from the Venice Conference was to pay him homage. I have before me an old letter which I wrote home at the time—

"My reception on my return has been most kind both here and in Cairo; I went up to the capital on Wednesday, and found Baring genial and pleasant, the Ministers cordial, the new Khedive gracious. The interview with his Highness was somewhat painful to me, for I could not so soon after my old friend's death bring myself actually to *congratulate* his Highness on his accession, but I told him he could rely on the same fidelity and loyalty as I had shown to his father.

"Happily I had been on friendly terms with the new Khedive during the previous summer, when, as a young student, he was in Egypt for his holidays.

"He therefore quite understood my emotion, and respected it, as he had himself seen on what good terms I had been with the late Khedive. His Highness replied to me—'I am sure I can always trust you, and I know how much my Government is indebted to you for services in the past.'

"I was told at the Palace that the last photograph the Khedive Tewfik gave away was the one he had given me in December.

"After my reception at Abdeen Palace, I visited all the Ministers, and then lunched with Tigrane Pasha, the Minister for Foreign Affairs. I returned to Alexandria on the evening of the 11th.

"As to leave this year, we must come home in May or November on account of the pilgrimage, which is, as you know, a movable feast. The *early* leave can probably be arranged for without any particular difficulty. The *late* leave is risky and doubtful, as, were cholera to get into Egypt *viâ* the Hedjaz—and of course we cannot expect *always* to *keep it out*—I should like to stop in the country ; though *stamping out cholera* has nothing to do with me or with the Quarantine Board, but is solely the duty of the *Interior*

Sanitary Service. Also if the Venice Convention is ratified this summer, it will be better that I should be here to set the new machinery in working order. So you may see us in May."

The next two months passed busily but pleasantly withal, as the delegates had at last become quite friendly to me. Then in the middle of April I went up to Cairo to attend the ceremony of the reading of the Sultan's Firman acknowledging his Highness Abbas II. Khedive of Egypt.

When I was summoned to Cairo, there happened to be with us in Alexandria a friend from London, who of course wanted to see the great ceremony. He was a cheery soul, always bubbling over with jests, was good-natured George. At the time of which I write he used to interlard his phrases with *single letters*. For instance, if he had said the wrong thing he would observe S.I.S. (sorry I spoke), or N.F. (no offence). Such tricks of speech are most catching, so (to his infinite chagrin) I called him B.K., meaning Bank Clerk, for he held an official position in or about Lombard Street.

Now when he asked me to get him an invitation for the Reading of the Firman, I at first told him that I thought it was not possible to do this so late—on the eve of the ceremony—then a happy thought struck me, and I exclaimed, " Eureka ! You shall go as a financial magnate or B.K."

I therefore took my friend to the Abdeen Palace, and leaving him in an ante-chamber preferred my request for a ticket for the morrow's *fantasia*. All the Assistant Masters of the Ceremonies with one accord said the thing was impossible, so I had to penetrate into the august presence of the Grand Master himself. Seated in his private room the Pasha looked much worried, and no wonder he was grumpy and gloomy, for a bomb-shell had just burst over his devoted head in the shape of a lively complaint from a group of big-wigs called " The Commissioners of the Public Debt," who, rightly or wrongly, insisted that they had not been allotted for the morrow's ceremony that position on the principal stand to which according to precedent they were entitled. You, kind reader, may in your wisdom qualify such a squabble as a "storm in a teacup," but the harassed Grand Master found it a mighty big teacup filled with terribly hot water, as he knew to his cost, for *he was in it.*

So I did not behave " like a bull in a china shop," but smilingly salaamed his Excellency, and said— " Don't mind *me*, Pasha, *I* do not wish to bother for tickets or to raise questions of precedence : I only thought you might like to hear the latest gossip from Alexandria."

The big man's face relaxed, he offered me a cigarette, lit another himself, and then said in French, " Sit down, mon Président." Soon I tickled his fancy with some yarn, and raised a laugh, then said I must not take up more of his Excellency's time, and finally ventured to add, " What a pity it is all the tickets are gone for to-morrow ; there's a friend of mine here, a *financier* from England, who would have been pleased to have been invited to the ceremony had he arrived earlier."

"One minute," said the great man; "what's your friend's name?" I handed the Pasha his card, and he said, "I don't seem to have heard the name before" (and between you and me and the bed-post this was scarcely to be wondered at); "but I will see what can be done."

That same evening on Shepheard's balcony a Palace orderly handed to my friend an official envelope containing a card inscribed with the following legend—

"By order of his Highness the Khedive, the Grand Master of Ceremonies begs Mr. B——k to be good enough to assist at the Reading of the Imperial Firman which will take place at Abdeen Palace."

I need not dwell on how we bought Mr. B——k a new top hat; nor on how, when the ceremony was over, he tried to get the shop to take it back, on the plea that *it did not fit;* nor on how we rigged him up at eight o'clock on the eventful morning in his dress clothes (which for civilians were *de rigueur*); nor on how after the ceremony we did a quick change and drove to the Pyramids, and had a capital lunch at Mena House, and a good time generally. But B.K. has had a great respect for English diplomacy ever since.

Having duly arranged with the Government to take a short holiday *before* the pilgrimage, the young Khedive granted me a fortnight later a private audience, at which I took leave of his Highness, and ten days later we left for Europe.

I returned in July; though, as it turned out, there was no real necessity for me to have done so, as cholera did not appear in the Hedjaz that year, and the pilgrims (18,161 in all) were spared the long detention at the Tor encampment.

I have made little mention in these pages of the many gala dinners and balls for which, as the head of a Government Department, I invariably received the Khedive's commands, but I well remember the first dinner-party given in Alexandria by Abbas II., to which I was invited, for it was on board the Khedive's magnificent yacht *Mahroussa*. It was midsummer, and I thought the idea a capital one, for Palace dinners as a rule were very warm functions, it being etiquette for *all* officials, European as well as native, to wear the " fez " in the Khedive's presence, even at banquets and balls. On board the *Mahroussa*, at anchor in the harbour, well away from all other vessels, it was comparatively cool and fresh. I recollect also that the guests were fewer in number than usual at State functions—though the yacht's spacious dining-saloon could have held many more. In fact we were but thirty in all, consisting of seven Princes, all the Ministers, and those Chiefs of the Government Administrations that had their headquarters in Alexandria. The *Mahroussa* was beautifully illuminated with hundreds of electric lights outside and in, and the decks and saloons tastefully decorated with flowers.

The next time I saw the Khedive I was on business bent, and my errand a far from pleasant one. The difficulty was this. The Sultan, fearful that cholera, which was still in some parts of Europe, might reach his capital, had induced, or ordered, the Constantinople Quarantine Board to impose stupidly vexatious quarantine on arrivals from Europe, namely, ten days against vessels coming from ports of Northern Europe (between Cronstadt and Cherbourg) ; five days against certain English ports ; and five days likewise against the Mediterranean ports of France, Italy, and Austria. Now, however exaggerated these measures may have seemed to me, it certainly was none of my business to criticize them, inasmuch as I fully admit that each country has a perfect right to protect itself by taking such precautions as it deems best, even though they be absurd. But the Sultan endeavoured to go a step further, for the Turkish delegate to the Alexandria Council was instructed *to ask that Egypt should follow Constantinople's example*, and, in case of refusal, he was to threaten that Turkey would enforce quarantine against Egypt. I was up in arms at once and ready for the fray. *The Times'* correspondent telegraphed the facts to London on September 21st, and concluded his message thus—

"The President of the Board, Mr. Miéville, refuses to submit the proposals for discussion on the ground that they overstep the terms of the regulations of the Alexandria Board. He adds that, though Turkey may arbitrarily impose quarantine against Egypt, the Alexandria Board can adopt such measures as are proposed only for valid reasons, and not from fear of reprisals. The cholera is abating in Europe, and there is the less reason, if indeed any previously existed, for such a wholesale and vexatious measure of quarantine."

The delegate's efforts having thus fallen very flat, the Sultan directed his Grand Vizier to telegraph to the Khedive, who at once sent for me. I explained to his Highness the attitude I had taken up, the which I most respectfully hoped I should not even be asked to abandon. The Khedive's position was, I admit, somewhat difficult, as Egypt is under the suzerainty of Turkey, but his good sense came to his aid.

When ultimately—for I had later on again to see the Khedive on the same subject—it had dawned on the Grand Vizier's mind that I was not to be brow-beaten, Turkey actually carried out her threat, *and imposed quarantine on all vessels from Egypt, though it was not even alleged that Egypt was infected.*

As a matter of fact we were a great deal healthier than Turkey in general, or Stamboul in particular. But, quarantine or no quarantine, I had the satisfaction of feeling that I had acted in accordance with the dictates of reason and common-sense, and I believe that the quarantine imposed against us fell more heavily on Turkey than on Egypt, and so " the threat went *home* to roost."

Two months later I was able again to take a short holiday, and had a most pleasant trip up the Nile on the steamer *Rameses the Great*, belonging to Cook's justly renowned Nile service. I went as the guest of the late Mr. John M. Cook, who for many hundreds of miles south of Cairo was known as the Uncrowned King of the River. Mr. Cook was unable himself to make the trip, but his pleasant genial son, Mr. Frank H. Cook, acted as host, and it goes without saying that I was most hospitably entertained.

Indeed there is no need to enlarge on this theme, for the many thousands who have taken passage in the vessels belonging to Messrs. Cook and Sons' Nile flotilla know how luxurious and comfortable the voyage to Luxor, Assouan, and beyond always is, when taken under the auspices of the famous World's Tourist Agents.

It was during this trip that I met a most refreshing old countryman, who, seeing that I could talk to the natives in their own tongue, and apparently knew also something about each temple, tomb, and so on, kept as near to me as possible on our excursions in order to overhear what information I had to impart to my own particular friends. For visiting ruins, even if they *are* from five to six thousand years old, is an amusement that is apt to pall unless one takes an intelligent interest in what one sees. Well, one day, at Denderah, I was pointing out how the capitals of the splendid columns of the Temple had been wantonly defaced by Vandals. "And how distressing," I added, "to think that the beautiful features of Hathor were disfigured by the early Christians."

"Aye," said the old countryman, who, as usual, was standing near me, "but canst tell if them Christians were *Church of England?*" (!)

CHAPTER XXV

A MEMORABLE EPIDEMIC

THE real number of the victims of the awful epidemic of cholera that raged in the Hedjaz in 1893 will never be known, but even the mortality among the pilgrims admitted officially by the Ottoman authorities was appalling.

A Reuter's telegram from Constantinople on the 9th of June heralded the tragedy with its usual grim curtness—

"Cholera is at Mecca, where sixty fatal cases occurred yesterday."

And *The Egyptian Gazette* made its comment at Alexandria on the 11th of June—

"The Quarantine Board has decided on putting in force at once the 'Regulations applicable to arrivals from Arabian ports in the Red Sea at the time of the return of the pilgrims,' and on considering all the coast of the Hedjaz as infected with cholera.

"The Quarantine Board has acted with a promptitude on which it and its President are to be congratulated. So far as it is concerned, we feel assured that all that is humanly possible will be done to protect Egypt from the scourge.

"Cholera having broken out so early in the season at Mecca adds to the gravity of the peril to Egypt. The pilgrims have not yet arrived at Mecca, and their number is unusually large this year. They will arrive at a hot-bed of cholera at the most favourable time for its propagation, and, though none will be permitted to enter Egypt until they have been subjected to a rigorous quarantine, there is always a chance of the disease being introduced into the country."

The Egyptian Gazette a couple of days later announced—

"Their Excellencies Riaz Pasha (Prime Minister) and Tigrane Pasha (Foreign Minister) arrived at Sidi-Gaber yesterday by the first morning express, in order to confer with his Highness the Khedive on the position of affairs created by the outbreak of cholera in Mecca. They had a private audience of his Highness the Khedive, and in the afternoon a long conference with Mr. W. F. Miéville, C.M.G., President of the Quarantine Board, on the preventive measures taken against the introduction of the disease into Egypt."

*   *   *   *   *   *   *

I may here give briefly a rough sketch of the measures adopted by the Council—

The encampment at Tor was organized to hold 12,000 pilgrims at a time.

A second camp was organized at a spot called Ras Mallap, which is roughly about half-way between Tor and Suez. Here, pilgrims whose destination was

Egypt, and who could not therefore be sent direct through the Suez Canal, were to be detained three days for medical inspection, notwithstanding having been twice disinfected at Tor, and having there purged *fifteen* days' quarantine. This was by way of extra precaution for Egyptian pilgrims. The great difficulty we had to contend with at Ras Mallap was the want of water, which necessitated a steamer being sent there for condensing purposes.

A third station was established at Nekhel, in the El Tih desert, half-way along the caravan route between Akaba and Suez.

Elaborate precautions were taken to prevent pilgrims returning to Egypt, either in sailing vessels across the Red Sea, or by any of the caravan routes, without having first purged their quarantine at Tor, Ras Mallap, or Nekhel. To this end cruisers patrolled the Egyptian waters of the Red Sea from Suez to Kosseir and on to Souakim. And on land a fleet dromedary service was instituted to keep close watch along the coast from Suez to Souakim, more especially near Kosseir and other possible landing-places. This was done by the Department for the Repression of the Slave Trade.

In the event of evasion, and on the assumption that it was possible that the fugitives might cross the desert from the Red Sea to the Nile, all the governors of provinces and towns in Upper Egypt were instructed to be on the look-out for returning pilgrims, and to cross-question, and, if necessary, arrest them.

It was even thought possible that pilgrims might

come by land, and, avoiding Nekhel, manage to reach the Suez Canal, and, watching their chance, swim, or be ferried, across.

To prevent this rather remote danger—for I personally held that such a long desert journey would most likely kill ailing pilgrims, and that the sun would disinfect the survivors—military and camel posts were, with the ready help of the Governor-General of the Canal, the Chief of the Coast-guard service, and the Governor of Suez, established all along the Suez Canal. This service was excellently carried out, though I remember that five small vessels had to be kept going in order to provision the various posts thus created.

And now let the newspapers continue the story.

The Egyptian Gazette of the 28th of June reported—

"The deaths from cholera among the pilgrims now in the Hedjaz are officially returned as follows by the Ottoman authorities—

"At Mecca, on the 20th instant, 231 deaths; on the 21st instant, 221 deaths; on the 22nd, 102 deaths. On the 23rd instant the pilgrims were on Mount Arafat, and there is no record of the mortality on that day.

"At Moona, on the 24th instant, 220 deaths; on the 25th, 455 deaths.

"It will be seen that the mortality returns from cholera in the Hedjaz are steadily increasing, as we supposed would be the case after the vast crowds of pilgrims had assembled in the Moona valley under the most unsanitary conditions. The number of pilgrims this year is far in excess of the average, and as no less than 50,000 are expected to have to be dealt with at the Tor Quarantine Station, the Quarantine Board's officials have not a very light task before them this summer. It is hoped, however, that the number in quarantine there at any one time will not exceed about 10,000."

And later, on the 1st July—

"The first batch of pilgrims may be expected to arrive at the Tor Quarantine Camp towards the end of next week, when the Quarantine Board's officials will have their hands full. Provision has been made for the simultaneous accommodation and victualling of 12,000 pilgrims, and one little detail will give some idea of the magnitude of the task, viz. that no less than 30,000 tent-pegs are among the camp equipment."

The Times, London—

"THE CHOLERA.

"*Alexandria, 6th July.*—With the departure of the pilgrims the cholera is decreasing at Mecca and Jeddah. The total amount of deaths at Mecca since 7th June is over 7000, and at Jeddah, since 29th June, 1450. Confidence is felt that the strict regulations, and the fifteen days' quarantine at El-Tor, imposed by the Quarantine Board, will prevent the epidemic from reaching Europe."

Le Phare d'Alexandrie, Alexandria, 7th July, 1893—

"THE PROTECTION OF EGYPT.

"The journals brought by the last mails are full of heartrending details of the cholera epidemic at Mecca, and the ravages committed by the disease during the pilgrimage. According to these accounts all quarters of the city suffered, and whole families were struck down.

"As was to have been foreseen, all the arrangements were insufficient, and it is said that bodies were left lying in the streets instead of being buried. All this is terribly sad, and no one can help feeling sorrowful and afflicted when contemplating the severity of calamities such as this which fall so mercilessly on suffering humanity.

"The first returning pilgrims are expected at Tor this very day, and we cannot but fear that cases of cholera will be brought to the camp, considering with what intensity the epidemic raged at Mecca.

"We cannot but acknowledge, however, that the Quarantine Council is fighting with great energy to prevent the disease from spreading, and with praiseworthy zeal has taken the necessary measures to save the country. For instance, all pilgrims are forced to bathe in the sea ; their clothes are taken from them and replaced by new garments provided by the Quarantine Service. The linen and clothing of healthy and bettermost pilgrims are passed through a disinfecting stove, while every article too foul for disinfection is ruthlessly burnt."

The Egyptian Gazette of the 12th July said—

" It is to be regretted that nothing whatever can be done in Egypt without political considerations coming into play, and we can only say that if a little more help and support were given to Mr. W. F. Miéville, the President of the Quarantine Board, in this time of trial, and if political animosity were buried before the common danger, that energetic official would have a fairer chance, and the burden of his responsibility would be thereby greatly lightened." [1]

The Times, London—

" THE CHOLERA.

" *Alexandria, 9th July.*—The medical delegate to Mecca of the Egyptian Quarantine Board gives a horrible account of the condition of the pilgrims. The deaths from cholera have been double the number officially reported. In the valley of Mouna it became impossible to bury the dead, and between Mecca and Mouna the road was strewn with corpses. In Mecca the victims lay decomposing where they died, and when the order was given for interment, several days elapsed before its execution for want of a sufficient number of grave-diggers.

" There are 7000 pilgrims now due at the Quarantine establishment of El-Tor, where the earliest arrivals have already brought cholera. As many as 50,000 in all are expected, but as El-Tor provides accommodation, provisions, and water only for 11,000 at a time,

---

[1] This article was evidently provoked by some scurrilous attack on me.—W. F. M.

the Quarantine Board has refused permission to land any pilgrims in excess of this number. These must, therefore, remain aboard, as they can neither land on Egyptian territory nor pass through the Suez Canal before performing fifteen days' quarantine at El-Tor. The Government provides food for the poorest pilgrims, and is doing its utmost to protect Europe from cholera."

* * * * * * *

Of course I need scarcely say that the jurisdiction of the Egyptian Board did not extend into Mecca, or any part of the Hedjaz, that country being *Ottoman* territory. All we were permitted to do by the Sultan was to send to that region our own delegate (a Moslem, of course) to report on what he saw; and this only on the understanding that he did not venture to interfere with the Turkish authorities. However, my chief object in here interrupting the narrative as told by the newspapers is not to record that the deplorable state of Mecca had nothing to do with the Khedive's Government, but is rather to relate the history of an incident which, though it must not be accorded a fresh chapter, may fittingly be given a separate title; and as this little book is throughout written in a familiar and colloquial style, I had better choose the head-line—

A ROUND WITH RIAZ.

His Excellency Riaz Pasha was, at the time of which I write, Regent of Egypt—in addition to being Prime Minister—the Khedive being absent in Europe.

Riaz is a wizen-faced, dried-up little man, of uncertain temper (due possibly to physical suffering), affable and courteous in private life, but, owing to his somewhat behind-the-times ideas and impatience on meeting opposition, often irritable, and nearly always difficult to get on with officially. He has, however, many good points, is strictly upright and honourable in his dealings, and a faithful, courageous servant of his country. He loves detail, and I have grave suspicions that he thought the Regency had added considerably to his stature, and that he could, with impunity, interfere in everything. The burning question during that hot summer was very naturally, " Will the Quarantine Council be able to ward off the cholera ? " So the Regent communed with himself, and resolved to be down on me if anything went wrong. His opportunity came when the Tor camp was full, and complaints were made that vessels were at anchor off Tor, with pilgrims on board who could not be landed.

Riaz summoned me to the Palace of Ras-el-Teen early on the 27th of July. After hearing the complaints, I explained that due notice had been given to the harbour authorities at Jeddah, and copies thereof duly posted in all the Jeddah shipping offices, to the effect that the Tor encampment could only hold 12,000 pilgrims at one time, and that consequently as soon as that number had left Jeddah for Tor, the remainder should only be despatched after a certain lapse of time, to be determined by circumstances.

But the Regent was not satisfied, and querulously and sharply inquired in a reproachful tone, " And pray why do you not organize the Camp to hold *more than* 12,000 at a time ? "

I was tired, worried, and over-wrought as it was, and this implied reproach made my blood boil. In my best French I let out—" Did his Excellency want me to put a quart of liquor into a pint bottle ? Did he desire a massacre of the innocents through a water-famine ? Did he think it wise to pump the Tor wells dry, and let thousands of his co-religionists die of thirst while they were re-filling ? Did he know what I had gone through in organizing and providing for even 12,000 ? Had any European Power ever created a quarantine station capable of containing so many souls at one time ? Did he not see the fear of creating a fresh home for the cholera by allowing agglomeration ? Did he think that disinfection could be carried out for an even greater number, when, as it was, the disinfecting stoves were working night and day ? Did he want to worry and harass instead of helping me ? If so, let him use his powers as Regent to appoint a new President of the Quarantine Board. And in any case let him accept my resignation, which I had the honour then and there to tender ! "

My language was fluent and forcible : I had not read the attacks made on me by my old friends in the French Press for nothing, and had mastered choice and biting expressions.

Riaz was astonished.

Happily a secretary entered the room at that moment and created a diversion, and without accepting, or declining to accept, my resignation, his

Excellency the Regent begged me to remain at the Palace, as he should probably like me to see the other Ministers.

A little later, a Cabinet Council presided over by Riaz himself was held, at the first part of which I was invited to be present, and I spoke very warmly about the Tor encampment, reiterating most of the arguments I had used to the Regent. My old Venice friend, Boutros Pasha Ghali, then Finance Minister and Acting Foreign Minister, kindly praised my work and took my side generally ; and when at last I left the Council Chamber to return to my duties, I knew that Riaz Pasha would never worry me again, and that I should hear no more of the resignation question. And on the evening of that very day the Regent wrote me a private note, addressing me as *Mon cher Miéville*, and ending his letter *Tout à vous, Riaz.*"

So my little outburst, which was natural enough, though perhaps unjustified, made of Riaz Pasha a good friend. And long may he remain so.

* * * * * * *

The Egyptian Gazette of the 27th of July contained the following—

"His Excellency the Regent came into Ras-el-Teen Palace this morning, and gave a private audience to Mr. W. F. Miéville, C.M.G. The position of affairs at the Tor Quarantine Camp was, we understand, the subject under discussion. As will be seen in the latest reports from the camp, there were upwards of 12,000 pilgrims in camp on Tuesday, and five vessels were lying in the roads with their pilgrims on board, it being impossible to disembark them in consequence of the limits of accommodation provided in the camp having been reached.

" In every country in the world when lazarettos are full, ships have to wait their turn. In like manner they will have to wait at Tor; and indeed very few quarantine stations in the world could put up over 10,000 persons simultaneously, and that with the comfort experienced at Tor."

British Medical Journal[1]—

" The first announcement officially made of what will be the memorable cholera epidemic of this year at Mecca was on the 7th of June, when the mortality was already eighteen per day, and deaths from 'ordinary diseases' seventy-two.

" The population of Mecca is estimated at about 60,000, while the number of pilgrims massed together there this year from all parts of the Moslem world is variously estimated at from 200,000 to 300,000 ; the latter figures I should consider considerably over the mark. As there are no means of estimating the number with even an approximation to certainty, it is a matter of guesswork, and it is well known how difficult it is even for experts to estimate crowds of very large numbers. It is certain, however, that the pilgrimage is very exceptionally large. The members of the Mahomedan faith joined it this year on account

---

[1] Extracts from an article on 'Cholera at Mecca and Quarantine in Egypt,' by J. Mackie, M.B., C.M.G., British Delegate at the Quarantine Board, Alexandria, July 1893.

of the Day of Sacrifice at Moona falling on a Friday, the 24th of June. The numbers arriving at Jeddah by sea might be pretty accurately controlled, but the arrivals by land cannot be estimated. The number of pilgrims shipped at Suez alone was 25,301, of whom 14,310 were Egyptians. Besides this number, 18,931 transited the Suez Canal, coming from the Mediterranean side, giving over 44,000 to be accounted for at the quarantine stations on their return. Deaths from cholera and other pilgrimage diseases will, however, have greatly thinned their ranks, whilst many remain in the Hedjaz to trade, or for other reasons, returning later or with next year's pilgrims. Up to the 13th of July over 10,000 deaths from cholera had been officially reported from Mecca and Jeddah, while there is no report of deaths from other diseases. That this number, though official, is under the mark, may be inferred from a report of Dr. Chaffy, an Egyptian Moslem, sent by the Quarantine Board as their sanitary correspondent to Mecca.

" This report (addressed to the President), of which I give a translation of some extracts, reveals a ghastly state of things happening one may say almost at the door of Europe, taking account of these days of rapid steam communication. Dr. Chaffy says—

" ' On arrival at Mecca I commenced at once an inspection in the town. The hospital, private houses, and tents were full of people suffering from cholera. I sent you by telegraph the number of deaths declared officially, but on account of the extraordinary mortality it must be admitted that the number of deaths could not be precisely known, and it may certainly be considered to have been double of that officially declared ; even more. At Moona it was impossible to bury all the dead, which lay here and there in heaps. Round about the Syrian caravan (Mahmal) there was a large number of bodies lying unburied.

"'Returning from Moona to Mecca, I found the route strewn with dead. In the town of Mecca itself, dead bodies were lying about in a state of putrefaction, and, when they were at last transported to the cemetery, they were thrown down there, and left lying for days unburied from want of a sufficient number of grave-diggers. The mortality from ordinary diseases at Mecca was caused by pernicious fever and diarrhœa.'

" One has only to read this and Burton's description of Mecca and pilgrim life there on ordinary occasions, to form some, but a very imperfect, idea of the state of things after the sacrifices at Moona, under the scorching heat of midsummer. After the sermon of many hours' duration on Mount Arafat, a stampede, graphically described by Burton, takes place down to the Moona valley, where the sacrifice of sheep takes place, the valley being converted for the time into a charnel-house. No one who knew these rites was astonished when the mortality after 'Moona' was officially reported to have mounted up from 220 and 455 to 1000 a day. I have seen no account of the mortality on the return journey of forty miles from Mecca to Jeddah, but one may infer that a good many must have died by the way, as cholera was declared amongst return pilgrims at Jeddah on the 29th of June, and only three days before they were dying at the rate of over 1000 a day in Mecca, whence they had come.

"The station at Tor is practically a desert, water being supplied from wells. There are no running streams to pollute, and the pilgrims are lodged in tents. Each ship as it arrives is assigned a section apart for its pilgrims, the sections being at a considerable distance from each other, with guards placed to prevent intercommunication. Healthy and infected sections are kept well apart. The period of quarantine is fifteen days, dating from time of arrival, if healthy, or dating from the last case of cholera in the section after arrival. During the quarantine the vessel bringing pilgrims is cleansed and disinfected, and the personal effects of the pilgrims are disinfected by steam under pressure, for which the Quarantine Board possess disinfecting machines established at the station.

"If considered necessary, the camping-ground of an infected section is changed. The number in a section varies from perhaps 300 to 900, according to the number brought by any one steamer. After having undergone the prescribed period of quarantine without a suspicious case, the foreign pilgrims are re-embarked on the steamer which brought them, and pass the Suez Canal in strict quarantine, and well guarded, to prevent communication with Egypt. In the case of Egyptian pilgrims, after having undergone the prescribed period of quarantine at Tor, and being declared healthy, they undergo a further three days' observation at a fresh camping-ground at Ras Mallap—a healthy spot at a considerable distance from the Tor—and are thence brought to Suez, generally in clean vessels sent by the Egyptian Government, and allowed to land in free *pratique*. Vessels leaving Jeddah with pilgrims receive their papers for Tor, and go straight to the quarantine station on the peninsula. The station is guarded by military sent by the Egyptian Government, and I believe there are about a thousand soldiers at present there on duty. All likely places where sambooks or other small craft might land pilgrims *en contravention* are strictly watched, and every precaution taken by camel patrol and coast-guard cruisers to prevent return pilgrims from landing in Egypt, except by the stations established by the Quarantine Board. Personal effects too worthless and dirty for disinfection are ordered to be burnt; the Egyptian Government at its own expense having sent a supply of clothing to draw upon to replace them. Communication is kept up with Suez by small steamers lent by the Egyptian Government, which take provisions if required, and mails, there being unfortunately no telegraph wire between Suez and Tor."

*   *   *   *   *   *   *

Of course the Tor encampment was far from perfect, but I honestly believe that everything possible had been done that could be accomplished, considering the want of funds; and evidently many others shared this view. The Khedive, when he returned from Europe, told me that the Sultan had expressed the

desire that I should be informed how greatly pleased
his Imperial Majesty had been to learn from his own
special commissioners that the Turkish pilgrims at
Tor were well cared for, and made quite comfortable.

The truth is that the changes had been the outcome
not of one individual brain, but the result of the
combined and cumulative working of many minds.

The Board's efforts to repel an invasion of cholera
were happily crowned with success, and immediately
the campaign had terminated, and the last pilgrim
had left the Tor encampment, I applied to be allowed
a two months' holiday, as my share in the work had
been rendered all the more arduous and fatiguing by
reason of the terrible damp heat which had prevailed
that summer.

CHAPTER XXVI

THE PARIS CONFERENCE

" His Excellency Ahmed Pasha Choucry, Governor-General of the Isthmus of Suez, and Mr. W. F. Miéville, C.M.G., President of the Quarantine Board, have been selected by the Khedivial Government to represent Egypt at the International Sanitary Conference which is to commence its sittings at Paris on the 7th February.

Such was the announcement made by the local Press in January 1894, and shortly afterwards the two delegates left Alexandria in the s.s. *Niger* for Marseilles.

The Paris Conference might well be called the *Pilgrimage Conference*, for it met solely for the purpose of coming to an understanding as to the best means of minimizing the danger of cholera being introduced into Egypt and Europe from the Hedjaz.

In my opinion the general plan adopted by the Paris Conference was intelligent and practical, and reflected great credit on its originators. The idea substantially was—To induce the authorities in

285

countries where cholera was prevalent to see that no pilgrim *set out for Mecca* unless healthy and cleanly, and to this end it was hoped that the health officers in the *port of departure* would inspect, and if necessary detain, and disinfect the baggage and clothing of every pilgrim before embarkation.

To organize stations at the southern end of the Red Sea, where pilgrims from India and the Far East should undergo a second inspection before being allowed to enter the Hedjaz.

To endeavour to establish some analogous control over pilgrim caravans journeying to Mecca by land.

To provide funds for the perfecting of the existing Quarantine Camp at Tor.

The Conference, which was held in the spacious and splendid saloon on the ground-floor of the French Foreign Office, began on the 7th February, as had been arranged, and I was present at the opening ceremony in the seat allotted to me between Mr. Michel de Giers, now Russian Minister to China, and my Egyptian colleague, Ahmed Pasha Choucry.

Monsieur Casimir Perier, Prime Minister and Foreign Minister in France, made a short speech welcoming the delegates in the name of the Republic, and wishing success to our labours.

Then Monsieur Camille Barrere, the *de facto* President, or Chairman, delivered the opening address, from which I give an extract—

"It seemed to the Government of the Republic that the time had come for Europe to crown the work accomplished by the last two Conferences, by resolutely entering on the examination of the serious sanitary problems raised by these pilgrimages.

"We have, in fact, in the last few years entered on an entirely new course, and one which will mark an epoch in the history of international prophylaxis; that of solutions—solutions, moreover, which respect all interests, those of public health and those of universal commerce. Formerly Sanitary Conferences met but to place on record the divergent views of the several members. To-day these fundamental differences no longer exist, or exist but in a very small degree. And this is owing, gentlemen, to two things: the first, and doubtless the principal, reason is the progress of the science and the development of the principles of hygiene, to both of which—and I am glad to say it—the Powers represented here have so largely contributed; the second reason is the new method of discussion recently adopted. For whilst formerly diplomates and scientific men kept, in assemblies of this sort, each to his own speciality, of late years they have intermingled and worked together for a common object. It was at Venice that for the first time this fusion was brought about, and you all know, gentlemen, the brilliant results of this collaboration. To attain that result it was only requisite that the doctors should practise a little diplomacy, and the diplomates a little medicine.

"At the Venice Conference the representatives of Europe substituted the condition of the vessel for the condition of the port, abolished vexatious and excessive quarantines for all ships which followed the rules laid down, replacing the old system by that of inspection and disinfection.

"At Venice were established the laws for the preservation of Egypt from the invasion of the epidemic, and for stopping it on the threshold of the Suez Canal. Now we must go deeper and further, and pursue the epidemic to where it is most dangerous, viz. to the places from where it enters. The members of this high assembly have therefore to labour together to discover a way of arriving at this result."

* * * * * * *

On the 9th February the delegates were received by the President of the Republic, the late Monsieur Carnot, and then, the usual visits of courtesy having been exchanged, work began in earnest. Personally, I was fully occupied, as I belonged to the two special committees, in addition to attending all the meetings of the Conference, both plenary and when sitting in committee.

The Paris Convention was signed on the 4th April, 1894. In addition to preventive measures to be taken in Indian and other ports, and on pilgrim vessels, the Conference organized a vast system of sanitary supervision in the Red Sea and in the Persian Gulf. As, however, the Convention has not yet been ratified, and as Turkey will seemingly never carry out in the Hedjaz in general, or Mecca and Moona in particular, adequate sanitary reforms, it unhappily looks as though the resolutions come to by

the Paris Conference will, as regards Turkey and
Persia, practically remain without effect.

But I cannot bring this chapter to a close without
the warmest possible mention of the princely hospitality shown by " La belle France " to the foreign
delegates. A sumptuously served buffet, with excellent champagne and other wines, was always open in a
room adjoining the Conference chamber. Then all
official Paris entertained us royally. Running through
the invitation cards, which I am glad to say I preserved,
I find that I attended officially nine banquets and five
balls during February and March, including two State
balls given by President Carnot.

Then of course we foreign delegates had to try
in some way to show our appreciation of all this
lavish hospitality, so we gave a banquet (and a most
successful function it was, thanks to the trouble taken
by our charming German colleague, Mr. de Schoen)
at the Restaurant Laurent in the Avenue Gabriel.

When I add that I went, during my stay in Paris,
to twenty-eight theatres, and to numberless private
luncheons, dances, and dinners—for I met many old
friends, and Lord Dufferin, whom I had known in
Cairo, was then at the Paris Embassy—I often wonder
how I lived through that most festive time. To let
my readers into a secret, I honestly believe I managed
to survive all the gaieties and feasting by *skating*
vigorously in my spare time at the Pôle Nord and
the Palais de Glace, of which last fashionable ice-rink
Lord Dufferin was also an almost daily frequenter.

I must not forget to add that the delegates were

officially received by the great Monsieur Pasteur, and had his wonderful institution thoroughly explained to them.

*   *   *   *   *   *   *

Once again did the s.s. *Niger* bear me across the Mediterranean, and in April I reported myself in Cairo as having fulfilled the mission confided to me.

CHAPTER XXVII

STRUCK DOWN

THE rest of the year 1894 passed quietly, the pilgrimage gave but little trouble, cholera not making its appearance at Mecca.

In July 1895 I was granted leave of absence, and after my departure I believe the Quarantine Board and the Acting President had much trouble with the returning pilgrims. I have by me no records for 1895, but, if I recollect rightly, the pilgrimage was a curious one, the authorities being apparently undecided as to whether cases of cholera had or had not occurred in the Hedjaz, and the Alexandrian Board seem to have had some difficulty in making up their minds as to whether to treat the pilgrims at Tor according to the mild rules prevailing in healthy times, or to apply the severe regulations applicable to cholera years.

Most of my holiday was spent on the Royal Isle of Wight Golf Links at Bembridge, and on the superb links at St. Andrews belonging to the " Royal and Ancient."

On 7th November work once more claimed me, but happily I entered on it feeling " like a giant refreshed."

Some time that winter a suspicious sickness made
its appearance in Egypt, which at first was designated
by a fancy name, " Fissikha," from the Arabic for a
preparation of rotten fish much relished by the natives
of certain districts, but the disease was speedily discovered to be our old enemy cholera. How the
scourge originated is hard to say. Happily the epidemic was nothing like so fatal as in 1883, and Alexandria once more enjoyed a comparative immunity—
an immunity even much greater than had been the
case thirteen years before. Though, as I have elsewhere stated, it was not part of the Quarantine
Council's work to grapple with disease when once it
had appeared in Egypt proper, I stayed on in Alexandria till the worst was over. The cholera of 1896
does not seem to have left much impression on my
mind, and I recollect it chiefly by reason of the work
I did (in my private capacity as a member of the
British colony) in connection with the " relief of
deserving Maltese," who, in consequence of the cholera
epidemic causing an exodus of the well-to-do, and
thereby bringing about stagnation in certain trades,
found themselves, through no fault of their own, in
destitute circumstances. I had been elected honor-
ary secretary to the committee for the collection and
distribution of funds, and, as is usual in all movements
of the sort, the secretary found his hands pretty full.

In June the Khedive sent for me as to arrangements
in connection with a trip his Highness intended
making through the Suez Canal. He wished all the
Quarantine authorities to be apprised of his coming,

that no delay might occur at the various ports of call.
After assuring his Highness that his commands should
be obeyed, I ventured to suggest that, as there was
no cholera in the Hedjaz or at Tor, it would be a
good opportunity for him to visit the pilgrim encampment at the latter place. This the Khedive
promised to do. Then I begged that, as a personal
favour, he would permit me *not* to tell the Director
of the Tor station of his Highness's intention to
inspect the camp, so that thus he might be sure of
seeing everything in its everyday garb, and not in
gala dress and freshly furbished up, as would be
the case were notice given. The Khedive was good
enough to approve of this idea also ; and as a matter
of fact, when he did ultimately visit Tor he took both
the village and camp officials most completely by
surprise. On returning from Tor his Highness once
again sent for me, expressed his great satisfaction at
everything he had seen, and, as a souvenir of his visit
to the camp, he presented me with his portrait, with
autograph.

And the third circumstance which I recall, is the
fact that I had in 1896 to detain Egyptian pilgrims
at Tor *on their way to the Hedjaz*, instead of as in
other years solely on their return from the holy
cities of Islam. This, of course, was because, Egypt
being infected, the pilgrims might otherwise have
taken the germs of cholera to Mecca, and so infected
the thousands of their co-religionists gathered together
from other parts of the earth. In other words, I
practically did for the Egyptians what the Paris

Conference desired should always be done for pilgrims leaving infected countries. If India, for instance, would each year isolate and inspect pilgrims from infected areas *before their embarkation*, cholera would be carried to the Hedjaz much less frequently than in the past.

As soon as the epidemic in Egypt had practically ceased (which happened about the end of July), I went to Europe to take a course of baths at St. Moritz in the Engadine, for I had been feeling very unwell, nervous, and run down.

I returned at the end of October 1896, and the pressure of work was terrible, owing chiefly to the presence of *plague* in India.

My name figured in the honour list published on or about the 8th of January, 1897, on the occasion of the anniversary of the Khedive's Accession, and I wrote home—" My latest news is a big decoration— Grand Officer of the Osmanieh ; the third highest honour in the Khedive's gift. It is gratifying, of course, but I want rest and change of post rather than honours, for the strain is killing me."

Eight of the clock on the morning of Thursday, 21st of January, saw me as usual at my desk in the President's office. A few days previously, Machell Bey, the head of the Coast-guard service, had come to me about some little difficulty which had occurred between one of his agents and one of mine at Ismailia. I had suggested that he should send for Purvis Bey, the Inspector of Coast-guards along the Suez Canal, that we three Englishmen might talk the matter over, and settle the difficulty without a lot of red tape and official correspondence. This had been agreed to, and nine on the morning of January 21st had been fixed upon as the hour for meeting in my office. Punctually my good friends Machell and Purvis arrived, and the question at issue was soon satisfactorily arranged. Then Machell remarked how ill I was looking, and I admitted I was worried and over-wrought. When they had gone I tried to tackle other work, but I found great difficulty in concentrating my attention, and at half-past ten, or thereabouts, I had a heart seizure, was taken home, and never again have I set foot in the President's room.

A few days later the doctors gave their final verdict, which set forth that I had been seized in my office with faintness, accompanied by extremely irregular heart's action, which had persisted for more than twenty-four hours, and was of such a serious and alarming nature that it ought to be regarded as a warning of my unfitness to continue in active service, and that therefore I ought not to retain my functions as President of the Quarantine Board.

CHAPTER XXVIII

VALEDICTORY

WHEN attacked and vilified in the foreign Press, I did not hesitate to lay before my readers faithful translations of even the most abusive articles. So I now venture to transcribe two or three of the flattering notices that appeared in both the English and foreign newspapers.

The old abusive *Bosphore Egyptien* had been long since suppressed, but its place had to a certain extent been taken by *La Réforme*, a French publication which could on occasion be just as virulent as the *Bosphore*. This paper, however, when I was struck down, buried the hatchet and published an article which so touched me that, though I had not the pleasure of knowing the editor, I wrote him a little note, as from man to man, thanking him for his too generous appreciation of a stricken foe.

"*La Réforme.*　　　　　　*Alexandria, 9th Feb.* 1897.

SILHOUETTE D'EGYPTE.

W. F. MIÉVILLE.

"When an official is promoted to an important post, such as the Presidency of the Quarantine

Council, one is somewhat diffident about according praise to him for fear of being suspected of time-serving, or even of toadying. But when it is a question of an official leaving his post, suspicion as to motives can no longer be entertained, and the reader cannot have any doubts as to the sincerity of the approval expressed, and the free spontaneity of the regret felt.

"And in listening to all those who have been able to form an opinion of Mr. Miéville, I felt that he was regretted. A man must be indeed of solid worth to be mourned by those whom but yesterday he ruled; above all, he must have that rare and special gift, concerning which much might be written, and which is named 'intellectual uprightness.'

"Mr. Miéville belonged to that old school of Egyptian officials who esteemed it a duty to be as urbane, as kindly, and as courteous towards the natives as towards the members of the European colonies. He was one of those men who, having received a brilliant education, knows how to make use of it for the honour of the nation to which they belong, as well as to their own private satisfaction as well-bred gentlemen. He had nothing aggressive about him, let us render him that justice.

"Since he was called to the Presidency he has always shown himself to be, what he is, a perfect gentleman. He has ever sought to conciliate those holding divergent views, and he has nearly always succeeded. He was truly a model President.

"I might catalogue the titles and decorations of

the ex-President, but in truth the enumeration would add nothing to what I have said of him. If I wished to sum up, I should say that Mr. Miéville was a well-liked man in a difficult position. And that is no small praise in the times we live in."

The Egyptian Gazette contained a long biographical sketch, from which the following extracts are taken—

" The career of Mr. Miéville is one of great interest, inasmuch as it is that of a man who, by his own talents and merits, succeeded in climbing the ladder of official favour until he had reached a very high rung on it. Had his health not unfortunately given way, we feel sure that he would have gone higher and occupied probably a prominent position in the conduct of the world's affairs.

" His brilliant record is that of a distinguished public servant who has done good service as Chairman of the Quarantine Board, an international body which requires to be dealt with most tactfully. That he was the right man in the right place is proved by the fact that, at the Venice Conference of 1892, Mr. Miéville was unanimously re-elected Chairman of the re-organized Quarantine Board for Egypt. On one occasion Lord Cromer paid a very high tribute to Mr. Miéville when he said that his work was 'of a nature to require the exercise of much tact and judgment, as also the display of considerable powers of organization. Mr. Miéville has carried out his difficult and responsible duties with skill and ability.'

" Sir Charles Cookson also acknowledged Mr. Miéville's 'great and natural capacity for business,' his faculty of gaining 'the confidence of different classes of people,' and the 'conscientiousness, energy, intelligence, and judgment' which distinguished him.

"And Mr. Gorst, who, as the English head of the Ministry of the Interior, has been in an exceptionally favourable position to appreciate the talents Mr. Miéville displayed in his delicate and arduous post, wrote to him—'No task requires more tact and knowledge of human nature than the management of an international body, and I can, from personal experience, testify to your success in that respect.'

"One of the few English officials who kept in close touch with members of other nationalities, he was admirably aided in the performance of his social duties by the lady whom he married on the 28th of March, 1882, and who has, through all these years, proved a worthy helpmate to him. Mr. and Mrs. Miéville will be missed by a wide circle of friends in Egypt, who will all join us in expressing the hope that rest and freedom from anxious cares may enable Mr. Miéville to completely recover his health and again take an active part in public life."

My successor was a Professor at the Cairo School of Medicine, Dr. M. A. Ruffer, an Englishman, of (oddly enough) Swiss extraction like myself. On taking his seat as President for the first time he, was good enough to allude to "the eloquence, tact, and diplomatic knowledge of my honoured predecessor," and at the same meeting the Council unanimously passed a vote of thanks to me "for the zeal, devotion, and courtesy always displayed in the performance of my delicate duties."

Being quite unable to leave my bed, I perforce had to bid farewell to the Members of the Council in a letter.

I wrote also a letter to each of the Heads of the many offices under my jurisdiction, thanking them, and the clerks under them, for their co-operation and loyalty. I felt very sad at leaving them, for if a measure of success had fallen to my lot, was it not for the most part due to the ready and staunch services of those under me?

The Staff presented me with my portrait in oils, and in the letter, which was signed by over sixty of the principal officials (including Austrians, Egyptians, Englishmen, Frenchmen, Greeks, Italians, Swiss, and Syrians), and which accompanied their most handsome gift, the following paragraph occurred—

"The kindness with which you have always treated the members of the Staff, without distinction of rank or nationality, the solicitude you have ever shown to the deserving, and the indulgence with which you have pardoned the weak, are to us but so many remembrances of you which will remain engraved on our memories. Thus it is but with your heart that you can understand the feelings which we entertain towards you, feelings that will accompany you throughout your life."

Then letters from public bodies with which I was in my private capacity connected, reached me.

My old friend Morice Pasha (now Sir George

Morice) wrote "on behalf of the committee and members in general of the Cercle Khédivial to express the deep regret" with which my resignation of my membership and of my post of Vice-President had been received, and the letter went on to say—" It is in a large measure due to the initiative taken by you and the confidence with which you inspired us, that we were induced to join you at a critical moment in the Club's affairs in taking charge of them. We are indebted to you in a great measure for the successful result attained, for your advice and influence have always been at our disposal, and have proved most valuable."

I was deeply touched, and all this spontaneous kindness and appreciation made the wrench of leaving Alexandria all the harder, and made it a pain indeed to part with the genial, jolly, kind, and affectionate friends in the land of my adoption.

One last word : I feel bound to place on record that in the matter of pension the Egyptian Government behaved just as generously as my colleagues and friends did in the matter of kindly sympathy, and in the expression of appreciation.

CHAPTER XXIX

WINDSOR

SLOWLY, very slowly did I struggle back to health. The last few weeks in Alexandria were so sad and trying that I sometimes wonder how I escaped a second heart seizure. The sale of the furniture; the shower of private letters; the offer (and necessary refusal) of a public farewell dinner; the last interviews with a few of my greatest friends and colleagues; and the most trying ordeal of all, the saying good-bye on board the s.s. *Equateur* to the shoals of friends of all degrees and nationalities who came to bid God-speed to my wife and myself; these things were not calculated to produce calm and tranquillity, nor did they permit me to indulge in what was so essential to my recuperation, namely, absolute rest.

However, that winter and the following were spent pleasantly and peacefully on the gloriously sunny, flower-bestrewn Riviera. It was in the lovely gardens of Cannes that I re-read the hundreds of touching letters which had been addressed to me by friends and colleagues and subordinates in Egypt.

It was at Nice that I received on the evening

of the last day of December 1897, the telegraphic message from Lord Salisbury, intimating that her Majesty the Queen (whom God preserve) had been graciously pleased to give directions for my promotion to a Knight Commandership of the Most Distinguished Order of St. Michael and St. George.

And it was at Nice likewise that on New Year's Day 1898 I had more cablegrams and telegrams from divers peoples and countries than I had ever before received in twenty-four hours.

The one sad note in this the hour of my triumph was the frequently recurring thought of how my old mother would have treasured these kind sayings in her heart.

Six months later the Queen held a private Investiture at Windsor Castle. We were then staying at Tunbridge Wells, from which pleasant retreat I went up to town.

At Paddington station I was pleased to find amongst the twenty-seven officers and civilians who had been summoned to Windsor to receive the honour of knighthood at the hand of their sovereign, several familiar faces—Frankfort de Montmorency, who commanded the British garrison at Alexandria, 1887—1889; General John Davis, who had been General Officer commanding in Egypt; Admiral Tracey, the President of the Royal Naval College; Admiral Compton Domvile, and Edward Leigh Pemberton.

On the journey down I talked chiefly to Sir Richard Martin, lately returned from Rhodesia, and we found we had mutual friends (Milner and Sivewright) in South Africa.   Looking round the saloon-carriage in which we travelled, I could not help being struck by the fact that I was seemingly the youngest man present by some ten years, whilst the great majority were my seniors by close on twenty years.

We reached Windsor station early in the afternoon, and found the royal carriages awaiting us. I drove to the Castle with Generals Davis and de Montmorency, and Sir George Morris.

We alighted at the Grand Entrance, catching as we did so a charming glimpse of the Long Walk, and were conducted to a large drawing-room leading out of St. George's Hall, where we were received by the ladies and gentlemen of the Household.

While waiting for luncheon we were asked to write our names in the Queen's Birthday-Book, which I did, adding, by request, the words " Windsor Castle," and the date.

The Lord Steward (the Earl of Pembroke and Montgomery) then asked me under which of my names I wished to be knighted, and of course I chose "Walter."

Luncheon was served in St. George's Hall—the display of gold plate was magnificent. My immediate neighbours at table were Generals John J. H. Gordon (Member of Council for India) and Viscount Frankfort de Montmorency.

The Investiture was held in the Green Drawing-room at three o'clock.

The Queen was accompanied by her daughter, the

Princess Helena (Princess Christian), and by her grandchildren Prince Christian Victor and Princess Victoria of Schleswig-Holstein, and her Majesty was attended by numerous members of her Household.

General Sir William Lockhart (Commander-in-Chief in India) was first introduced into the presence of the sovereign, and received a G.C.B. He was followed by several Knights Commander of the Bath, and by one K.C.S.I.

My turn came next, and I was introduced into her Majesty's presence by the Hon. Sir Spencer Ponsonby Fane (Comptroller in the Lord Chamberlain's Department) on my right, and by the Hon. Charles Barrington (Gentleman Usher acting for Sir Albert Woods, Garter King of Arms, indisposed) on my left. The latter carried on a red velvet cushion the Insignia of a Knight Commander of the Most Distinguished Order of St. Michael and St. George.

I bowed on entering, again in the middle of the room, and again on approaching the Queen. I then knelt on my right knee on a footstool placed close in front of her Majesty. The sovereign then dubbed me " Sir Walter " by placing her sword on *both* my shoulders. I then raised my right arm horizontally, the Queen placed her hand on my wrist, and I raised it to my lips. I remained kneeling, and her Majesty proceeded to my Investiture by placing the Riband and the Badge of the Order round my neck, and by affixing the Star to my breast. During this part of the ceremony I was much moved. The Queen spoke very softly, though quite clearly. She looked very tired. Once again in the same manner her Majesty presented her hand for me to kiss, and then I retired from the Royal Presence with the usual three reverences.

We left the Castle as soon as the Investiture was over, and were driven to the station (in the same state as on our arrival) to the strains of "God save the Queen," the sentries saluting, and the people who lined the streets bowing to us.

I wore *levée* dress *without* any of my other decorations or medals.

In the Statutes of the Order of St. Michael and St. George it is laid down that the Ensigns of a Knight Commander shall serve as evidence of a Knight's great Merit, Virtue, and Loyalty—and the Motto of the Order is—

"AUSPICIUM MELIORIS ÆVI."

Thus therefore did my Queen give me

"A PLEDGE OF BETTER TIMES."

THE END